2023: ✓

The Patron Saint of Lost Dogs

ALSO BY NICK TROUT

Tell Me Where It Hurts
Love Is the Best Medicine
Ever By My Side

The Patron Saint of Lost Dogs

NICK TROUT

**Doubleday Large Print
Home Library Edition**

HYPERION

NEW YORK

**This Large Print Book carries the
Seal of Approval of N.A.V.H.**

For Emily

Dum spiro spero
—Cicero

While I breathe,
I hope.

≪ CONTENTS ≫

Monday

« 1 »

The jingle of the old shopkeeper's doorbell makes me jump—not least because my first customer of the evening happens to be my first customer in fourteen years.

"Can I help you?" I ask, realizing too late my tone probably sounds more annoyed than inviting. I guess I need to brush up on my customer service skills.

On the far side of the waiting room stands a man in a funereal charcoal suit, tethered, by way of a nylon cord, to a golden retriever. The dog seems intent on getting to me—her tail up and aflutter, nails scratching for traction on the linoleum. The man on the makeshift leash has other ideas, though. Barely audible curse words form on his clenched lips as he yanks on the cord.

"You the doctor?" he asks.

I look down at my white coat, which looks (and feels) more like a costume than a uniform. It's a little tight in the pits, a little shy in the wrists, but I did remember to drape a stethoscope around my neck like a scarf. Still, I almost feel like an imposter. Maybe that's because I am a bit of an imposter.

"Yes," I say, nodding. Slowly stretching out the syllable does little to improve my credibility. "I'm the doctor." The man squints past me, over my shoulder, at the plaque screwed to the examination room door— DR. ROBERT COBB, DVM.

"I thought Doc Cobb was dead?"

"He is. I'm Dr. Mills."

The man raises an eyebrow. If he thinks I'm going to elaborate, he's mistaken.

"Whatever," he says with an exaggerated sigh that sends a cloud of alcohol fumes my way. "I just need someone to put her to sleep." He jabs a cocked thumb and index finger downward, in the general direction of the dog, but keeps his eyes on me.

Unbelievable. Back in town for fewer than four hours, and working on a living, breathing, creature for the first time in fourteen years, and what's the first task I'm asked to perform? An elective euthanasia. Doesn't it figure.

"Okay," I say, but without conviction. "You'd best come on through to the exam room."

I lead the way, and to my horror, the man lets go of the cord, and a supercharged golden linebacker barrels toward my groin.

"Frieda, God damn it," he mutters as he stumbles after her.

My outstretched hand is meant to fend off fangs, fur, and drool, or at the very least slow her momentum, but Frieda treats my rebuttal as a welcome greeting, her graying snout rooting under my palm as she begins to rub her entire body back and forth across my legs. Dark corduroy pants and golden retrievers are not a good combination.

Frieda then charges past me, and I corral her down the short hall into the exam room, which hasn't changed one iota in almost half a century—dull and scratched stainless steel examination table taking center stage, chipped Formica counters, unlabeled drawers, and cabinets built into institutional green walls. There's a wooden bench for the owners, a wooden stool for the doctor. The passage of time may have made this space shrink, but right now it feels austere, more claustrophobic than cozy, a pervasive tang of antiseptic in the air.

"So Frieda is . . . was . . . one of Cobb's patients?" I ask.

"No."

"I don't understand."

"She's not his patient. This is probably her first time at a vet's office."

Probably? What does *probably* mean?

The man blinks slowly as he speaks. He has a receding hairline, leaving plenty of forehead real estate for worry creases. His necktie is slack, top button of his shirt undone, and I can see red chafing around his throat—probably not used to being constrained by a starched collar. But at that moment, what strikes me most is that, as far as I can tell, not a single strand of blond golden retriever hair clings to any surface of his dark suit.

"Is she sick?" I ask, looking down at Frieda. She has settled, and by settled I mean she has become an appendage glued to the side of my right leg. It's as if we are conjoined, like contestants bracing for a man-dog, six-legged race. And she refuses to be calm unless one of my hands is touching the top of her head. I poke the fur on her head gently. So what if my contact looks more like a wary blessing than a friendly pat?

"She's having accidents." The man ratchets up the volume and furrows his brow, as though this is more than enough justification to terminate her life. "Every morning. Exact same spot. I just had the floors redone, and they're already ruined. You know it's not like I wanna do this or nothing."

His bluster sails past me. Instinctively, I latch on to the details.

"Accidents? Urination or defecation?"

"She pees in the kitchen. A lot."

"What's a lot? A normal adult dog in a normal environment produces anywhere between twenty and forty milliliters of urine for every kilogram of body weight in a twenty-four-hour period. Assuming she weighs . . . let's say ninety pounds, or roughly forty kilos, then a volume of—"

"All I know is she's peeing like a race-horse."

I remove the coarse nylon collar from around Frieda's neck. She's not going any-where.

"Is she spayed?"

"Dunno." He glances down at the cell phone in his hand and begins keying some-thing into the phone.

"You have no idea?" I say.

He stops moving his thumbs and looks up with a glare. I decide to change tack.

"Eating okay?"

"Sure."

"Any vomiting?"

He shakes his head.

"Is she always looking for water? Drink-ing from the toilet bowl?"

"That's disgusting."

Now I raise my eyebrows.

"Not so as I've noticed."

I take a step closer to the man and am once again bowled over by the smell of booze. My golden shadow follows suit.

"Well, I'm sorry to be so blunt but something isn't adding up."

The man rocks back a little in his stance, twists his face into a frown of incredulity. I have stopped petting Frieda, and judging by the frenzy of her busy snout in and around my crotch she's not pleased. She barks and I relent.

"Let's review the facts," I say, feeling more confident on firmer ground. "For starters, your dog is obese, there's no evidence of weight loss, and therefore inappropriate urination secondary to underlying cancer seems unlikely. Absence of bilaterally symmetrical alopecia tends to rule out Cushing's disease, and your history doesn't fit with kidney disease or diabetes. From a purely physiological standpoint a dog simply cannot have a normal water intake and excessive urination in one specific location and at only one specific time of the day."

His features stretch back into place. "What are you talking about?"

I take a deep breath. Unfortunately for me, my entire professional career has left me unprepared to discuss the intricacies of polydipsia and polyuria with . . . to put it politely . . . inebriated laypeople. Then again, there's not much call for small talk and insightful conversation when your patients are dead and never show up with an owner. Which is absolutely fine by me.

"Where you from?" asks the man before I can answer his apparently rhetorical question. "Down south?"

Given our current latitude in the northernmost reaches of Vermont, I could point out that "down south" is pretty much everywhere else in the lower forty-eight.

"Yes, sir, Charleston, South Carolina."

"Long way from home."

I manage a fake smile and keep quiet. Nothing could be further from the truth.

"You're new, you're a stranger, so let me offer you a piece of free advice," he says, leaning in with a hard liquor–soused whisper. "Your fancy medical-speak won't mean nothing to the folks of this town." He leans back. "I'm not here for a lecture. I'm here to get done with my dog."

Get done with my dog. It's been nearly a decade and a half since I graduated from veterinary school, determined to follow in my late mother's footsteps, to became an expert in one specific and, for most pet owners, undervalued discipline—veterinary pathology. When you want to know the name of the disease that made your pet sick, I'm your guy—a veterinary pathologist. We're the doctors who spend our days staring into microscopes, looking at slides, examining wafer-thin slices of diseased tissue so you can have a diagnosis. Sexy? Maybe not. Essential? Like William H. Macy says in *Fargo*, "You're darn tootin'." Literally translated, *pathology* means the study of suffering, and if my training has taught me anything, it's a healthy respect for life. *Get done with my dog*. What a jerk. I may be accustomed to the clinical aspects of death, but this guy's cavalier attitude makes even me bristle.

"Just so as we're clear," I say. "You have absolutely no interest in trying to resolve your dog's problem?"

The man gives me a withering look and works his fingertips into his forehead, as if he might manually iron out some of the creases.

"Look, I feel bad about this."

I pause and will myself to lock eyes before I say, "Only not bad enough."

He stiffens. "You vets are all the same.

Always trying to test for this. Medicate for that. Never know when to quit."

"I thought you said your dog had never been to see a vet?"

He inhales, air whistling through clenched teeth. "It's simple math. I can't afford to find out what's wrong with her. I can't afford to fix her. And right now I can't afford to live with her. Just the way it is."

I look down at Frieda. She's unnaturally clingy, obviously promiscuous with her affection, and thanks to her my sweaty palms look like I'm wearing golden mittens. Fabulous. Even so, as far as I can tell she seems to be happy. I look up at the man, hoping to see nothing but evil in his eyes, and yet, for all his remote, hard-nosed logic, something tells me he's having a tougher time with this decision than he's letting on. I don't want to do this, but if I refuse I'm sure he'll go somewhere else. It feels like Hobson's choice, in other words, no choice at all.

"Very well," I say, after a significant pause. "It's your call, but I am going to need you to sign a consent form." Assuming I can find a consent form.

"Is that really necessary?" he asks.

I pull on a drawer—boxes of needles of different gauges and lengths. The one below contains syringes. The third is home to all manner of paperwork—consent forms for surgery, pharmacy scrips for medication, rabies vaccine certificates—but no euthanasia consent forms.

"You know I'd rather not stay for the . . . for the, uh . . . injection," he says, suddenly contrite and backing toward the door. "Okay to leave her with you?"

"Sir, I need you to sign a consent form."

I continue to rifle papers and feel beads of sweat forming on my upper lip.

"Why don't I just swing by tomorrow morning, I'll sign it then."

"First thing?" I ask. He nods and is almost out the door before I remember the reason I'm in this mess, why I find myself in an ill-fitting white jacket, a thousand miles away from home. "Hey, before you go, there is the matter of the bill."

He stops in his tracks.

"Of course," he says, reaching inside his breast pocket, fumbling with a wallet.

I know what you're thinking—how can you be so cold as to discuss money at a time like this? Well, two things—Mr.

Charcoal Suit clearly isn't feeling sentimental. And given my current circumstance, it's imperative.

"How much?"

I have no idea how much to charge. I pick a number.

"Forty."

"I've only got a twenty."

"You want me to give her half the dose?"

That one got away from me, and the man looks like I might be serious.

"Can I settle up tomorrow, when I come back to sign the form?"

My shoulders slump forward in surrender. "I suppose so," I say, and he presses the bill into my hand, like he's tipping the executioner, before backing away. No good-bye to me, but more importantly, no good-bye to Frieda.

I wait for the jingle of the shopkeeper's brass bell as he leaves through the front door and allow myself a deep exhalation. Combine what I am about to do with my disturbing lack of experience, and it might be best if Frieda and I are left alone.

Despite the neediness of my feathery side-kick, I manage to locate a 12 cc syringe, a

20-gauge needle, a tourniquet to raise a vein, and a transparent plastic bottle containing a cobalt blue liquid bearing the disturbing label BEAUTHANASIA. Stupid name. Where's the beauty in an overdose of barbiturates?

I look down at my patient. Or perhaps victim would be a better word. Her age has to be around twelve, maybe thirteen years. I base this estimate on several observations. Beyond the obvious gray muzzle, her elbows are thick and calloused, like leather patches on a threadbare jacket, worn thin from lying down too much. Her breath has a distinctive and frankly disagreeable bouquet—thanks to extensive dental disease—and, from what little I've seen, she has a proclivity for shaking her ears, probably the result of a chronic affinity to swimming in ponds and lakes. Right now she's panting. Not surprising, given this strange environment. I guess we're both riding a wave of adrenaline—only hers looks like excitement and mine looks like nervous anticipation.

Snap out of it. You've got a job to do. Time to balance compassion with bone-chilling coldness.

The thing is, to deliver my poison I must access a vein, and that means getting up close and personal, which means getting Frieda on the exam table. I begin patting the metal surface of the exam table. What am I thinking? Even polite society might label her proportions as, well, plus sized—maybe not quite muumuu material, but one would definitely advise against a bikini. She's not going to hop up there. How best to do this?

I have my hand on top of her head. Slowly I reduce this contact to a single finger, like she's a chess piece and I'm still debating my move. She remains calm, so I take a careful step backward. I consider my options. Do I use the element of surprise: rush at her, arms open wide? Or do I try to win her over, lull her into a false sense of security, and then pounce: pin her limbs, secure her head, and guard against snapping enamel? Curious chocolate eyes look up.

I make my move—one arm in front of her shoulders, one arm around her butt, and, despite an unsanitary mouthful of golden hair, with a scoop, a shove, and a scramble, somehow I get her up and onto the table.

While I'm cursing the shooting pain in my lower back, I reel at my reflection in the metallic surface. It's the glare from ghostly white cheeks and chin, my having shaved off my beard yesterday for the first time in ages. It looks as weird as it feels. I'd be looking at a stranger were it not for the recognition of my hair and nose. Forget dirty blond, the unruly mop is boring brown; however, I do try to think of my nose as more Romanesque than prominent. Meanwhile Frieda, wholly disinterested in my new look, lies on the table like a canine version of Superman in flight, front legs outstretched, back legs outstretched, and that feathery tail won't stop swishing.

"I'm going to need you to stay as calm and still as possible." The warble in my voice is amplified in the small room and my pitch is wrong—too formal—as though I'm talking to another person and not a dog. Maybe it's better if I keep quiet. I already know it's better not to look into her eyes.

Be detached, regimented, and mechanical. Sadly, I'm guessing not that different from how some people might already describe me.

I take a minute to walk through the entire process in my mind, step by step. Everything is ready. I am prepared, but there's still a nervous judder in my every breath.

I plug in an electric clipper, turn it on, and startle at the harsh chatter of the blade.

"It's okay," I say, more to myself than to Frieda. I reach out for a front leg and, without hesitation, Frieda does something so natural it stops me in my tracks—she offers up her paw. Believe me, anthropomorphic mumbo jumbo has no place in my vocabulary, but I'm at a loss for another way to describe a simple gesture that screams "I trust you."

And what an interesting oversize paw it is, great tufts of fur crammed between the webs like she's wearing fuzzy golden slippers. Against my better judgment, and only because we are alone, I take it and tentatively shake it. My hand is still moving up and down when I notice the contracture of certain muscle groups around

Frieda's lips. This makes no sense. Is this dog smiling?

I let go of her foot. What's happening to me? Dogs can't smile and "giving paw" is a learned response rewarded with food or physical attention. Reminding myself of these facts helps me regain a little composure, then I'm struck by something improbable—a few tiny flecks of what appears to be cracked pink nail polish clinging to her nail beds. This is unlikely to be the work of the man in the charcoal suit. Clearly, there is more to this dog's story.

Frieda paws the air between us for a second time. I groan. This proximity to a living creature is as unfamiliar as it is disturbing. It is precisely why I have spent my entire veterinary career avoiding this kind of awkward encounter. Of course I can do this, all of this, everything it takes to be a general practice veterinarian (hey, finishing top of my class at veterinary school should count for something). Trouble is, the last time I worked on an animal with a heartbeat was the week before graduation, and with the passage of time I may have underestimated a certain . . . I don't know . . . sentimentality . . . messing with the process.

"Let me clip a little fur, there we go."

Frieda's panting has ceased, and the rhythm of her tail is beginning to slow. I return the clippers to the counter, pick up the rubber tourniquet, lasso her forelimb, and tighten it in place. I sense her head starting to relax and feel the warm air of her sigh whistle past my cheek as she settles her chin across her free front paw.

Guess I'm not going to need that muzzle after all. Somehow, in spite of this alien encounter, Frieda remains content. Me, I can't stop my hands from shaking.

I focus on the bald swatch of skin, wipe the surface with alcohol, and watch as the vein declares itself—plump and straight.

Golden retrievers are consistently one of the most popular breeds of dog, ranking fourth behind Labs, German shepherds, and beagles.

The rapid thud of blood pulsing in my ears begins to slow. It's a trick that rarely fails; a secret shared by an old anatomy instructor as a way to remain calm before an exam—the recitation of facts and observations. Always useful in high-pressure situations.

Arguably, golden retrievers have had more leading roles in movies than any other breed.

Okay, so some of my factoids are not clinically relevant.

Roughly 60 percent of golden retrievers will die of cancer, a rate about twice as high as most other breeds.

Perhaps I could tell myself that Frieda's alleged incontinence stems from bladder cancer, an aggressive transitional cell carcinoma—inoperable and painful. If it were cancer, if I knew for sure, then I'd be doing her a favor by ending her suffering. I frown and shake my head. The truth is I'll never know. I'm just trying to make myself feel better. If I'm going to pretend to be a real vet, even for a short time, then I must learn to embrace what for me is a totally foreign concept—clinical ambiguity.

Needle and syringe in hand, I risk a look into Frieda's eyes. Big mistake. Though her head remains perfectly still, her tail picks up the pace.

"Good girl," I manage, patting her head,

betraying everything she sees in me as my trembling hand inserts the needle into the cephalic vein. She doesn't flinch. She doesn't pull away. She doesn't make a sound. I pull back on the plunger, just like I was taught to do as a student, and a swirl of purple blood spins inside the syringe. I can't believe it, I'm in on the first try.

This is it. Now, I may not be the most sentimental guy in the world, but even I understand that this is a moment when Frieda should hear the comforting words of a familiar voice, feel the comforting touch of a loved one. Thoughts of my late mother's passing fill my head, the comparisons impossible to ignore. I shake the recollection from my head in an attempt to focus.

A golden retriever has never won Best in Show at Westminster.

Standing in front of her I lean forward, move in close, middle and index finger stabilizing the plastic barrel, thumb extended, ready to drive the plunger home, and for the first time since we have met, Frieda's tail has gone completely still.

I lift my head ever so slightly, and this time the tip of Frieda's tongue licks me squarely on my nose. And that's it. That's all it takes for me to finally accept I can't do this. I quickly pull out the needle and squeeze my thumb over the vein. I'd totally forgotten about the way this sort of inter- action makes me feel. No, *forgotten* is not the right word. *Forgotten* suggests something that faded over time, and, to be honest, I've followed a career path that sidestepped or suppressed precisely this kind of intense emotional confrontation. I guess I was never meant to be the kind of veterinarian who's ready with a comforting word or a shoulder to cry on.

Ten thousand cats and dogs are eu- thanized in the United States every day.

Best make that ten thousand minus one.

"This does not bode well," I say out loud, my mind moving beyond this specific fiasco to everything else I will have to en- dure in order to get out of the mess I'm in. How I crave the soothing dead silence of my regular audience.

What am I going to do? This crisis just shifted from tricky to disastrous. It's more than the golden fur ball staring up at me expectantly; it's the bigger problem of what forced me back to this very room, to this very town, for the first time in twenty-five years.

Suddenly Frieda's tail stops wagging, like she's tuned in to something. And that's when we both hear it—the jingle of the bell over the front door.

Is Mr. Charcoal Suit back to see the deed is done?

« 2 »

We hear the sound of approaching foot-falls. There's nowhere to hide, and I can't think of a good explanation.

A cursory double tap, the examination room door swings open, and Frieda and I stare back like thieves with our hands (and paws) in the till.

"Evening, Dr. Mills. You're still here? How was your first night? Who's your golden oldie?"

Frieda is unwilling to wait for a formal introduction and goes straight into an un-restrained and physical greeting similar to the one she bestowed upon me.

"Lewis, meet Frieda. My one and only case of the evening."

Dr. Fielding Lewis is an odd little man—ebullient, a close-talker sporting a ridiculously full head of gray hair for a seventy-three-year-old and, despite the late hour, obviously inclined to wearing colorful, silk bow ties. According to Lewis, he and the late Dr. Robert Cobb were best friends and professional rivals for the last fifteen years. And though he only works part-time, Lewis is the saving grace of this veterinary practice, a practice still burdened with the preposterous name The Bedside Manor for Sick Animals. What remains of this business may be on life support, but without the selfless dedication of Dr. Fielding Lewis, I have no doubt it would have flatlined long ago.

Lewis tries to tear himself away from Frieda's embrace. "What's she in for?"

I work an imaginary itch at the back of my head.

"Well, I was having a hard time processing what I was asked to do."

Lewis stops patting Frieda and considers me. "What exactly were you asked to do?"

Frieda tolerates his dereliction of duty

for no more than two seconds. She barks, and it is his turn to relent.

I wince. "Put her to sleep."

He stops patting Frieda again. I can't tell whether the dog is incredulous or offended. Either way, she circles back to settle beneath my right palm.

"It can be tricky working alone on a rambunctious animal," says Lewis. "I'd be more than happy to restrain her while you give the injection."

"That's not the problem."

I hesitate and watch Lewis cant his head ever so slightly to one side, pushing his lips forward into a pensive pucker.

"Then what is?"

He's waiting for an answer, but at the same time, I can tell he doesn't expect to get one. How do I put the feelings into words? Answer: don't even try. Stick with what you know best.

"The problem is killing a dog charged with bouts of inappropriate urination based on nothing more than hearsay and circumstantial evidence."

Lewis flashes a wry smile. "But, Cyrus, I thought you of all people would be used to death and detachment."

"I am," I say, though this synopsis of my career as a pathologist feels a little harsh.

"Our profession has an enormous responsibility when it comes to euthanasia. We're a service industry, and sadly, in the eyes of the law, pets are still considered property. Of course there are times when I wish I could convince an owner not to put an animal to sleep, but once the decision's been made, and we've accepted the task, our duty is to see it through. We're not in the animal rescue business. We simply can't afford to be."

Lewis puts the lecture on hold as he considers me. "Is there something else you're not telling me?"

I sense he's pushing buttons, continuing to probe, trying to crack me open. Perhaps I can get away with something evasive but still true.

"You see, Fielding . . . the thing is . . . um . . . I've never been the person actually responsible for the act of taking a life."

Lewis leans back. "You've never performed a euthanasia?"

I shake my head.

"Do you want me to do it?"

The creature remains content below my hand, gently panting, eyes closed. "Certainly not."

"Then what the hell are you going to do?" I think this is the first time I have heard Lewis raise his voice. "I mean this does not exactly constitute exemplary professional conduct, and for a man in your, how shall I put it, *delicate* situation, I'm pretty sure any hint of misrepresentation or deceit is the last thing we need."

I wipe my palms down my face and rest my fingertips over my lips. He's absolutely right. The word *delicate* is an understatement. You see, in order to practice veterinary medicine at Bedside Manor, I need to be licensed in the state of Vermont, which should be a formality for an appropriately credentialed doctor of good standing. However, for a doctor whose out-of-state license has been suspended, pending a hearing, it's a major problem. Lewis is the only person who knows. It doesn't matter that the charges against me are a total fabrication, a vendetta by a former employer for filing a wrongful termination lawsuit. It doesn't matter that this has nothing to do with clinical negligence or malpractice. What does matter (more than I can tell him to his face) is that Lewis believes and supports me, 100 percent. That's why I explained to him that I would keep my head down, make sure my reputation remains unsullied and beyond reproach, and no one will be the wiser. At least until I achieve what I set out to do with Bedside Manor. What could possibly go wrong?

"Thing is, there's something not right about this dog."

Lewis scoffs, realizes I'm serious, and comes over to squeeze my shoulder. He's way too touchy-feely for my liking.

"Cyrus, I don't mean to be critical, but *you* were the one who said you'd never worked a single day as a *real* veterinarian. Real was your word, not mine. Suddenly, with your very first case, you're telling me you have acquired a sixth sense about a maligned golden retriever."

I force a smile. "Indulge me. Let's give this dog the benefit of my doubt."

"What doubt?"

"Doubt about the owner's motive for getting rid of her."

Lewis releases his grip. "Who is the owner?"

The realization of my rookie mistake paralyzes the muscles of the old man's face.

"I'm sorry," I say, annoyed at the whiny high pitch of my voice. "He walked right in, demanding to put her to sleep. I've been in town one night, I've no idea what I'm doing, and my first customer demands I kill his dog. I wasn't thinking straight."

Lewis looks at the retriever. "I don't recognize her. Are we sure this is Frieda? I don't see a collar or a name tag."

"Frieda," I call. Frieda twitches her ears and stares directly at me. *"Quod erat demonstrandum."*

Lewis rolls his eyes, shakes his head. "Brandy," he calls. The dog formerly known as Frieda twitches her ears and stares directly at Lewis.

"Point taken," I say, "but I don't think he would have made up a name like Frieda."

Lewis does not look convinced. He begins to pace. Suddenly he stops. "Where's the consent form?"

My hesitation, raised finger, and slow inhalation tell him everything.

"So I'll assume you never discussed the disposition of the body, general or private cremation, the type of urn required, etcetera."

"I couldn't find the paperwork. I told you, it's been a long, long time since any of this stuff even crossed my mind."

"Cyrus, this is bad. This is exactly the sort of thing that will sink us before we even get started. I mean what if the dog has been stolen? What if she doesn't belong to the man who brought her in? What if he's a disgruntled neighbor who hates dogs? What if the dog is part of a custody dispute, and he's trying to punish his ex-wife by killing off her beloved retriever? You've got to wake up to the real world of veterinary medicine. The pet-owning public can be your conduit to the truth. If you want to keep this practice alive, you must learn to interact with them, you must learn to interpret their meaning, and you must learn that they are not always telling the truth."

I look away to stop myself from spilling the awful secret I'm keeping inside. "Who said anything about keeping this practice alive?"

*   *   *

Utterly discredited, I grab a can of weight-loss prescription dog food from a shelf in the waiting room and let Frieda drag me by her cord across the main work area, through a door out back, and up a stairway to the living quarters on the second floor. In the right hands this house might have been a fine sprawling Victorian, but as far as I can tell, it's a dilapidated husk of its former self—rotted siding, loose gutters, missing shingles, the list goes on and on. Household chores and maintenance were clearly low priorities for the late Doc Cobb. Bedside Manor may not be the house all the kids fear on Halloween, but I'm pretty sure its restoration lies beyond the budget of most TV home improvement shows.

At the top of the stairs there's a heavy door, meant to ensure privacy and help muffle the sounds of barking dogs. Frieda barges through, slips her leash, and takes off down the central hallway. She seems to know exactly what she is looking for—the kitchen. I follow her, ignoring the bubbling and peeling floral wallpaper as I pass the spare room that was deemed Dr. Robert

Cobb's office. The door is closed, and I have no desire to go inside. It's uncomfortable enough to be here in this part of the building. It's like I've been left alone in a stranger's home, and even though its smells, its settling creaks and moans, its chill, and its shadows spark many memories, I feel like a trespasser.

The golden sits on the cracked tile floor in front of a purple Post-it note stuck to the refrigerator door. It's from Mrs. Lewis. She's too kind. Knowing I was arriving today, this woman I've never met warmed up the house, made my bed, and stocked the refrigerator with a few basic provisions. A few? I open the door and discover the fridge is full, packed with enough labeled Tupperware containers of precooked meals for a week.

"I'm not sure you really need a last supper, but let's see if I can find . . ."

Am I talking to the dog? Of course not. I'm merely thinking aloud as I locate a can opener and an empty bowl. Frieda eats as you might expect, like she was headed for the electric chair.

While the retriever makes a thorough inspection of the rest of the house I take a seat at the dining room table, its hand-crafted oak surface obscured by a paper-work volcano overflowing with bills and statements and final notices. This flagrant disorganization is as physically unbearable as it is mind-boggling. Earlier in the day, I started to organize things into what's been paid and what's come due. So far, there's nothing in the paid pile. Lewis told me Cobb had been sick for months, but he and I both know the fiscal and managerial neglect of this practice has been years in the making. Cobb may have been lauded as a great veterinarian, but he was a lousy businessman. So far everything is so over-due that accounts have been closed and lines of credit canceled. It looks like the practice has not been able to purchase or restock any basic medications for several months. The service contract for the X-ray equipment has not been renewed and the company will no longer supply radiographic films or chemicals. All unopened envelopes bearing the name Green State Bank in their top left-hand corner have been stockpiled to create a precarious tower.

I rock forward and suddenly there's fur underneath my right hand. Frieda is back.

In less than an hour she's already become a creature of habit. "And you're not helping matters." Okay, this time I admit it, I'm talking directly to the dog. She watches the words leave my lips, and though she cannot possibly understand me my mind provides her with a silent comeback: "And whose fault is that?"

I look at her. I look at the pile of bills. It's an easy call. "You want to go for a walk?"

Despite a hint of a low-country accent infecting my vowels, a new round of excitement tells me Frieda picked up on the *w* word. We head to the hallway closet. I find her a decent collar and leash and borrow some winter attire, which I am thankfully unaccustomed to wearing— duck boots, a winter coat, and a plaid cap with faux fur earflaps.

Having spent the better part of my life living well below the Mason-Dixon line, my expectation of winter means digging out a windbreaker and the possibility of a light frost. Stepping outside, I pine for the South. This cold is breathtaking. Lewis suggested I shave off my beard, saying, "Doctors shouldn't look like Grizzly Adams, even in Vermont." Now I wish I'd kept the facial hair. Someone has inserted tiny stiff frozen straws inside my nostrils, and I can feel the chill licking around my teeth and permeating bone. Did I mention how much snow they get up here? It's only January and they've already cracked one hundred inches.

It's a cloudy moonless night, so I'm reluctant to enter the cross-country ski trails through the woodlands out back. This leaves us with two options. Turn left out of the practice lot or turn right. Left takes you toward the center of town, not necessarily a good thing when you're walking a Lazarus dog. And I can't risk running into Frieda's mystery owner until I figure out what to do with her. So I turn right, toward the outskirts of suburban sprawl, Frieda intent on dislocating my shoulder.

I've always been a fast walker. Hate to dawdle. If you need to get from A to B, why not do it as quickly and efficiently as possible. But here in Siberia I discover a problem. The sidewalks offer about as much grip as a slick bobsled run. In patches, hand-tossed salt has cut through to asphalt or concrete, but for the most part I'm inclined to shuffle along like an old man with a bad case of hemorrhoids. Frieda has other ideas. She appears to have nails like crampons, clawing at the ice, driving forward while I windmill and flail in order to keep up. "Easy, Frieda, easy."

Two things become apparent. Frieda is not used to being walked on a leash and Frieda is inordinately fussy about going to the bathroom. Although a number of telephone poles and lampposts require careful consideration, she drags me a good five hundred yards up the street before finding a spot she deems acceptable. I wonder if this has something to do with her urinary problems. Ignoring a glance that implores me to avert my eyes and respect her privacy, I pay attention for straining, urine flow, urine volume, and the presence of a "clean finish." Her buildup and preparation may be more froufrou lapdog than hardy gundog, but as far as I can tell everything seems to be working just fine.

"All done?" Damn, there I go again. Worse still, I repeat the question in a whisper, as though fewer decibels will make this one-sided conversation acceptable.

Frieda scratches up a couple of icy stripes with her back paws, and to her dismay, I begin to head back in the direction we came. I'm not going to apologize—it's so cold I've lost all sensation in my face, and that pile of paperwork isn't going anywhere without me.

About halfway back to the house I notice something in front of us twinkling in the darkness. Before long it's become a concentrated spot of light, hovering, arcing back and forth, and then there's a figure, a woman, swinging a flashlight with each step she takes, a stocky four-legged creature by her side.

I turn up the collar on my winter coat, tug down on the brim of my hat, and rein in Frieda's leash a little tighter. By the time I've realized that the woman's disturbing Princess Leia haircut is actually a pair of bulky earmuffs, they are upon us, a black Labrador intent on saying hello. Like a novice water-skier behind a speedboat, the woman hangs on for dear life until the ice underfoot gets the better of her, the leash slips, and before I know it she is literally crashing into me.

"I'm so sorry," she exclaims, clutching me tightly. It's as if an enormous leech has glommed onto my body. And then, shining the beam of her flashlight in my face, she says, "Well, well. Lucky me, saved by a knight in shining armor."

Though it's hard to make out her features in the darkness, her tone of voice is distinctly frisky, and she's still holding on to my arm as we turn our attention to our dogs.

What's with encounters between unfamiliar dogs? Skip the handshake, the small talk, they are straight into "you sniff my naughty bits and I'll sniff yours."

"Now that's what I call speed dating," says the woman, leaning into me and uncomfortably eager to share her thoughts on the subject. "I'm Crystal, and the black Lab engaged in foreplay is—"

"Um . . . nice to meet you," I say, shucking myself from her grip as I try to pull Frieda away. "Come on . . . boy. We've got to get home." Did I really say *we*?

"At least tell me your name. You staying in Eden Falls?"

"You might say that," I say as I am walking away. "I'm"—I cough out the word— "Cyrus" as I wish her a good night, increasing my pace, eager to avoid any more inquiries. I don't look back, and thanks to my faux fur earflaps, I can't be sure, but I think I hear "Hey, that looks just like Frieda."

Everybody knows everybody in this town. But thankfully only 48 percent of eyewitnesses choose the right criminal.

Most anywhere else Frieda and I could sneak into some cheap motel with a pair of scissors and a bottle of Just for Men and I'd clip and dye the golden retriever into another black Labrador. But this is Eden Falls, Vermont, population 2,053, and based on this brief encounter, an allegation of dog-napping may be the least of my worries. The residents of this tiny backwater have always been hungry for any drama that might titillate their quiet existence. For fourteen years I've moved on with a modest, simple life, content to let my past fade into a forgotten darkness I never intended to disturb. Bedside Manor insists I take a look back. It's bad enough that I have to be here. It's bad enough that in order to see my money I must act like a regular animal doctor. It's bad enough that I'm working illegally on a suspended license from another state. But these concerns are nothing compared to the shameful truth lurking in my DNA. I have worked too hard to delete its existence, to get beyond the anger and disappointment, but now, back in Eden Falls, curious minds are poised to scrutinize me, expose me, and worst of all, make me accountable for who I really am—the only son of Dr. Robert Cobb.

Tuesday

At precisely eight o'clock the next morning I hear the after-hours doorbell—old-fashioned, shrill, and insistent—ringing in the second-floor hallway. I suppose it could be my first customer of the day. Then again, it could be Mr. Charcoal Suit, here to sign his consent form and pay off his bill for services I have totally failed to render.

I find Frieda lying down in front of the refrigerator. Perhaps by worshiping this appliance she thinks she will be rewarded with a tasty morsel trapped within.

The bell ringing intensifies from intermittent Morse code to a continuous electric trill. It seems the person pressing the door-bell will not be denied. This cannot be good. I lock the dog in the kitchen (just in case) and race downstairs to the front door.

"Can I help you?"

There's a tall thin gentleman in a suit and tie and a long cashmere coat clutching a leather briefcase, standing on the stoop. "Dr. Mills?"

The voice is familiar.

"Yes, I'm Dr. Mills."

The man allows a hint of relief to taint his stern expression.

"Mr. Critchley. Green State Bank. You stopped answering my e-mails and phone calls."

His tone is clipped, and he makes no attempt to shake my hand, as though he's only here to state facts.

"There's been some . . . developments . . . concerning your father's will. I thought it prudent to meet with you, face-to-face. There are still papers to be signed, details to clarify. I trust my timing is not too inconvenient."

His words hang in cartoon bubbles of frosty condensation. Oh yes, the last will and testament of one Dr. Robert Cobb, which arrived at my Charleston apartment ten days ago. Let's be honest, in the twenty-first century, it's strange to learn of your father's death by tearing open a real paper envelope. Sure, it was a shock, but our relationship was, to put it politely, problematic. Still, where the discovery of my mother's passing sucked all the air from my chest, the loss of Bobby Cobb did fill me with a certain sense of regret. Snail mail had taken a while to find me, and though the circumstances were totally different, for the second time in my life, I had missed burying a parent.

The details of the will are quite straightforward. Cobb has left me Bedside Manor, the property and the business. And, despite the somber circumstances, the timing was fortuitous. Without my license to practice, I can't get another job in South Carolina or anywhere else for that matter. In order to get my license reinstated, to defend my actions, prove my innocence, and restore my professional reputation, I need money for legal fees. I'd already blown through the contents of my 401K and was forced to sell my condo and move into a rental, so when Bedside Manor fell into my lap, there was nothing to think about—sell the building, sell the practice, take the money, and run back to Charleston as fast as I can, where I can resolve my license issues, clear my name, and start over.

"No, come in," I say and lead him upstairs to the dining room and my unsightly pile of paperwork. "Sorry, but I don't seem to be able to get Internet service up here." I pull out my cell phone, flip it open—dead. I offer up an apologetic smile, flash him the blank screen. "Forgot to charge it again."

The bank's attorney ignores my excuses. He's focused on my Green State Bank envelope tower.

"It's . . . well . . . a little overwhelming," I say, trying to ignore the contempt mounting in his twitching lips. "Please, have a seat."

Critchley is a gangly praying mantis of a man, all pointy knees and elbows as he tries to cross his legs and get comfortable. He keeps his coat wrapped tightly around him as he sits, as if he wants to insulate himself from this contagious fiscal irresponsibility.

Frieda lets out a wary bark, begins to scratch, and Critchley turns toward the closed kitchen door.

"It's only the dog," I say.

"What kind of a dog?"

Critchley places his briefcase on his lap, somewhat defensively. I wonder if he's had a previous run-in with a canine in his job as a well-dressed repo man. After my close call with the owner of the black Labrador last night, best to be misleading with the truth.

"Rottweiler." I might have stopped there, but I've been dealing with snooty lawyers for months and his uppity attitude gets to me. "One hundred and forty pounds of pure steel. Hates strangers, but old . . . Typhoon . . . will be fine so long as he doesn't catch a whiff of fear. And hopefully that kitchen door will hold up. You have dogs of your own, Mr. Critchley?"

Critchley shakes his head. I can tell I've unnerved him. He pops the latch on his briefcase and lets me stew in silent dis-comfort before making a show of remov-ing a single piece of paper. His features tend toward gaunt rather than chiseled and he sports a haircut cropped to near military specifications. It suits his take-no-prisoners coldness.

"Before I get to the will proper, I thought it might be helpful to see, in actual dollars and cents, the enormity of the challenge that lies before you. This document summarizes the various liens against both this property and the veterinary business operated by the late Dr. Robert Cobb, the . . . Bedside Manor for Sick Animals?" He pretends to have difficulty focusing on the words.

I shrug. "It's a long story."

But Critchley eases back in his chair, like he's got all the time in the world.

I force a little laugh through my nose. "It's stupid," I say, willing him to read my discomfort as I try to fold into myself.

"Now I'm curious."

I find that imaginary itch at the back of my head. Body language accounts for between 50 and 70 percent of all communication. Clearly, for Mr. Critchley, it may as well be Mandarin.

"This house was originally going to be called Benton Manor after Jack Benton, the guy who wanted it built as his Vermont retreat. It was never completed."

"Jack Benton, as in Benton Copper and Gold Incorporated, the mining company?"

I nod. "According to my mother, Benton had elaborate homes across the country, but he was a fanatical leaf-peeper, came up here every fall, always brought his Labradors. Inevitably his dogs needed a vet."

At this point I half expect Critchley to interject "Dr. Robert Cobb," but the attorney says nothing. It seems I must continue.

"This was back when Cobb had graduated from veterinary school. He was in debt, renting an apartment, and trying to earn a living making house calls. He and Benton hit it off. Benton gets sick, cuts back on his travels, decides to give the property away."

"For free?"

"Not quite. He insisted it be used as a veterinary clinic and be named Bedside Manor."

Critchley appears more pained than confused.

"That's ridiculous. Nobody gives away substantial equity like this without ensuring recognition for the name of the donor at the very least."

"I don't know what to tell you. All I know is, before he died, Jack Benton already had a library, an oncology wing at Johns Hopkins, a regional airport, and a highway named after him. Apparently he didn't want a veterinary hospital."

Critchley appears to mull this over.

"I've no pets of my own, but I've heard from several reliable sources that your late father was a well-loved member of the community and had quite a gift for communication."

Though I manage a curt smile, I'm amazed at how much it hurts to hear this compliment, even after all these years. It spotlights one of the saddest keepsakes of my childhood. Sure, Cobb had a knack for mixing charm and compassion, no doubt about it, but at what price? If you're always there for your patients, how can you be there for your son? It smarts to hear Critchley's praise, like bumping an old bruise that's refused to fade away. Growing up I would have killed for a father with a gift for communication *with me.*

"Yeah, well it's complicated," I say instead of what I'm thinking.

Thankfully, Critchley appears no more interested in hearing about said complications than I am willing to share. "Before I go any further, Dr. Mills," he stresses my last name, "I need to see official proof of your relationship with the deceased?"

I reach into my wallet, pull out my South Carolina driver's license, and hand it over. Then I pick up the FedEx package on the table next to the envelope tower. Inside, together with my copy of the will, there's my birth certificate, and a notarized copy of the court order approving the change in my last name.

He scrutinizes everything, going all TSA on me. He takes his time with the birth certificate. "Mills was your late mother's maiden name? Ruth Mills?"

"Correct," I say, stamping a little authority on the word in the hopes that I will shut him down before he asks the obvious question about the name change—why?

Thankfully Critchley makes no further comment, returns the proof, and hands over his summary. "As you can see, at the time of his death Dr. Cobb owed money to virtually every company with which he did business, from purveyors of pet food through to disposal of biohazardous material. I've listed the dollar amount for each, and the total is at the bottom of the page."

"I'm led to believe Cobb was quite ill for the last few months of his life."

Critchley hesitates but doesn't blink an eye. "Not my problem."

But the way he looks at me makes me feel like he's also saying, *and clearly not your problem, either.*

"Dr. Cobb did apply for a second mortgage on this property," he says.

"A second mortgage? But this house was a gift. When did he get his *first* mortgage?"

"About twenty years ago. Not sure how it got approved. Probably back when he was filing joint tax returns with your late mother."

Mom worked from home. As I said, she was a veterinary pathologist like me. Stained slides of diseased tissue arrived in the post in the morning, were read under a microscope, and a written report was sent out in the afternoon mail.

"Naturally this second mortgage application was denied. We did, however, offer to consolidate his debt, at, I might add, an extremely competitive and reasonable rate of interest."

With this he hands over a second sheet of paper. I see the figure the bank requires the practice to pay off on a monthly basis. The neon pink highlight only makes the number seem even more ridiculous.

"You sure this is correct? From what I've seen of the books, the practice hasn't come close to *ever* making that kind of a minimum monthly interest payment."

"Again, Dr. Mills, not my problem."

Sensing Critchley's eyes upon me as I scan the numbers, I look up. He may not be gloating but I can tell he's enjoying himself.

"That brings me to the will." He pauses for effect. "I regret to inform you that the original offer to buy the practice has been withdrawn."

I feel like there's a trapdoor where my diaphragm used to be. It flies open and my heart drops through.

"What?"

"As we previously discussed, the buyer

always had reservations based on the practice barely sustaining even a part-time veterinarian in Dr. Cobb's associate, Dr. Lewis."

"Yes, but you said if I plug the holes in the schedule, fill in the gaps, demonstrate there's enough business for one full-time vet, the sale shouldn't be a problem. You made it sound like it was a done deal. You even promised it would take no more than two weeks to go through."

Critchley remains impassive, gently pushing his open palm in my direction, ordering me to stop.

"I have, however, secured an alternative buyer."

Any rush of relief is tempered by my irritation at the way he is dragging this out and a sense that he is still holding something back.

"Ever heard of a publicly owned company called Healthy Paws? They operate veterinary practices in thirty-six states?"

"Yes," I say. "Doc Lewis mentioned them to me. They're the big practice across the valley and our nearest competitor. Doc Lewis sneered at the very mention of Healthy Paws, a practice obsessed with what he called *conveyor belt medicine*, where everyone complains they never see the same vet twice. No pet ever gets out of there without a shot or a blood test. Nickel-and-dime you as soon as you set foot in the place, his words not mine."

"Well, whatever the case, I ran some of your figures past one of their managers." Critchley shakes his head in disgust. "In the past Healthy Paws would buy up pretty much any practice on its last legs, but in this economy, they are becoming increas-ingly risk averse. Bear this in mind when considering their offer."

He hands over another sheet of paper. Healthy Paws—*for those on all fours*. Hate that.

My eyes flick through the details, reach-ing the bottom line before my mind actu-ally registers the bottom line. "This can't be right."

"That's the offer."

"You're telling me Healthy Paws will only buy the practice if I can prove my monthly production figures meet their definition of an 'acceptable minimum.' Otherwise there's no deal."

"If it's any consolation, they are prepared to take the average over several months."

"But I don't have several months." Or a license to practice in Vermont. Or a license to practice anywhere for that matter. "And this monthly production figure"—I slap it with the back of my hand—"is pretty much the same as the minimum monthly interest payment you want me to pay the bank. It can't be done."

Critchley eases back in his chair, reaches into his briefcase one more time. It's obvious everything is going according to plan.

"That's why I took the liberty of having an alternative proposal drawn up."

"What's this?"

"It's the simplest solution, given your circumstances. The will places everything in your name and you sign everything over to the bank. We'd be more than happy to liquidate what assets remain in the practice together with the building and the associated land. It won't nearly cover all of your father's debt but at least *you* will be free and clear."

"You're saying I'd get absolutely nothing, no money whatsoever."

"Correct. But think of it this way, you won't be losing any of your own money either."

I get to my feet. I have a habit of pacing when I'm trying to think.

"How long do I have to decide?"

Critchley can barely conceal his glee.

"I'm supposed to call Healthy Paws at nine this morning, let them know either way. Their deadline, not mine. That's why I came over first thing."

I look past him to the bay window with the view of the shrunken backyard and the hiking trails behind the property. The snow's crust sparkles in the low morning sunlight, but it's the two trees in the foreground that have my attention. One is a mature apple tree, a Cortland, Mom's favorite, and I still remember the day she and I planted it as a sapling. The other is a huge oak. For months I begged Robert Cobb to help me build a tree house in its branches. For months he made excuses. Eventually I stopped asking. I told Mom I'd discovered I was afraid of heights. We both knew the real reason—I didn't have any friends to share it with.

I raise an index finger, hoping for a few minutes to decide, striding back and forth between the fireplace and an empty win-dowed curio cabinet. The cabinet used to be home to a collection of Lenox china. Cobb must have sold it when the bills began to mount.

There's clawing at the kitchen door. Frieda sounds like an enormous and highly motivated rodent.

"Dr. Mills?"

This is ridiculous. Bedside Manor is supposed to be a windfall, a financial lifeline to professional vindication, not a shortcut to personal bankruptcy.

Then I notice something faint etched onto the plaster wall, lost in the shadows next to the barren dresser. I take a step closer and see a series of short faded horizontal lines, seven or eight of them, one above the other, each scratchy pencil mark accompanied with a date, handwritten by my mother.

"Dr. Mills?"

The fog inside my head clears enough for me to hear Ruth Mills say, "Shoulders back, head straight. There you go. Almost two inches taller than last year."

"I must insist, Dr. Mills. I have other business to attend to."

I come back. "Let me get this straight," I say to the man studying his watch. "If I turn this business back around, prove I can make their minimum monthly profit, Healthy Paws will buy it as a going concern."

"In theory, that's correct."

"So, in theory, I can sell in the next thirty days."

"Yes, but as you said yourself, it's impossible. If you want my opinion, I'd grab a few keepsakes, pack my bags, and head back to—"

"Where do I sign?"

Finally I appear to have taken Critchley off script.

"Man has a choice," I say, "and it's a choice that makes him a man."

Critchley's expression switches from incredulous to mystified.

"It's a quote. From *East of Eden*. Cal Trask, James Dean's first big role."

The man from Green State appears none the wiser. Not that I care. I can convince myself that this has nothing to do with sentiment and everything to do with Critchley's provocation. How dare he tell me what's possible and what's not. And besides, I really don't have anything more to lose.

"What makes you think you could do better than your father?" he asks.

I've got nothing, no idea, but I'm determined to finagle some sort of a reply. "I'll be using a completely different business model," I say with unabashed confidence.

"Really? Different how?"

It's obvious he's humoring me.

"For starters," I say, "billing for services rendered has always been slack and tardy. Stuff gets overlooked and forgotten and bad debt ignored. As soon as I've worked my way through that lot I'll have a better sense of where things have gone wrong and how I can put them right."

Critchley waits for more. "That's it?" he says, looking pleased that his low expectations of me were correct. "You've never run a veterinary practice before, have you?"

This is not a line of questioning I want him to pursue. I brace, but he changes course. "If I were in charge, I'd start making cuts right now."

I nod, say nothing.

"For example, your health insurance costs are ridiculous."

"They are?"

"Yes, they are. You have only two employees, and yet you offer one of the most expensive health care plans in the state."

Two employees? Other than Lewis, who else is on the payroll?

"Choose a cheaper plan and you'll save yourself some money right there."

Frieda lets loose with a sequence of booming barks that cause the kitchen door to reverberate. If Mr. Critchley does have other thoughts on the matter, he no longer wants to share them. He gets to his feet.

"Dr. Mills, by refusing to sign over Bedside Manor to the bank this morning, whether or not you sell to a prospective buyer, your minimum monthly payment on your consolidated debt comes due thirty days from today. However, given the nature of this speculation, my boss will insist on some sort of a . . . good faith payment . . . long before that date. Let's say twenty-five percent. Something to prove you're on track. Something to prove we are not about to throw more good money after bad. You understand?"

"When?"

Critchley hesitates, and I can't help but wonder if he's making this up as he goes along.

"End of business this week."

"But that's only four days from now."

"Best I can do, given the circumstances." He pulls out an imposing document, I presume a contract. "You don't have to sign this. It's not too late to change your mind."

I clear a little space on the table and my Green State Bank envelope tower comes crashing down. Critchley shakes his head, passes me the contract, and he's about to hand over a pen when he catches himself.

"Do you understand what you are doing? With the business transferred to your name, you become personally responsible for every bill and every angry creditor who demands their money. In essence, you will have to pay for the sins of your father."

Too late, I think. It's one thing to go ignored by your father growing up, but the wrong he did to me when I lost my mother was *his* sin and I've already been paying these last fourteen years.

"What do you say we make it Saturday, not Friday? Five days from now. You can't deposit the money until Monday either way. Call it part of my new business model, expanding hours to include the weekend."

Critchley shakes his head. "You really think the extra day will make a difference?"

"Definitely. Swing by on Saturday to pick up your check. I guarantee the folks from Healthy Paws will make me an offer in less than three weeks," I say, trying but failing to sound confident as I sign on the dotted line.

"Let's hope so, Dr. Mills. Though I think you're making a colossal mistake, I applaud your desire to keep your father's legacy alive."

I finish the *s* in Mills with a flourish and look up.

"Trust me, Mr. Critchley, this venture has nothing to do with him." I stop short of adding "and everything to do with solving my legal troubles and getting back to an uncomplicated life."

I have time to catch the mischief in his eyes, a glint that says, *you're not fooling me,* before Frieda begins to bark again—Critchley's discomfort around dogs my only consolation.

"Typhoon's hungry," I say. "He wants his breakfast."

Critchley snatches up the signed form

and takes it with him rather than returning it to his briefcase.

"See you at week's end, Dr. Mills."

He's already halfway out of the dining room, but he knows where I am headed.

"Thanks," I say. "Now if you don't mind letting yourself out."

I time Frieda's release to perfection— her body slams into the door at the top of stairs, right on his heels.

<< **4** >>

"See anything like this before?"

The question feels like an accusation, hissing between the clenched dentures of a wizened old woman, one Mrs. Silverman, currently regarding me with unconcealed hostility. I'm grateful for the six-month-old husky by her side who ignores me altogether. His sudden focus on scratching off certain portions of his flesh has rendered me invisible. Virtually reptilian, the skin around the poor creature's eyes, muzzle, ears, and feet has been replaced by thick and crusty scales that exude the aroma of fermenting yeast.

"Doc Lewis has been trying to fix up Kai for months and I can already tell"—at this point Mrs. Silverman narrows her steely eyes and juts a hairy, powdery chin in my direction—"you're no Doc Lewis. Or Doc Cobb for that matter."

She said, Doc Cobb, not "your father." I can't tell whether she's being crafty or clueless. Either way, she'll get no argument from me. Not counting last night's failed attempt at Frieda's euthanasia, it is now Kai who has the dubious honor of being my first clinical conundrum as a *real* veterinarian.

"Well," I say, "I'd like to give it a shot, if that's okay, ma'am."

It's hard to know whether she recoils from my "foreign" accent or me. Ridiculous. Live in the South for a while and even a die-hard Yankee will pick up a subtle lilt and an occasional drawl. My inflection has a hint of Rhett Butler at most. She acts like all she hears is pure hillbilly. Perhaps I should let her know I was born in nearby Burlington.

Mrs. Silverman huffs as I come around the examination table to take a closer look at Kai. I notice how she avoids physical contact with him, as though feeling sorry for him does not entail actually touching him. Kai, it seems, is the leper who deserves a cure but until such time remains unsightly.

Despite their appearance, Siberian huskies are not actually wolves. Wolves survived the Ice Age, whereas huskies only came to the States in the early twentieth century. Predatory menace has been traded for big periwinkle eyes reaching out to me, begging for a scratch. I look over at Mrs. Silverman—she's acting hawkish, ready to attack my professional shortcomings. It seems I have no choice. I command my lips to smile, take a step forward, press my fingertips into the skin between his shoulder blades, and begin to scratch.

It's disgusting—greasy keratin, fungi, and all manner of secondary bacteria infesting my cuticles. Why didn't I put on a pair of gloves? The only upside, and it's minor, is Kai's response—arching his spine into the contact, tail wagging, obviously thrilled by my manual exfoliation technique.

As soon as I offered to see appointments last night, Lewis insisted on giving me a crash course in the art of a thorough physical examination. *It's like riding a bike, once you learn you never forget.* The thing is I feel as though I am going through the motions, petting rather than palpating. I try my best to remember the highlights from Lewis's lesson in bedside manner. *When you're listening to the chest with your stethoscope, be sure to let your eyes drift around the room like you're concentrating.* My attempt at rolling my eyes probably looks as though I'm about to faint. *Nod every now and then, and don't forget to smile. Owners like that sort of thing. Makes them think you can actually hear something.* My nod is more of a spasm, my smile distinctly nervous, and the frown on Mrs. Silverman's face suggests she is far from impressed.

However, I do know that Kai likes when I scratch any crusty area of his skin because he melts and thanks me for the distraction and temporary relief. He dislikes, though, when I examine the cracked and ulcerated webs of his footpads, pulling away and showing me his teeth. Trouble is I can't tell if he's actually going to bite me or giving me fair warning. I'm totally out of practice interpreting the message in his coarse communication, and as a result, I'm hopelessly jumpy. I must look like I'm ready to run screaming from the room, jazz hands fluttering overhead.

"Well?" says Mrs. Silverman.

I make a show of the raised eyebrows and the stern countenance of someone who is clearly impressed and not someone who is clearly clueless. *If you don't know what to say or do, take a rectal temperature, it will give you a few extra minutes to think.*

"Let me take his temperature."

Thermometer in place, I consider the dog's age.

"Inherited diseases of the husky. What have I got? Hip dysplasia. Genetic eye diseases: juvenile cataracts, corneal dystrophy, and progressive retinal atrophy. These can occur with any eye color. Then there is . . ."

"What are you mumbling on about?"

Her question brings me back into the moment. The dog's age has to be important, the distribution of lesions, and the fact that they involve very specific parts of the body. And that's when a picture forms in my mind. As usual, I've jumped straight to a conclusion and a strange one at that. For some reason I see the black-and-white image of a child, eyes letterboxed for anonymity, from a textbook of, of all things, *human* skin disorders.

"I'm assuming Doc Lewis ruled out the possibility of parasites?"

I check Kai's temperature—perfectly normal.

Mrs. Silverman stares through me, offers her dog a pitying glance, and shakes her head.

"Course he has," she says, and under her breath I hear her add, "you damned fool." My fingers begin to twitch, and Mrs. Silverman notices, forcing me to shove my hands under my armpits.

"Look, if you ain't seen nothing like it, speak up and we'll be on our way. And don't be thinking I'm paying for this visit. I'm only here out of loyalty to Doc Cobb and Doc Lewis. Just as easy for me to go to that fancy new practice in Patton. Bet they'd have the answer for me."

She makes a grab for Kai's leash and gets out of her chair, surprisingly spry for her years. After my conversation with Mr.

Critchley from Green State Bank and his insistence on a good faith payment, I can't afford to lose a single client.

And if you are totally clueless, try, "This thermometer must be broken. I'm going to grab a new one," then head out back and try to look up what's wrong.

"No, please." I snap, the desperation in my voice giving her pause. "If you could bear with me for one more minute, Mrs. Silverman." I pat the air between us, hoping she will sit back down. "I think my thermometer might be broken. I'll be right back."

I exit the examination room by a side door marked PRIVATE and enter the large work area containing a bank of cages, two dog runs, an old soapstone sink, and a wall of cabinets, counters, and drawers, home to pills, capsules, ointments, and syrups.

"Ah, Cyrus, good morning. Decide what you're going to do with that golden retriever of yours?"

Fielding Lewis watches me over the rim of his coffee cup, leaning into the counter-top, the *Eden Falls Gazette* spread out before him. Today's bow tie has a New Orleans feel—purple, gold, and green fleurs-de-lys.

"Not exactly," I say, scanning the room for a hard drive or a monitor. "Has the man who brought her in been back to sign the paperwork?"

Lewis shakes his head.

"Someone recognized her last night when I took her for a walk."

"Really," says Lewis. "Well, I've never seen her before. Maybe her vet's in Patton?"

"Maybe. What d'you think of me taking her to an adoption center? Or a retriever rescue group?"

"Fine. Do it. Too bad you can't use the 'Wall of Fame.'"

Lewis reads my confusion and explains. "Don't tell me you haven't noticed the wall next to the front door? The one covered with dog photos?"

I shake my head.

"It's like a lasting tribute to all the dogs Bobby Cobb found homes for over the years. If someone came across a stray dog, if a dog needed to be adopted because its owner was relocating or lost a job or died,

Cobb posted the pet's picture on the wall. Made sure they found a good home. People even joked about him being the Patron Saint of Lost Dogs."

"Wait a minute," I say, "last night you told me we're not in the animal rescue business, that we can't afford to be."

"We can't. Who do you think was providing food for these dogs while they were waiting to be adopted? Let alone paying for vaccines, worm, flea, and tick treatments?"

"He did it all for free?"

Lewis nodded. "There's not even a donation box up front. Don't look so surprised. You've seen the figures for this practice. Cobb was running it into the ground through kindness."

I'm not in the least bit surprised. Bad business labeled as one more saintly act by the pet lovers of Eden Falls sounded about right. What Lewis was misreading was my look of irritation. Yet again, Cobb would go out of his way to provide you with a good home, befriend a lost soul, so long as you had four legs.

"Take my advice," says Lewis, "when it comes to Frieda and finding a rescue center, you'd best stay outside of a thirty-mile radius from Eden Falls."

Good idea, everybody knows everybody in this town. "You know, I'm pretty sure the owner was lying about her urination problem."

I catch the distressed look on Lewis's face.

"Act fast, young man. Your good conscience will not save you from the disciplinary committee of the Vermont State Veterinary Board."

"Uh-huh," I manage.

"How's the charming Ethel Silverman?" Lewis takes a sip from his cup, but it does nothing to hide his smile.

"Fabulous. Where's your computer?"

"You'll find what you need in that cabinet, over there." Lewis gestures with his eyes.

I open the doors. There are three shelves on each side containing neatly organized textbooks, periodicals, and magazines. I'm paralyzed. "Bedside Manor doesn't have a computer?"

I hear a page being turned, a pause, and then, "Nope."

My hands are still attached to the door

handles. "No Wi-Fi, no Internet, no Google, nothing." I must remember to call Verizon and hook up some broadband for my laptop.

"What d'you mean, nothing? There are gold standard tomes in there."

I notice a sheet of paper taped to the inside of the cabinet's door. The blue ink of the neat copperplate may have faded over time, but I instantly recognize my mother's handwriting and begin reading a detailed outline of her filing system, followed by a plea to keep things tidy. Visualizing this order, this discipline, I feel an instant sensation of reassurance. It's soothing, but at the same time heavy.

I consult Mom's guide, reach in, and remove a textbook entitled *Veterinary Dermatology*. "I think Mrs. Silverman pretty much hates my guts."

"Of course she does," Lewis says in a quieter voice. "Ethel can be a cantankerous old bird on her best days. Finds something bad to say about everyone."

This remark stops me in my tracks. "Really," I say, turning to face him. "Does she know who I am?"

"No idea," says Lewis, swallowing his final mouthful of coffee. "Nice job with the beard, by the way."

I huff, wanting to let him know that life was easier without the need for facial grooming. Shaving is supposed to turn me into someone I never wanted to be.

"Did she recognize you?" asks Lewis.

"If she did she never said."

Lewis puts his mug down. "When were you last in Eden Falls?"

It's a tough question, not least because it points out a brazen and damning fact—I never returned for Bobby Cobb's funeral. "Fourteen years ago, three weeks before my mother died. But I didn't come back to Bedside Manor. I was at the hospital in Patton the whole time."

I can see her sitting up in bed, a red bandanna almost bright against her pale skin. She was joking, upbeat, and eager to get home. Together, we reviewed her blood work. She was in remission. She was going to be fine. This was never going to be my last visit.

Lewis fingers the handle of the mug. "And before that?"

"Not sure," I lie, knowing exactly when it

was. "It might have been the summer before my sophomore year of high school."

Lewis does this thing with his mouth, a chipped upper incisor worrying his lower lip. I've noticed this when he gets serious. "Was that when you moved down south?"

"Let's just say I was sent."

"You make it sound like you were deported."

I bite my tongue and choose my words carefully. "Mom never wanted me to go away. Cobb had the final word. He swore it was all about my education. Run-down regional high school versus an elite private school. Free tuition sealed the deal, thanks to my aunt Rachel."

"Your mom's sister, right?"

I nod. "She was the headmistress. Beaufort, South Carolina. From a purely academic standpoint it made perfect sense." I wait a moment and add, "At least it did to Cobb."

"So the pimply teenager never got back?"

I hesitate, the reasons beginning to stack up in the back of my throat like bile.

"Mom preferred to come down," I say and hope I can leave it at that.

Lewis nods, and I can't tell whether or not he knows he's on dangerous territory.

"Okay. Then the last time you were in Eden Falls you were maybe fourteen, fifteen, and now you're what?"

"Forty."

"Forty. Twenty-five years later, you've got a different last name and you speak with a funny accent. I'd say there's a reasonable chance Ethel Silverman has no clue that her new veterinarian is Bobby Cobb's son."

I think about this. I love the idea that I can maintain a sense of anonymity while I am in town, but it'll never happen, not in Eden Falls. And there's no way the estranged son can pretend to be keeping the Cobb legacy alive. So that means my only hope is to make money and sell the practice faster than the fierce scrutiny and the inevitable dissent.

I go back to *Veterinary Dermatology* and work my way down the *A*'s in the book's index.

"To be fair, not every word that comes out of Ethel Silverman's mouth is bad," says Lewis, turning over another page. "Think about what might happen if the new doctor in this little town of ours were to solve poor Kai's relentless skin disease when everybody else has been stumped? That's the kind of gossip this practice could use."

I shake my head. "Ever heard of 'acrodermatitis enteropathica'?"

"Never," says Lewis, "but it sounds good to me. You think that's what Kai has?"

My finger reaches the *B*'s in the index. Nothing.

"Damn, I can see this photograph of a child, a baby, from an Armed Forces Institute of Pathology textbook, and he's got exactly the same kind of crusty scabs on his face and hands as Kai. And I can even see the name of the disease—acrodermatitis enteropathica—and I'm fairly certain it's caused by a dietary deficiency."

"Of what?"

I grit my teeth, willing the answer to shake loose from somewhere deep inside my brain. Incredibly, nothing happens. How can that be? This new job has my synapses turned inside out. "Can't remember."

Lewis moves into my personal space and doesn't give it a second thought. "How d'you do that?" he asks.

"Do what?"

"Recall that kind of obscure detail."

"It's what I do," I say.

"But why study human disease?"

I'm confused. "Disease is disease, whether you're human or a duck-billed platypus. There's a lot of overlap. Besides, I like comparative pathology."

Lewis flashes his bushy gray brows. "Hey, if it helps find a cure for Kai."

"Yeah, but don't forget what they say about hearing the sound of hoofbeats?"

Lewis nods. "A good clinician should think horses and not zebras."

"Exactly—well, I think unicorns. Why do you think I have the term *acrodermatitis enteropathica* stuck in my head?"

"At least you've got something to go on. Of all the possible causes of skin disease, you've already narrowed it down to diet. From there, how hard can it be?"

Lewis is right. Most deficiencies are caused by a lack of vitamins or minerals. Once more I reach for *Veterinary Dermatology,* find *V* in the index, and within seconds, Vitamin A deficiency is starting to look good. Then I catch the phrase "generalized scaling." Kai's lesions are in very specific locations of his body. The jarring "incorrect answer" buzzer sounds in my head and I'm about to move on when a list of differential diagnoses catches my eye. I flick back to the index, to the letter Z, flick forward to the appropriate text, and discover the clinical signs of zinc-responsive dermatosis. And there it is, the canine equivalent of a disease of children called "acrodermatitis enteropathica," a congenital zinc deficiency causing characteristic skin lesions in infants as they discontinue breast milk.

"Whatever you think you've discovered, whatever you think the cure might be, there will always be a certain client who needs to see actions and not just hear long words. Ethel Silverman is the kind of client who needs something . . . how shall I best put this . . . tangible."

Lewis's rant yanks me from my page.

"Round these parts, people prefer honesty to pussyfooting and bull, if you get my meaning. Let them have it. I promise you they'll respect you all the more."

Newspaper abandoned, Lewis is in the process of drawing up some white fluid from a glass bottle into a needle and syringe.

"Okay," I say, reluctantly, "so what you got there?"

Lewis grins, flicks the barrel with his finger, and recaps the needle. "Steroids. Kai will thank you for them and, if nothing else, for the next twenty-four to forty-eight hours, Ethel might even think you're going to restore her dog's skin to its former glory."

He makes a show of presenting the medication with two hands, like a sommelier proffering a bottle of fine wine for approval.

"I am," I say, accepting his injectable snake oil as I make for the examination room.

"Oh, and Cyrus," says Lewis. "Did you meet Doris this morning?"

"Doris?"

"Our receptionist."

Ah, the second employee on the payroll. "There was no one here."

Lewis does not look surprised. "You'll meet her later. She must have turned up when you were in with Mrs. Silverman."

"Where is she now?"

"She had some errands to run. We were quiet. She'll be back later. Oh, and she had a couple of messages for you."

I wait a beat.

"Well, she said there were two messages on the practice answering machine."

"She didn't tell you what they were? She didn't write them down before she left?"

Lewis laughs at my naïveté. "When you meet Doris, you'll understand."

I say nothing but think, *Can't wait.*

Back in my exam room I'm greeted by, "You took your time."

Whoa, tough customer.

"Sorry, just a few more questions, Mrs. Silverman, and I'll have you on your way."

Mrs. Silverman rolls her eyes, and suddenly I'm struck by her misplaced aggravation and Lewis's words of wisdom, and it is all the encouragement I need to harden my inquiry.

"You don't feed Kai regular dog food, do you?"

"Why?" she barks.

I will myself to keep going. "Because I'm betting you feed him something you concocted yourself, some kind of home-made diet."

Ethel Silverman fastens her eyes on mine. "I checked with his breeder first," she says, sounding way too uptight. "He said it would be okay, so long as I added a vitamin supplement, especially calcium for growing bones."

I've never played poker. Maybe I should take it up. Inside a fist-pump is brewing because this is exactly what I am looking for. Perhaps I can do assertive after all. "So what *does* he eat?"

Ethel sucks on her fake teeth, as though she can almost taste the answer. "Cottage cheese and cornflakes. It was meant to be temporary. Dog's a finicky eater."

"Well," I say. "I very much appreciate your honesty, ma'am, but here's the thing. Kai's diet is all wrong—too much calcium, too much cereal, and it's causing a deficiency in an essential mineral—zinc." I gesture to Kai. "That's why your dog's skin looks more like a crocodile than a husky."

Mrs. Silverman pulls out a practiced sideways glance. "How do we treat it, bearing in mind he'll turn his nose up at almost everything?"

"Simple," I say, "stop the cottage cheese, the cornflakes, and the supplements and begin feeding Kai regular dog food."

"You're not listening. I told you he don't like regular dog food."

She eases back in her chair, letting her chin fold into the tired wattle of her neck, and smirks.

What to do? I should have a decisive comeback. Instead I'm dumbstruck. I go with a sweaty forefinger and thumb stroking my naked chin, hoping this might pass as meaningful contemplation. *Veterinary Dermatology* didn't say anything about the patient with a sensitive palate and an owner with an attitude.

Eventually I ask, "You try dry or canned food?"

"Dry, of course. Canned food's messy, bulky, and besides, it's more expensive. You ever lived on Social Security?"

"Okay then," I say, rushing past her, out in the waiting room (still empty), to a shelf containing a selection of canned and dry dog food on display. I grab half a dozen cans, cradle them, and offer them to Mrs. Silverman.

"Told you, can't afford them."

I look down at Kai and he looks up at me, tail sweeping back and forth. He's not thinking about the food, he's thinking about the possibility of another scratch. It's that simple, and his need reaches out to grab

me. I look back at Ethel. She's still scowling, and I can't help but let loose with a
genuine smile as I shake my head.

"What?" she says after a beat, but her
tone tells me she's actually more curious
than annoyed.

I choose my words carefully. "Mrs.
Silverman, you don't know me and I doubt
you know what kind of doctor I am, but I'm
hoping that you trust Doc Lewis, that you
appreciate Doc Lewis must have some
faith in me, and that if nothing else, I truly
want to fix your dog's horrible skin problem
so that you and I will not have to see one
another again for a long, long time."

For a few seconds, the grimace distorting Ethel's face tells me this brutally honest approach may have backfired. Time to
backpedal.

"Look, I'll pay for the food," I say. "Let
me grab you a bag."

"Here," says Ethel, quick to root through
the pocket of her winter coat and pull out a
plastic shopping bag, no doubt previously
destined for a date with Kai's poop. I deposit my cache. "Now, you'll pay for them?"
she repeats.

"This is the deal," I say. "You try the diet,

Kai likes it, his skin gets better, and you find a way to pay me back. Preferably before the end of this week. Kai won't eat it or his skin fails to improve, we'll say we're even."

To my amazement, despite my offer and my plea, the inimitable Ethel Silverman still looks unconvinced. Then I remember the steroid shot.

"And before you go, I need to give Kai a quick injection. Make him feel better."

And like that, just as Lewis predicted, this obstinate old woman thaws enough to offer a nod of approval to my plan.

« 5 »

Like a dutiful Sherpa I lug Kai's food out to
Mrs. Silverman's salt-licked Subaru, her
appreciation little more than a grunt when
I wish her a good day.

"Nicely done, Cyrus," says Lewis, taking me by the arm before I can even wipe
my snowy shoes on the waiting room
doormat. "Now, I have another challenge
for you."

I'm in a daze as he leads me toward the
reception desk in the waiting room. It's still
unmanned. Time to look into Doris's job
description.

"I just gave away a boatload of free dog

food," I confess, embarrassed that I'm setting such a bad example. "Somehow we're going to have to get totally ruthless about making money."

Lewis is busy with a pen and paper, blithe to the particulars of my transaction with Ethel Silverman, as though finagling such deals with difficult clients comes with the territory. He stops writing and looks up at me. "And how d'you propose to do that?" he says. "Drive around the streets, trying to hit passing cats and dogs?"

"No idea, but if Bedside Manor is going to be"—I think about saying *sellable* but settle on—"profitable . . . then you and I are going to have to come up with ways to make that stupid doorbell chime more frequently. By the way, you okay if we work this Saturday? Try to pick up some extra business."

"Of course," says Lewis, "but right now I need you to go on a house call."

"Whoa there, I'm not ready to fly solo. At least here I've got you to back me up and a library of out-of-date textbooks. If my experience with Ethel Silverman is anything to go by, I've underestimated how different this work is from what I'm used to."

Lewis meets my eyes. "Rubbish. It's one more sick animal in search of a cure."

"Yeah, but you and I are used to looking at the same disease from a completely different perspective."

"I'm not with you," he says.

I hesitate. What's the best way to explain? "See, it may be the same disease, but you're used to being at one end, and I'm used to being at the other. You're the clinician, the hands-on guy, caught up with the client and the animal in the now. You're trying to define the disease and stop it in its tracks. As a pathologist, if I'm involved in a case, more often than not, it's already too late."

Lewis frowns. "I don't agree. Same disease, same treasure hunt. Whether you're a pathologist looking down a microscope or a clinician listening to a chest, you're hunting for clues that will yield the exact same prize—a diagnosis."

"But when you're a pathologist, time is on your side. Think about it, it's not as though the outcome can get any worse. A corpse rarely requires a prognosis."

"You're still searching for clues about

a particular disease, working backward is all."

"Yeah, but in a treasure hunt you need to follow the clues in a logical sequence, and sometimes my mind is like a frog on speed, it jumps all over the place."

Lewis scoffs. "Don't sell yourself short. You're a smart man. You're just rusty."

"No, I'm not, I wish it were that simple. In my final year of veterinary school I was assigned a dachshund with a digestive disorder. Every morning, before rounds, I'd find a colossal turd sitting in the dog's cage, almost as big as the dog itself. It made no sense. I became obsessed, trying to figure out how this tiny dog could possibly generate such a humongous stool."

"What was the dog's problem?"

"The dog's problem was me. The joker in our group eventually confessed to transplanting a fresh turd from *his* patient to *my* dachshund."

"And what kind of a dog was his patient?"

My cheeks grow warm. "Great Dane. As soon as I knew, it seemed so obvious."

"You're simply too trusting."

I shake my head. "I have a weakness for the obscure diagnosis. Can't help it. My training has me attentive to the smallest details. General practitioners don't need my help nailing down the easy stuff. They need me to unmask the weird and the wonderful. In my world a vomiting dog puts me on high alert for gastric ulcers, stomach cancer, *Helicobacter,* Zollinger-Ellison syndrome, and a whole lot more. I'm never going to see simple food poisoning or motion sickness, or likes to lick frogs, or needs to be wormed."

"Hey, you play to your strengths." He pauses. "I'm told your mother was the same way," he says in a softer voice, as though he knows he's taking a risk broaching the subject.

I take in Bobby Cobb's best friend. There's not a hint of retribution or malice in the old man's eyes. Quite the opposite in fact. It's like he's pleading, begging me to clear the air. I can only imagine what Cobb must have told him about his son. For that matter, how much did Cobb share with the devoted pet owners of Eden Falls?

"I wanted to be a pathologist, like her," I say. "She always taught me to relish order, logic, and the challenge of working a case from back to front, long before I discovered the upside of *not* being face-to-face with the person who loves a sick animal."

Lewis looks into me, and I notice his eyes smile before his lips.

"You get used to it. You do. Give it time."

"There's a lot less pressure when a disease has had its fun. Everything is in the past tense. It's like reading a murder mystery and going straight to the end to find out whodunit. It's like standing at the bottom of a cliff with the dead body and all you have to do is look up and wonder, *did he fall or was he pushed* and why. No one's going to ask you to save him."

Lewis squeezes my upper arm, and I shy away as politely as possible. "What matters is you're here, that you came back to accept the terms of your father's will."

I should point out that I have not been exactly forthcoming about my plans for Bedside Manor, but I say nothing. I know, I know, but right now I don't have the heart to tell Lewis that, one way or another, I'm determined to sell the place and he's going to be out of a job. Truth is, I still need him to show me the ropes.

"Don't give me that look," he says.

"What look?"

"Like you just sucked on a lemon. Eden Falls isn't such a bad place to hang your hat. You like to ski?"

"Not really."

"Spectacular hiking. Especially in the fall."

"I prefer to be near the ocean."

"If you like culture, Burlington's not far."

"I live in Charleston, one of the most cultural small cities in the country."

Lewis regards me like a teacher regarding a student who's always armed with a surly comeback. "I'm not going to lie," he says, "the residents of this town are an odd, wary bunch, slow to warm up to visitors. But I promise you, once they do, a more genuine, straightforward but kind group of folks you will not meet."

I breathe out. The sound is something between a growl and an exasperated sigh. Lewis means well, but he should know that Eden Falls ranks somewhere between the Strait of Hormuz and the Korengal Valley as places in the world I would least like to visit, let alone "hang my hat." Fourteen years and a thousand miles away was morphine for my past. Back in Eden Falls, my father's will (what an apt term) promises nothing but flashbacks, ghosts, and whispers behind cupped hands. Trouble is, the only way out is through.

"Look," Lewis releases his grip but remains close by, "this house call is for one of my favorite clients. I told him all about you. I am drawing you a map."

Lewis scribbles lines and the names of certain landmarks as points of reference. He doesn't notice my concern over the phrase, *I told him all about you.*

"How much did you tell him?"

Fielding stops his map making and looks at me. Though his shaggy gray thatch of hair defies his years, time has furrowed the leather of his face into creases and crow's-feet that beg to differ. He has to angle his head up to make eye contact, but when he does the wisdom wrinkles create an expression verging on disappointment.

"I told him you were a good man," he says, his tone soft but even. "I told him I'd trust you to look after my own dog. Should I have said more?"

My eyes fall to the floor. Like I said, I tend to jump to conclusions, and they're not always the right ones. I shake my head and come back with a weak, "No."

There's that reassuring squeeze on my upper arm again. I wince with a whistling inhalation. I can't help it. I'm not into gratuitous physical contact with anyone. It's just the way I am. It's not personal. I happen to like this man and I can see why Robert Cobb liked him as well. Lewis exudes so much more than professional geniality. Somehow he makes you know that he really cares. Yes, I'm tuning in to the difference between Lewis and Cobb. I can't help it. Perhaps I should be asking a bigger question—why didn't Cobb care as much about me?

"Hate to break it to you," says Lewis, "but if you want to make this practice work, you need to earn some trust. This client is very different from Ethel Silverman. A perfect opportunity to develop your communication skills."

"Diagnoses and cures will earn trust. I'm looking to do my job, not get friendly with pet owners. I don't engage in irrelevant verbal fluff. Ideally, in my opinion, information about a case should be concise, pertinent, detailed and, best of all, written."

Lewis shakes his head. "Let me tell you something—animal health care has always been about choice. It used to be about choosing which veterinarian best fit your personality. Back in the day, when Doc Cobb and I competed for business, it wasn't enough to be a decent clinician. You had to connect with the client. You had to connect with the patient. You had to make them want to see you again. These days there's another ugly dynamic in the mix—money. Take Healthy Paws, the competition across the valley in Patton— they care more about making money than they do about making their patients better. They've totally lost sight of the honor and altruism of our profession. Only the other day they had an ad in the paper offering half price spays on Wednesday and pay for two vaccines, get one free. It's tacky, it's demeaning, but some of your customers will buy into it. Listen to me, Cyrus, to win them over, they're going to have to find something about you that they really, really like."

I don't know what to say. How can I tell Lewis I'm all about making money as well? How do I let him know the rival practice he despises will soon be the new owners of Bedside Manor? And let's not forget, I chose to be a pathologist because I prefer to work in silence and alone. Which is not to say I'm antisocial. I want to make friends. I'm just not very good at it. Boarding school may have been great for my education but it stunted my communication skills. I was a shy Yankee boy dropped in the heart of Dixie. When kids think you sound funny, you keep your mouth shut. It's a lot less painful to become a loner.

"Here's your map. His name's Harry Carp. His dog's called Clint."

I take the scrap of paper and work out in my head roughly where I'm going.

"He's good for the price of the house call?" I ask.

Lewis's sharp intake of breath is not what I want to hear.

"Harry will pay. His checks don't bounce. Takes his time writing them is all."

Great, more bad debt. "Hope he won't mind if I ask for cash up front," I say.

Lewis's pout says, "Come on, have a heart," but his expression slowly twists into a smile. "Think of this as part of your edu-cation, an investment in acquiring the type of skills that will pay big dividends down the line. Pet owners like sharing their concerns with fellow animal lovers. This has nothing to do with you as an individual. Here's an opportunity to work on your . . . rapport."

Unfortunately they don't teach "rapport" in vet school, and if they did, I suspect it wouldn't have been an easy A for me.

"You should take Doc Cobb's old truck."

"That dilapidated Silverado out back?" I ask.

"Yep," says Lewis. "Though bear in mind it does have a minor problem."

I lower my chin, let my eyes roll up to meet his, fearing the modifier *minor*.

"No reverse."

"What?"

"Be careful how you park. Make sure you can drive straight out. Harry's driveway has a big turnaround. You'll be fine."

"Maybe it'd be better if you go instead?"

Lewis consults his wristwatch, does that chewing thing with his lower lip.

"I've got an appointment," he says. "A haircut, in twenty minutes."

He makes this information sound serious.

"There's a barbershop in town?"

Lewis grabs his coat from behind the counter. "No, of course not," he says. "Mrs. Lewis has been cutting my hair on the first Tuesday of every month since we got married. Take my bag of tricks, okay?"

He turns to leave but spins back around to face me. "Strive for a friendly chat, not an interrogation. Try to make more eye contact and stop fidgeting so much with your hands. Acting distant and detached might suit you, but it can come across as disinterested. And when that happens, mark my words, clients will go elsewhere."

Warning delivered, he walks out the front door, leaving me to work on that imaginary itch at the back of my neck.

Before I head off to Harry Carp's, I check in on my desperado retriever. I find Frieda in the living room, sprawled across the couch. Presumably her disregard for getting up on furniture is a relic of her former life with Mr. Charcoal Suit. I ignore her greeting—rooting snout, wagging tail, and tap dance moves that are more Tin Man than Fred Astaire—brush golden tumbleweeds off the cushions, and scrutinize their surface for evidence of any accidents. Not a wet patch in sight. Why does she go crazy when I try to stop petting her?

Fearing a repeat of last night's unwanted publicity I take her out for a covert pee via the small deck off the second-floor kitchen and a wooden outdoor stairway that leads down to the backyard. Instinctively Frieda goes all mountain goat on me, negotiating the icy steps, cautious with her footing, perforating the crusty layer of frost topping the snow like she's traversing crisp meringue. It's obvious Frieda loves being off leash, bounding around and digging to China. I, on the other hand, am miserable— shivering as the biting wind paralyzes my face, convinced the tip of my nose has already succumbed to frostbite. What I wouldn't give for a warm, briny breeze, the sound of lapping waves, or the smell of magnolias. I admit it: I'm weak, indoctrinated by a climate that doesn't require you to put on enough clothes for thirty minutes so that you can withstand the elements for thirty seconds. Sure, all this snow can be pretty to look at and festive for the holidays, but what do you do when your barren white world refuses to turn green for another five months? Give me the stifling humidity of a Charleston July any day.

Once again it takes Frieda forever to find the perfect spot, but once again she performs her ablutions without a flaw. There's been no evidence of excessive or inappropriate urination whatsoever. In different circumstances I'd suggest a blood test, analyze a sample of urine, but I don't have the time, the money, or the inclination. Taking her to a retriever rescue group is the best I can do. And here's the kicker—I have to do it anonymously, which means no chance of any business-boosting chit-chat from fanatical dog lovers touched by the dedication of the new vet in town. At most I get a little good karma, and last time I checked, good karma won't pay my bills.

Clearly old Doc Cobb didn't care for his truck. It's mostly rust with patches of black paint here and there. The muffler is held in place by bungee cords, and there are 178,000 miles on the clock. It does boast four-wheel drive, but as I climb into the cab I'm forced to acknowledge how I don't have to adjust the position of the seat or the steering wheel—a perfect fit. The engine turns over first time. I haven't driven a stick in years and as I depress the clutch and slip it into first, I note the letter *R*. How will I ever remember this vehicle can only move forward?

Turning left out of the practice's lot I head toward town, passing a bullet-ridden sign that confirms I have entered Eden Falls. Not to put too fine a point on it, but the name Eden Falls is a glaring misnomer. For starters, there's nothing remotely divine, idyllic, or biblical about the place (not counting a white wooden Rockwellian church). There's not a park or a playing field let alone a fabled garden. And technically speaking the word *Falls,* plural, is incorrect, thanks to a rockslide nearly eighty years ago, which reduced a mediocre tourist attraction to a disappointing and forgettable "Fall," singular.

Main Street is a twenty-five-mile-per-hour two-lane without a single traffic light or stop sign. In a vehicle, keeping to the speed limit, a driver can sneeze, wipe his nose, and cruise straight through, missing it all and missing nothing. This is the first time I've driven through town since coming back and I doubt much has changed since I was last here—there's an art gallery, a couple of antiques stores, a full-service gas station, and a convenience store located in a converted red barn. At the heart of the metropolis lies the Miss Eden Falls Diner. Last time I was there was with my mom when I was fifteen, one week before I was sent away to boarding school. I still remember my order: grilled cheese, French fries, and a hot fudge sundae. Mom had a Reuben, apple pie à la mode.

That Eden Falls still exists is mainly due to its proximity to the most northerly private school in the lower forty-eight, Eden Falls Academy. The school provides jobs, and the traffic of visiting parents has ensured the survival of a number of questionable lodging and dining facilities that, in a more competitive environment, probably should have gone out of business. These include Vera's Bed and Breakfast, the Harlequin Inn and Cottages (which sounds so much better than what it really is—The Checkerboard Motel), and the Inn at Falls View Farm, which, though the fanciest of a bad bunch, now offers vistas of something akin to a quarry rather than cascading water.

I suppose some might describe the town as quaint, even cozy. It does boast a covered wooden bridge that crosses the Missiquoi River as it meanders along the southern edge of town. And just beyond the bridge lies Garvey's Nursery and Garden Center. I have fond childhood memories of Garvey's. For a kid with no interest in fishing, hunting, or skiing, Garvey's was like going to Disney World. I'm talking about a miniature golf course, a miniature railway, a corn maze in the fall, and a petting zoo complete with cows, llamas, potbellied pig, miniature horse, goats, and chickens. Not that I ever engaged in the act of petting. I was quite content to observe the behavior of the different species, especially around precocious children. Now, a lifetime later, this menagerie fills me with dread because, according to Lewis, Garvey's farm animals are overseen by the doctors of Bedside Manor. I have my hands full with dogs and cats. What am I supposed to do with a llama?

It's about a mile drive to the center of town and, though I'm loath to admit it, the surrounding countryside is a winter wonderland postcard. Vistas of perfect blue meet a white-feathered forest that basks in liquid sunshine. I forgot to bring sunglasses. Instinctively I reach for the visor. What visor? Funny, I'm squinting, it's ten below, and the truck's heater is all about noise not heat, and still, there's something pleasing about the novelty of going out into the world to attend to a patient.

I notice a woman and a child loitering by a lamppost and slow down to see what they are doing. The two of them are duct-taping a poster in place.

MISSING:
Frieda Fuzzypaws

There's a picture of a golden retriever, there's an offer of a reward, and there's a phone number to call.

I pull over, watching them in my cracked rearview mirror. The little girl and the woman get into a car, head to the next lamppost, and put up another poster. Frieda Fuzzypaws is a name that could only have come from a little girl who likes to paint pink nail polish on her best friend's paws.

I turn around and look down the street

in the direction the pair is walking from. There is a poster plastered to every pole.

I pull out my cell phone, read the number, and dial.

As the number rings I stare into the mirror, waiting for the call to go through, for me to see the woman in the reflection rustle in her coat pocket and pick up.

"Hello. Hello."

I hear a voice but the woman in the mirror continues to help the girl tape another poster in place.

"Who is this?"

I can't speak.

"Is this about the dog?"

I hang up. In the mirror the woman moves closer to the girl and gives her a hug. My fingers begin tapping out a nervous rhythm against the steering wheel. I recognized the voice straightaway. The man in the charcoal suit.

Calm down, I think. *Weigh the facts.*

Obviously the number on the poster is not the woman's cell phone number, but probably her home phone number. I call the number and charcoal suit man picks up, meaning this woman, this child, and Frieda Fuzzypaws live together. The poster says "MISSING," as in lost or escaped, therefore the woman and the little girl believe this to be true, which means charcoal suit man created this lie.

Now what am I supposed to do? How do I hide a dog everybody is looking for and how can I come forward with a dog I'm supposed to have put to sleep?

≪ 6 ≫

Heading out of town, I see the last of the residential properties slipstream behind me as the truck lumbers toward a series of switchbacks. A man who never learned to drive in snow should be concentrating on the road, but my mind is elsewhere. I don't do impetuous acts, but there's a part of me that wants to forget this house call. It wants to find out where the woman and the little girl live, deposit Frieda at their front door, ring the doorbell, and run. But the analytical, investigative part of me says not so fast. This is a case begging to be worked in the wrong direction, from back to front. Isn't this what I'm supposed to be good at? Like I said to Lewis, my mind naturally prefers starting at the last chapter. I already know whodunit, or rather, who wanted it done. Frieda is our victim and, as far as I can tell, blameless of the crime she's supposed to have committed. Everybody's looking for her. Now, if I take her to an adoption center or a rescue group, chances are she'll be returned to the man who wants her destroyed. I doubt he'll risk another visit to a veterinarian. He'll probably take her out into the woods and do it himself. No, the man in the charcoal suit is our wannabe killer. He and I are the only people who know what would have happened. To prevent it from happening again, I need the answer to a far more complicated question. Why?

I miss the turnoff to Harry Carp's. It's easily done. All that marks the address are hand-painted numbers on a solitary mailbox bearing baseball bat bruises. The unplowed driveway hidden among the evergreens was completely obscured. I check the cracked rearview mirror of the truck before making a U-turn. The fairground fun house reflection plays tricks with my features, but it cannot hide the dark circles of unease and insomnia around my eyes.

Wheels spinning and back end fishtailing, I work my way up a narrow tree-lined driveway, locking onto a previous set of tire tracks, following them to an A-frame cabin that has all but disappeared into its woodsy surroundings. Lewis was right, there is plenty of room. Who needs reverse?

I grab the trusty bag of tricks, Lewis's "doctorin' bag," from the passenger seat, jump down from the cab, and trudge through the snow. A path has been shoveled to the front door, a good six feet of snowbank on either side, but there's no doorbell. Somewhere inside I can hear the sound of conversation and then gunfire, from a television. I rap hard on the wood. Nothing. I try again. Still nothing. How old is Harry Carp? And what kind of a guard dog is Clint?

I don't see as I have much choice. I wade, waist deep in powder, toward a window, hoping it is a kitchen or living room, hoping someone or something will see me. I have to tap on the glass before man or beast register they have a visitor. Harry Carp makes a show of his apology as something moves in the shadows, barking in either welcome or disapproval—I can't tell which. I wade back to the door and dust myself down before it swings open.

"Easy, Clint," says a man who has to be in his eighties, one hand pressed firmly into the grip of a walking cane as he leans in for support. Once upon a time he was probably a formidable man, but now his chest is more barrel than broad, as if transformed by diseases in his heart or lungs. His spine has succumbed to the weight and curvature of time, his scalp bears more liver spots than wispy remnants of hair, and myopia has left his cloudy blue eyes magnified in buggy frames. "I'm Harry. You must be Cyrus. Come on in." Harry extends his free hand and we shake, the grip dry and firm. But it's his fingernails that get my attention. The beds are bruised. One or two and I might excuse a clumsy blow from a hammer, but not all of them. I can't help myself. My brain begins to rev.

"Sorry I didn't hear you, Clint and I were watching our movie."

Harry talks between breaths, regaining control after the exertion of his trek to the front door, but I'm surprised by how much genuine pleasure he appears to derive from our encounter. It's more than smiling; he's beaming, lit up and alive, as though I might have crossed an ocean to get here. I wonder if he lives alone. I wonder about the tire tracks in the driveway. I wonder when the last time he had a visitor was.

"Okay, Mr. Carp," I say. "I assume this is Clint?"

The dog takes a tentative step toward me. I stand my ground and try not to look afraid. Clint is a black, short-haired mutt and based on his body shape and head he's definitely got some Labrador retriever somewhere in the mix. But his legs and his tail are not right. His legs are way too short and bowed, like a basset hound's, and his tail is long and curls into a bold and brazen *C*, like something better suited to an arctic breed.

"Hello . . . Clint."

Clint begins sniffing the hem of my pants. I look up at Harry, who seems puzzled by my hesitation. I should say something. I should do something.

"Bet he can't swim?"

My question, admittedly out of left field, goes unanswered, and I can't tell if Harry didn't hear it or thinks it's so stupid it's best ignored.

"The basset hound in Clint," I explain. "Basset hounds can't swim. Or not very well. Same with bulldogs, pugs, dachshunds . . ."

"You going to say hello to the dog or not?"

I nod, as though appreciative of the advice, and deliver a couple of halfhearted pats. Fortunately Clint circles back to his master's side before I have a chance.

"See, right there. Normally Clint would be all over you. You'd have to peel *her* off."

"Her?"

Harry grins. "Come on through to the living room and you can take a look."

I stamp out a couple of snow waffles with my boots and step into a dark hallway. To my left is a kitchen, tight but tidy, and straight ahead is a set of wooden stairs leading to a second floor that I doubt Harry has seen in quite some time. We head right, the heat from a wood-burning stove upon me long before I enter a small sitting room. There's a run-down couch, a shabby La-Z-Boy chair, and between the two what appears to be a large and noticeably pristine dog bed. The seating arrangements are angled toward a television, and on the screen I recognize the iconic frozen picture.

"The man himself," I say.

"Of course," says Harry, "but do you recognize which movie?"

The picture is of Clint Eastwood in a Stetson and poncho, cigarillo between his lips.

"Well, based on his age and outfit, he's playing The Man with No Name, so it's from the Sergio Leone spaghetti western trilogy. But with only this single frame, I'd still be guessing."

Harry looks pleased. "Movie buff?"

"You betcha," I reply, though an ever-tightening budget forced me to drop Netflix and I can't afford basic cable, which means no Turner Classic Movies.

"The first," he says. "The original. *A Fistful of Dollars.*"

I nod. *A Fistful of Dollars* was actually a remake of Akira Kurosawa's *Yojimbo.* But I keep quiet.

"You ever want to see a Clint Eastwood movie, they're all there."

Harry gestures to a wall taken over with

row upon row of VHS tapes with hand-labeled stickers on their spines. It's the kind of collection that would have given Blockbuster a run for their money in the days when schlepping back and forth in a car for a movie seemed like a good idea.

"You got *Rawhide*?"

"Of course."

"Gran Torino?"

"Yep."

I wait a beat, but have to ask, *"Bridges of Madison County*?"

Harry's smile vanishes.

Oops.

"Perhaps we should get back to talking about Clint. Clint the *female* dog."

She's on her bed, curled up. She seems friendly enough, but then they always do, don't they? I place my bag off to one side and squat down, nice and slow, like I'm trying to interact with a gorilla not a dog. I register the spring in my knees, feel the muscles coiling tight, ready to leap for cover at the first sign of trouble. Clint closes her eyes.

"She's my sixth Clint."

My hand hovers, finally makes contact with fur. She doesn't flinch.

"It's only a name, you know. I'm pretty sure she doesn't have a problem with it."

I nod, looking up and past him over at a table on the other side of the room. It's covered in prescription bottles, presumably his. Next to it, standing at attention, is a portable green oxygen cylinder.

"What's going on?"

Suddenly I see the shift in the man, a certain clarity taking shape in those big blue eyes as we get down to it. "Well, she's about to turn eleven. She's always had a good appetite. The Labrador in her, I guess. But she's off her food. I had chicken last night, and she normally helps me out when I can't finish up. She managed a sniff, but that was about it. All she wants to do is sleep. That's not my Clint."

"How often does she get table scraps?" There's enough accusation in the question for him to know I don't approve.

"Not often," says Harry, but he's not fooling me.

I hear Lewis inside my head, *Strive for a friendly chat, not an interrogation.*

"What about going to the bathroom?" I ask, inwardly cringing at being so nonscientific.

"She's not had a bowel movement for days. Is that bad?"

For a few difficult seconds I'm the actor who hasn't even read the script let alone forgotten his lines. Where's Lewis when I need him? My audience of one is waiting, and Harry's apprehension is tangible. I feel the heat in my cheeks, claustrophobic from the imposing coziness of the room, and oppressed by the weight of a strange responsibility to a frail old man.

"Not necessarily." I should fess up and tell him I'm in over my head. "You still take her for walks?"

"I wish," says Harry. "My granddaughter takes care of that. She lives with us. Looks after us. These days I'm lucky if I can manage to watch from the back door."

I nod. *The tire tracks on the driveway.* My uncertainty about what other questions to ask leaves me hanging in another awkward silence. And that's when the letters *ADR* pop into my head. ADR is an acronym students learn at veterinary school, a term applied to an animal with a vague, nonspecific illness. Yes, it could be said that Clint is ADR but, to a trained patholo- gist who craves scientific accuracy, the label ADR is distressingly vague. That's because ADR means, of all things, "Ain't Doin' Right!" ADR is not a disease. ADR produces no characteristic changes in the body. I cannot see, find, or palpate ADR. ADR is all about an owner's gut feeling, and I prefer facts to hunches.

Only one thing to do: gather information, pass it on to Lewis, and leave it in his capable hands.

"Right then. Um . . . up you come." To my surprise, Clint gets to her feet. She even concedes a swish of her tail but not much more. I pull out my stethoscope and listen.

Resting heart rate, normal dog, 60 to 160 beats per minute. I consult my wristwatch. Check. Lub-dub, lub-dub, even rhythm, synchronous pulses. Check.

As soon as everything sounds what I would consider to be normal, the doubt starts up, questioning how, after fourteen years, can I possibly conclude that a canine heart sounds normal? *But there is a normal rhythm and no audible murmurs.*

I move on to Clint's belly, and here, to my surprise, I make a discovery in which I have confidence.

"She's definitely tender in her abdomen."

High up under the rib cage Clint lets me dig deep, tickling her liver and spleen, but in the core of her belly, her abdominal muscles tighten into a six-pack worthy of an Abercrombie & Fitch model, guarding against inquisitive fingers.

"Any diarrhea?" I ask.

"No."

I invite Harry to lay a hand on her head, pull out a rectal thermometer, a tube of K-Y gel, make my apologies, and take her temperature.

Normal canine body temperature ranges from about 100 to 103 degrees Fahrenheit. "One oh two point four," I say, "perfectly acceptable." I get to my feet.

"What do you think? Can you tell me what's wrong?"

I recall Doc Lewis's advice about handling the clientele of Eden Falls, and honesty feels like the least this man deserves. "No, Harry, I can't."

Harry nods, disappointed but still with me.

"Though it's obvious Clint doesn't feel great. I think I should take a blood sample, send it off to a lab, see if we can get some answers via that route. Have a seat, and I'd appreciate you securing her head while I take a sample."

Harry comes around, negotiating the La-Z-Boy. He catches me as I help him into his chair. "I promise you, she won't bite."

I want to tell him how I've heard that one before, but there's a flinty conviction in his eyes. I'm obliged to believe him as Harry gets comfy, trailing a hand, playing with her ear. Clint seems to melt into Harry's familiar touch. I can't help but think about how even alligators can be hypnotized.

I find a sterile needle and syringe, a small bottle of alcohol and a cotton ball, appropriate collection tubes, and a thick elastic band to wrap around Clint's front leg as a tourniquet. I take a deep breath, stick the vein, brace for the scream, snap, and fury. Nothing happens. She never even notices. But the smile on Harry's face tells me he has.

"Uh . . . well done," I say, transferring my sample of fresh venous blood to the tubes. "I'll have these mailed off as soon as I get back to Bedside Manor."

Harry gets up with difficulty. I return everything to the bag and pick it up.

"Hope you don't mind, I'll let you see yourself out."

"Not at all," I say. "I'll be in touch."

Harry does not make to shake hands.

"Can I say something?" he asks.

Uh-oh. Lewis said all they want is a friendly chat.

"Sure."

Harry Carp looks away and works those bruised fingers on the silver stubble of his chin. Then his hands drop to his sides as he looks me directly in the eye. The expression on his face is serious, sincere. I want to look away as my heartbeat begins to quicken.

"You a religious man?"

The question catches me off guard, and I'm trapped in an agnostic moment of hesitation. "Not really."

"But you believe in God?"

"I guess."

My deliberation has him worried.

"Put it this way, you like the idea of there being some kind of higher power out there, somewhere, capable of giving you unconditional love no matter what?"

"Yes, yes I do."

Harry regards his dog, and his dog continues to stare up at him. "Me too," he says, nodding into a tight-lipped smile. "Only I've been blessed with that kind of love every day from this crazy-looking mutt! You reckon our pets are tuned in to God?"

I try to hide my skepticism in an appreciative nasal laugh.

"See, time moves fast when you get to be my age. The rest of the world has better places to be, better company to keep." Harry tries to touch Clint's head, his arthritic spine keeping him at bay until Clint reads the situation, rears up on her back legs, and completes the physical connection. "But this particular young lady is totally tuned in to yours truly. I am her world and she is mine, the constant of my life, the reminder that nothing else matters if we have each other."

Once again I feel the flush in my cheeks and I can't tell whether it's the oppressive warmth of the room or my discomfort at being privy to Harry's candor. I'm worried it might be the latter.

"You can tell I'm not a well man. My granddaughter's an angel, and I really mean that. Does everything for me, but hey, there's only so much you can do for a heart that's ready to quit. Look . . ." Harry pauses. A tremor has crept into his voice. He swallows hard. "If I die tomorrow, I know Clint will be well taken care of. I know she will cope. But . . . but if my Clint goes before me . . ."

Fear dances on his tongue, constricting his vocal cords, and I watch as a proud old man tries to keep it together. For a while, I think he might make it, but Clint, sensing her master's need, roots for his touch, and that's all it takes. Eighty years vanish in an instant and Harry is crying like a little boy. His shoulders are heaving and he is barely managing jerky breaths.

I just stand there, unable to move. It's hard enough for me to be a real veterinarian let alone a psychiatrist or a grief counselor. I'm reminded why I chose a career path that avoids these . . . sentimental encounters. In fact it's why I've avoided all manner of emotional confrontations for my entire adult life. My heart is where it's supposed to be. Buried deep and well protected in my chest.

"I can't think about living a single day

without her. When my lights go out, I ask for one thing and one thing only."

Harry is silent for several seconds, and I know I'm supposed to respond, but it's a struggle to find my voice. It's a whole lot easier to scratch my imaginary itch. "What's that, Harry?" I say, in a dry whisper.

"I want to be looking into the eyes of my last best friend. That's what I'm saying. You're a veterinarian. You know what I mean."

He winces as tears run anew down his cheeks. I turn away. I try to focus on the dog and not the prickle of sweat on my forehead. I hear Harry sniff back a jagged breath and I'm pretty sure he is regaining control. I look back at him.

"Doc Lewis tells me you're a clever man, with special training. I think God brought you to Eden Falls for a reason."

My body cringes.

"Okay, okay, let's say fate brought you here to fix my Clint."

"Sorry, Mr. Carp, but I don't believe in fate. I guess I'm too much of a scientist."

Harry wipes his eyes. "Really? My priest came to visit me the other day, never a good sign, right, and we got to talking about life, you know, the choices you make, the path you take, the things you'd do different if you could do it over."

Why will some people never understand that introspection changes nothing? Harry continues, "You say you don't believe in fate, but what if you're working on a dog and you discover a bump on her head, and then on her neck, her back, and her tail. There must be times when you say to yourself, *this can't be a coincidence*."

"Of course."

Harry beams. "See, this priest told me something that's stuck with me. 'Coincidence is God's way of remaining anonymous.'"

He pauses, giving the lesson time to resonate in my head. "Know who said that? Another pretty good scientist by the name of Albert Einstein. Believe me, you're back in Eden Falls for a reason. You might not know it yet, but give it time."

Back in Eden Falls.

He knows.

"If Lewis trusts you, then so do I."

I don't know what to say. I've rarely felt less worthy of someone's trust.

"You know the doctors tried to put me in

a hospital." Harry shakes his head. "Ask anyone my age where they'd prefer to die and they'll say at home." He takes a deep breath. "Well, let me leave you with this thought . . . Clint *is* my home."

It's hard not to be struck by this plain man, standing in his modest home, wielding his passion like a crowbar. At this close range he threatens to break open everything I have so carefully locked away. I grit my teeth and slowly reach for Harry's hand. I hope he reads my silent determination, and we shake on it.

"One more thing before I go," I say, relieved to be changing the subject. "Are you on blood thinners?"

"Yes, why do you . . ."

"Then you might want to tell your doctor to back off on the Coumadin."

Harry pulls out a handkerchief to wipe his nose, and I can tell he's intrigued. "How did you . . . ?"

"The bruising under your fingernails. I pick up on the weirdest things."

And with that I head for the front door.

To my surprise, Clint follows. She keeps her distance, her pace more of a plod than a trot. I can't help thinking that she's like the concerned relative who wants to take the doctor aside and have a word in private. In unison, we glance back at Harry. But he's not looking at us. He's staring at the empty dog bed, and I have the feeling he's imagining a future he hopes he never has to see.

The blast of cold air is like a slap.

Unbelievable. I forgot to give Harry a bill.

Lewis is pulling out of the practice's lot as I pull in. We align our vehicles for conversation, like police cruisers outside a Dunkin' Donuts. He powers down the window on his truck, I crank the handle on mine.

"How did it go?"

"Okay," I say.

Lewis looks puzzled. "Just okay?"

"Don't get me wrong, Harry seems like a nice guy, but the man's a wreck about losing his dog. All that emotion . . . it's disturbing."

Lewis shakes his head. "This is not like dropping off your car at the local garage and leaving it to be fixed. Owners need *you* to know why they are so invested in their animal's well-being."

"But don't you see, all it does is increases the pressure on the doctor to succeed. It's not helpful. I saw what it did to Doc Cobb."

Something changes in Lewis's features, like he sees a door open, just a crack, and leans in to see if it will give. "What did you see it do . . . to your *father* . . . exactly?"

"You know how he was," I say. "Work was his obsession. Owners would call at all hours of the day and night. He never said no. He never refused to go out on a call. Sometimes I wonder if they took advantage of his dedication, knowing it was his weakness. Whatever. All I know is Cobb had a hard time juggling veterinary medicine and his role as a husband, let alone as a father."

I'm grateful we're separated by glass and steel, otherwise I'm sure Lewis would be encroaching on my personal space. I change the subject. "I'm not sure what's going on with Clint." I recite Clint's history and clinical signs to see if the maestro has any pearls of wisdom he's willing to share.

"Sounds to me like a case of something

and nothing. Probably work itself out. But the blood test was a good idea. Package it up and have Doris call FedEx."

"She's back?"

Lewis nods.

"How long before we get the results?"

"They'll fax them over this time tomorrow." And then, seeing my surprise, he adds, "We're not that backward, you know. Hey, would you mind taking my afternoon appointments? It shouldn't be too busy."

"Sure," I say, waiting for the excuse or the explanation, but there's nothing except his charming grin. He's about to slip his truck into drive when I ask, "Not much of a haircut?"

"What? Oh, yeah. It was a trim is all, tidy up the back." He reaches a hand round to his neck where hair meets skin, as though he can feel the difference, even if it looks the same as when I last saw him. "Catch you later."

The dry electric heat is cranking inside, and there's a woman standing in front of the examination room door who appears to be trapped in 1958. Maybe it's the beehive haircut (tinted a yellow not found in nature). Maybe it's the sticky orange lips surrounded by a halo of permanent wrinkle lines, almost certainly the result of a life-time dedicated to sucking on cigarettes. Despite the warmth she wears a ski jacket, there's a screwdriver in her hand, and she is in the process of taking down the DR. ROBERT COBB DVM plaque from the door.

"Um . . . you must be Doris. Pleased to meet you."

"Ah, you must be Dr. Mills. I'm sorry, I thought I'd have this off before you got back."

"You can call me Cyrus."

Doris smiles. "That's nice of you, but I'd prefer to stick to Dr. Mills. I did the same with Dr. Cobb. More professional. Reminds the public that you have earned a title, don't you think?"

"Well, I suppose so." I wait a beat. "Can I help?"

The plastic rectangular plaque pivots on the final loose screw, and for a few seconds it rocks back and forth like the broken hand on a clock.

"Thank you but I'm nearly . . . there."

Now that she has it in her hand she

takes a moment to study it, as though it is something entirely new.

"Here. It's yours," she says, offering the plaque to me.

I hesitate to take it, for reasons other than the trace of reluctance in her voice.

"No." I fake a smile. "You keep it."

She reciprocates with a fake smile of her own, there's the briefest sparkle in her eyes, and the plaque disappears into her jacket pocket.

"Would you like me to order another one?"

Another Doc Cobb plaque? Though I graduated veterinary school as "Dr. Cyrus Cobb, DVM," I switched to my mother's maiden name as soon as I could. After what he put me through when she died, I needed to sever all ties, and that included ditching his last name.

"Another one?" I ask.

"Yes, another plaque?"

"No, thank you, that won't be necessary." I'll be back in Charleston before it arrives.

Doris arches her penciled-in suit-yourself brows, crosses the room to her desk, and deposits the screws in a trash can. "There were two messages for you on the answering machine this morning."

"Yes, Doc Lewis told me. Doris, I, um . . . in the future, I wonder if you could write down any messages for me on a piece of paper. Especially if you are going to be away from the desk for an extended period of time."

Doris stops sifting through her pile of case records. Seconds pass, she keeps her head down, and then, quick as a chicken, her head jerks up, eyes meeting mine.

"Of course, Dr Mills." And then, "It's just that . . . no . . . it was wrong of me to assume . . ."

"Assume what?"

Doris regards me with the kind of pained expression she might reserve for a simpleton who couldn't possibly know better. "Let's just say Dr. Cobb and I had an understanding. He was busy and he appreciated me filtering out the pet owners who simply needed their hand held, leaving him to get on with the real problem cases."

"I see. And the messages from this morning?"

"The first was from Crystal Haggerty. She said she enjoyed bumping into you last night and asked if you would call her." Doris pauses for effect and then adds, "About her black Lab."

Crystal. Black Lab. The woman who lunged at me and wouldn't let go. The woman who may have recognized Frieda. Everybody knows everybody in this town and clearly it took this "Crystal Haggerty" no time to track me down. How long before someone tracks down Frieda?

"Don't look so worried," says Doris, though her grin suggests she is enjoying my discomfort. "I sorted her out. I know these clients. I know their history. I know their . . . reputations."

I sense Doris has much more to say on the subject of Crystal Haggerty, but she's distracted by some loose papers on her desk. "Here, see, I wrote this one down. Anne Small, calling to see if anyone reported finding a golden retriever missing from last night. I've never heard of her, but I checked through our records. The dog's no patient of ours. She probably goes to that new place across the valley in Patton."

Anne Small, presumably the woman out and about putting up posters with, I imagine, her daughter. Probably called the local police as well. They are doing everything by the book to find their lost dog. If only I could tell them Frieda had simply gone missing.

"Did she leave a number?"

Doris hands over the slip of paper, making no attempt to conceal her glee.

I take it, pull out my cell phone, and thumb to recent calls. It is the same number I called earlier. Charcoal suit man.

"If you'd prefer to know about every single call I'm more than happy to oblige. No skin off my nose."

I consider. I'm sure she did make Doc Cobb's life a whole lot easier, but then again, how many genuinely sick animals and how much business fell through the cracks? "Perhaps, for now, it would be best, okay?"

This seems as good a time as any to institute some crucial managerial changes. "Do you happen to have a Sharpie and two pieces of paper?"

Doris says nothing, pulls open a drawer

below her desk, and hands over the marker and two sheets of A4.

In bold block capitals I write: *New Hours: Now Open Saturday 9:00 AM to 5:00 PM.*

"Here you go," I say, handing it over. "Please tape this to the front door. I know it's short notice, but I hope you're available to help out."

Doris takes the sheet of paper. "I'm available. But it'll cost you. Time and a half."

Wow, contract negotiations straight off the bat. "Fine," I say, like I've got money to burn.

On the second sheet of paper I write: *Payment in full is expected at the time of service.*

"Hang this up in the waiting room. Somewhere everyone will see it."

I'm treated to a slow single nod of acquiescence. "Will that be all?"

"Thank you, I'll let you go. I've got some blood samples to package up. You think you could let FedEx know I've got a shipment?"

"Of course."

I leave her standing there and head for

the work area in the back. I don't quite make it.

"It's been quite a while, hasn't it?"

I turn to face her. There's that smile again. "I beg your pardon."

"Since you were last here, in Eden Falls."

Doris appears genuinely interested, but she's not fooling me. I reckon Robert Cobb's receptionist knows much more than she's prepared to let on.

"Many, many years, Doris."

"At least twenty," she says.

"That's how long you worked for him?"

"That's right. A finer man you will not meet."

She says this as though I never knew him. I'm betting Doris knows about the will and the unhappy details of my estrangement from this so-called fine man.

"Notice any changes in the place?" she asks.

"To be honest I haven't had much of a chance to look around. But I will."

Doris begins to nod, excessively, as though she can hardly wait to get where she wants to go with this line of questioning. I try again to reach the door. My hand makes it to the handle.

"I wonder if anyone will recognize you after all this time?"

I spin around, struggling to keep the tetchy edge from my voice. "What are you implying, Doris?"

Doris twists her lines and wrinkles and somehow produces a look approaching surprise. "Nothing, nothing at all. Only, I imagine you've lost some hair, gained a few pounds, and these days you talk with a bit of an accent. Plenty of folks might think you're a complete stranger to town."

My turn, but my surprise is genuine. I've become used to Lewis and his tactful dance around the subjects of Ruth Mills and Bobby Cobb. Clearly, Doris has a different approach. I straighten up and try to stand a little taller. (Hey, you sit in front of a microscope every day and see what it does to your posture.) Time to clarify my situation. "If someone recognizes me as the son of Robert Cobb, so be it."

"Really? You think that's best for the practice?"

My mouth hangs open.

"I mean, it's bound to raise questions," she says. "The name change, the no-show at your mother's funeral, the no-show at your father's funeral?"

She sounds as though she's lamenting my shortcomings, like I forgot to turn up for a dental appointment. My tongue remains paralyzed as the waiting room door swings open and in walks a teenage girl carrying a cardboard cat carrier.

There's an awkward silence, as if she may have interrupted a married couple engaged in a squabble.

I lean in to Doris and breathe in the nicotine-infused beehive. "There are two sides to every story." I turn to face the newcomer. "I'm sorry but I don't start seeing appointments again until one thirty."

The girl looks surprised and makes a show of consulting her watch.

Doris inches a little closer to me. "Dr. Cobb always made a point of never turning away a sick animal." And the fixed expression she leaves me with is totally, *but that's up to you.*

Boy, I'm using up my quota of fake smiles for one day. "Won't you join me in the examination room while Doris locates your file."

The girl can't be more than eighteen years old, if that, with the kind of piercings guaranteed to draw the eye—nasal, septum, and lip—and cause the un-pierced among us to think about what happens to the metal and mucus when you catch a cold. Her hair has to be dyed, it's simply too black in contrast to skin so white she looks like she's ready for a cameo in another vampire movie. Her unzipped and ratty coat falls open to reveal an enormous bulge under a T-shirt that reads FAT PEOPLE ARE HARD TO KIDNAP!

"When's your due date?" Though there's a risk my question is politically incorrect, when something is so patently obvious my mouth usually betrays me.

"Last Tuesday."

No rings on any fingers. Some might think it's a precaution against perinatal swelling. I'm thinking she's a single mom.

"They didn't want to induce you?" I ask, placing the surprisingly heavy carrier on the examination table, closing the door behind us, and helping the girl take a seat.

"Next Monday, but I'm like, hoping to have him on Friday."

"Why Friday?"

"Because it's a full moon and it's the thirteenth."

She says this in all seriousness, with an innocence that is almost as refreshing as it is scary.

I nod, as though this makes perfect sense to me too.

"How far is it to the nearest delivery room?"

"Like fifteen miles, but this time of year with the snow and the ice it's literally going to take me an hour."

I nod. "Induction might be the best way to go."

She studies me and says, "You talk a bit like Forrest Gump. You're not from round here, are you?"

"No," I say. "No, I'm not."

"You work for the little old man?"

"Kind of. We're working together. I'm Dr. Mills, from South Carolina."

"I'm Denise," she says, "and this is my little Tina."

"And what's going on with your . . . little . . . Tina?"

"You tell me, Doctor Gump," she says, reaching a hand to her lips too late, as though she is not in the least bit sorry.

But you ain't got no legs, Lieutenant Dan.

I can't help but laugh. I open the carrier, reach inside, and pull out a large black cat. Tina may be shy and a little frightened, but she is wonderfully compliant. She stays where I place her, pressing her many love handles flat to the metallic table. I'm guessing she weighs around twenty pounds but to be fair, there's more to Tina than can be explained by an excess of canned tuna. I risk the same assumption twice in one day.

"Is she pregnant too?"

Denise nods. "I'm pretty sure she's at, like, day sixty-six," she says. "Doc Lewis told me to check back."

Day sixty-six is the feline equivalent of nine months. I whip out my stethoscope, listen to Tina's chest, take her temperature, gently palpate her Buddha belly. Everything seems to be in order.

Pedigree cats have a much higher

risk of a difficult labor than cats of mixed breeding.

"What was that?" asks Denise.

I chance a peek under her tail—prominent genitalia but no discharge.

"Oh, nothing. What makes Doc Lewis so concerned?"

"Her broken pelvis," says Denise. She stands up, takes the cat's pointy face in her hands, and plants a kiss on its black nose. "She's, like, an indoor cat. Or supposed to be. She escaped, years ago, gone for, like, a week and when she came back she was all, like, skin and bones and dragging her legs. Doc Cobb, you know, the vet who died, he looked at Tina for me, even though I had no money and he was like, 'ah, she'll heal just fine.' Guess he was right.

"Thing is, he said to get her *sprayed*." Denise works a little attitude into her eyes.

Sprayed. I'm pretty sure that's not quite what he said, but I don't interrupt.

"Yeah right, like, how was I supposed to do that? I was a kid and my old man wasn't going to pay for it. So I'd lock her in my room when she got horny. Worked fine, 'til

I got roommates. They're all in and out all day, you know."

"And Tina got out and got pregnant?"

"Right. Bit like me, I guess."

This conversation is becoming increasingly disturbing. It ignites the familiar itch at the back of my head.

"Doc Lewis took an X-ray of Tina's belly two weeks ago. There's only one kitten. He says it's like, really big, and Tina's pelvis healed crooked. She might not pass it on her own and I can't afford a C-section. I don't have a job and"—she taps her belly, flashes a phony smile—"guess who ain't gettin' one any time soon. Don't have the money for my own baby let alone my cat's baby. But I'm here, seeing you, ready to pay, 'cause she's like my little sister, and right now, she's the only family I got."

Denise stares up at me with big, green, wet eyes. What's with this preemptive crying over pets? Chances are Tina will be fine. Last thing I need right now is a reputation for reducing an impoverished pregnant teenager to tears. I grab a wad of tissues from a box on the counter, just in case.

"My old man kicked me out when he

found out I was pregnant. There's no father for the baby. This little cat has listened to my crap for years. She never once tried to get one over on me, never burst my bubble, she don't give me lip, and she lets me think I know best, even if we both know I don't. I need Tina and Tina needs me. I won't let her down."

Somehow she keeps the tears in check. Denise notices the unemployed tissues in my hand and appears to be puzzled.

"You gonna cry on me?"

I drop the tissues in the trash.

"Of course not. Don't you have anyone to help you out? What about your room-mates?"

"They're all in Cancún. Planned the trip before I got pregnant. Guess who lost her deposit?"

I look at Denise and then look at Tina. "You two make quite the pair," I say, running my hand along the cat's spine and getting a little "up periscope" action from Tina's tail. "Best keep our fingers crossed that neither one of you has to worry about a C-section."

If Tina the cat gets into distress as she

goes into labor, Doc Lewis is going to have to be the one to cut her open and deliver her kitten. As a veterinary student I never performed even the most minor of feline surgeries, let alone something complex like a C-section.

"Don't worry, I'll check in with Doc Lewis and let him know we've met. You have our number, and remember you can call us anytime, day or night, if anything starts to be a problem."

"What am I looking for, again?"

Okay, I think I can rattle off some of the general signs of pending labor but I promise to check in on the veterinary textbooks and call Denise if I discover something useful. "Vaginal discharge. Pushing and straining without success. You know, bearing down. Getting weak, trembling, or vomiting."

"Pretty much like me?"

"Correct. But I'm sure you'll both be fine." I offer Tina one more gentle pat to the head, pick her up, grunt at her weight as I place her back in the carrier.

"Let me walk you out to your car," I say, carrier in one hand, offering Denise my arm for support as we waddle out to the waiting room, straight past a scowling Doris.

Denise points toward a surprisingly new, if dirty, VW Beetle. "I'm borrowing it while my friend's in Mexico. It's crap in the snow but it beats walking."

I smile. I like Denise's no-nonsense, what-you-see-is-what-you-get attitude. Or maybe I relate to the pigheaded, stubborn spirit that has helped her to survive this much and get this far.

"Call me if I can help," I say. And I actually mean it.

"Thanks," says Denise. She looks up at me. "But what about paying for today's appointment?"

After my encounter with Mr. Critchley, his grim fiscal forecasts and the clock ticking on my good faith payment, I can hardly believe that I'm standing here with this pregnant girl and her pregnant cat and the concept of money could not be further from my mind. I can almost hear Dr. Robert Cobb saying, *Not so easy now, is it?*

"Let's sort it out next time. Promise to visit with Tina's kitten and your new baby."

Denise beams at me with so much pleasure it hurts me to watch, and I can tell, for the first time since we've met, Denise is vulnerable. In seconds, though, she's scrambling for the car keys, confirming that she will visit, and rushing, as best she can, for the sanctuary of the bug.

Back inside the empty waiting room, Doris is still glaring. "She coming back in to pay or what?"

"Uh, no . . . she's . . . in a hurry to get to a doctor's appointment herself. I said we'd bill her. I'll make sure Lewis knows."

Doris has her arms folded across her chest, and I follow her eyes to the far wall, where she posted my payment in full notice. If only Doris had had the same attitude with Dr. Cobb.

"You probably noticed that she's very, very pregnant. In her state, if she's in a hurry to see her doctor, I thought it best to let her go."

Doris's eyes bore into mine, and there's an unsettling grumble emanating from her throat. It is not of this world and it scares me.

I beam, to no avail, and back away, back through the exam room to the main workspace and "the library," check up on dystocia in cats, and discover that everything I told Denise is accurate.

Doris pops her head around the door. "I'll be back at two."

"Thanks, Doris."

"And this came for you."

She hands over a large sealed envelope bearing my name. *No stamps, no postmark. It's been hand delivered.*

"Who dropped it off?"

"No idea. Found it on the doorstep when you were visiting Harry Carp."

She doesn't wait around for me to ask why she didn't give it to me sooner.

I tear it open, reach inside, and it's like a jolt of electricity sizzles through my chest. I pull out a single sheet of paper, a printed online article, familiar and damning, pulled from the pages of an old issue of the Charleston *Post and Courier*.

CHARLESTON, S.C. (AP) — A Charleston man was forcibly removed from his place of employment after a skirmish with security.

Forty-year-old Cyrus Mills was terminated late Friday afternoon from McCall and Rand Pharmaceuticals, where Dr.

Mills, DVM, had been working as their chief pathologist for the past two years. Deputies were called when Mills refused to be escorted from the premises. Neither Mills nor McCall and Rand would comment on the reasons behind the dismissal, however the South Carolina State Veterinary Board has suspended Mills's license to practice pending further inquiries. No charges are expected.

I feel the boom of blood pulsing in my ears.

That's it. No accompanying note, just a single sheet of paper. Five humiliating sentences marking the darkest moment of my professional career and a death sentence for Bedside Manor.

❮ 8 ❯

Eating lunch is out of the question, and why won't Lewis pick up his phone? I'm pacing outside among the confetti of scorched dead butts, and it's five after two before Doris strolls up the driveway. As soon as she's in range she shouts, "Can't find a file? Someone waiting to see you?"

There's that wicked smile again.

"I need to reach Lewis. It's urgent. You know where he went?"

Doris takes one last slow drag and holds it in deep. The crinkles around her eyes begin to spasm. "The private lives of the doctors of Bedside Manor are none of my business."

Then she wipes the snow off her shoes and opens the front door. I join her in the empty waiting room.

"The word must be out," she says, removing scarf and mittens. "Tell you what, if anyone does show up, I'll come and find you. Fair enough?"

I'm speechless. Not only does everybody know everybody in this town, they know everything that's going on, and that includes me covering afternoon appointments for Lewis. For a second I wonder if Doris is behind the anonymous newspaper article. No, doesn't make sense. If Bedside Manor fails she'd be out of a job, and from what I've seen so far she might have a hard time getting another one.

"I'll be upstairs if you need me."

Even though I've acquired a golden shadow (Frieda insists we maintain some form of physical contact at all times), I pace the dining room, head swimming with candidates and motivation for bribery or revenge. I've got to keep it together, think rationally, and consider the evidence. The newspaper article was obviously downloaded from the *Post and Courier*'s Web site. Anyone with access to the Internet could have found it. No note. Maybe someone's playing games, being vindictive, or wants to send a warning? Why not go straight to the State Veterinary Board? Two possibilities. First, the sender has no interest in the specifics of my license because he or she is simply after any dirt that will emasculate me and any prospect I have of selling Bedside Manor. Second, most blackmailers don't go through the appropriate channels.

The package was hand delivered, so it is probably from someone local, and given the fact that this is only my second day on the job, it's someone who's been expecting me to turn up. Mr. Critchley from Green State Bank knew where to find me and he seemed disappointed not to be getting his claws into the property, but he never struck me as the extortion type. That leaves just about every pet owner in Eden Falls to whom Cobb bad-mouthed his only son. There must be plenty of his loyal clients out there—smarting from the way I abandoned him during his decline, convinced I boycotted his funeral, only turning up with an eye to making money—who would love to make me squirm before running me out of town.

Frieda catches my eye, like a kid making sure I'm watching what she's up to. I remove my hand from her head, pause, and allow her a few seconds of disbelief before scratching her backside, my delinquent petting duty apparently forgiven because her tail perks up. I hate to admit it but it feels good to have the company of someone I can trust. She gives me her smile, and I wonder if she's a dog who will always "seem" happy, no matter the circumstances. I can't reciprocate, and it's not just because of the anonymous article. For me to share Frieda's happiness, I need to know she will be safe back where she belongs. Now seems as good a time as any. I pull out my cell phone and press redial.

I'm greeted by a different, smaller voice on the other end of the line, reciting the number before adding, ". . . This is Emily, speaking."

"Hello, would it be possible to speak to Mrs. Small."

"Mommy's not here right now."

There's a silence because Emily knows it is my turn.

"Is your daddy around?"

"My daddy's dead."

I hesitate, missing my turn.

"Brendon's in the shower. You want me to get him?"

Emily splits the syllables in Brendon, placing the emphasis on "don." Is this Mr. Charcoal Suit? It could be a relative or a boyfriend but given my line of questioning, I'm betting the man in the shower is Emily's stepfather.

"That's okay."

"Mommy went to Wal-Mart to put up some posters."

I hate to ask the next question but I sense Emily hopes I will.

"What posters?"

"Posters of my dog, Frieda, Frieda Fuzzypaws. She's a golden retriever."

"What does she look like?"

Emily takes her time, as though she wants to get this just right.

"She's eleven years old, golden, with gray around her mouth and eyes. She's fat. That's my fault. She has enormous fuzzy paws and that's why I call her Frieda Fuzzypaws. Daddy brought me a picture book when I was little called *Frieda Fuzzypaws,* which is about a cat, but it turns out I'm allergic to cats, so we adopted a dog instead and Daddy let me name her."

"I see."

"She has a pink collar. It has her name on it. She's very, very friendly. Mommy says someone will find her very soon."

"Where is Wal-Mart?" I'm wondering if Mrs. Small will get back before "Bren-Don" gets himself toweled off.

"It's in Patton. She should be home soon." And then, as though she realized she has gone off script, Emily asks, "May I ask who is calling, please?"

I take a deep breath. It's time to give Emily my cell phone number and have her mom call me back. It's time for Anne Small to hear how the man of the house does not share her daughter's love of Ms. Fuzzypaws.

"Emily, I need you to write down my number for your mom. Do you have a pen and paper?"

"Just one moment, please."

The line goes silent and then she's back. I recite the number.

"Have your mom call as soon as she returns, okay?"

"Okay."

There's a knock on what passes for my front door, and instinctively Frieda lets loose with a series of short inquisitive barks. I can tell Emily's still listening and slowly the little voice gets even smaller as she says, "That sounds like . . ."

Though it pains me to do it, I hang up, lock Frieda behind the kitchen door, and find Doris, still wearing her ski jacket, standing at the top of the private stairway to the second floor.

"Do I have a patient waiting?"

Doris huffs in disbelief, "I didn't know you brought a dog with you."

I want to tell her there are a lot of things she doesn't know about me but she's already moved on. "Doc Lewis dropped by and left these for you."

She hands over two items, a folded piece of paper and a digital pager. I hesitate to take them, wondering why wouldn't he deliver them in person. Then I read his note, written in chicken scratch cursive.

Dear Cyrus,

Sorry about the late notice but the wife suggested we treat ourselves, get out of town, catch dinner and a movie. To be honest, it's been a long time since we've escaped from the practice, even for a few hours. We should be back by ten, eleven at the latest. I'm leaving you with the on-call pager. Doubt there will be anything to worry about. Most nights I forget I'm even carrying it. I'll switch the hospital answering machine back to my home number when I get back.

Have a quiet night and many thanks,
Fielding
PS. See all the posters around town—now what?

I turn on the pager and slip it into my pocket. I can't believe the way Lewis has abandoned me so early in my veterinary rehabilitation.

"As per your new instructions, Dr. Mills,

these are for you." She passes me a handful of "while you were out" phone messages. There's one from Tidy Town Refuse Collection informing me that they will no longer collect our trash; one from Bank of New England offering the practice a platinum credit card; and one from Yankee Golden Retriever Rescue, suggesting I "be on lookout for a dog answering to the name 'Fritter Frosty Pause'!"

"That's their phone number for the last one," she says. "Hope you can make sense of it."

"That's okay, Doris. I don't suppose anyone stopped by to sign a euthanasia consent form?"

Doris's glare makes me feel sorry I asked. "Naturally I would have informed you, Dr. Mills."

She pretends to grovel, which only heightens my discomfort. We stare at one another. Maybe she's hoping for an explanation, but at that precise moment I realize I must find a way to work with this woman, to use the talents Cobb saw in her to my advantage.

"After twenty years, I expect you know better than most how to separate the gen-

uinely strapped for cash from the gratuitously delinquent. I wonder if you could
compile a list of our clients with bad debt,
dividing them into these two groups. And
when I do see a case, maybe you could
warn me which group the owner belongs
to so I know whether to get on them for
money *before* they leave the building."

Doris eyes me with even greater suspicion, mutters "uh-huh" as though she
will be pleased to consider my request,
and disappears down the stairs, Zippo
and Marlboro in hand before she hits the
bottom step.

I read the message in my hand one
more time. For now Fritter Frosty Pause is
safer staying with me than being reunited
with certain members of her extended
family. And then my cell phone rings.

"Lewis?"

After a pause a gravelly voice I recognize
says, "You're in this as much as me." There's
a slow click, the line goes dead, and in my
mind I see the man in the charcoal suit finding a note addressed to "Mom" with a number to call. Brendon Small is clearly a man
on edge, a man who knows he's made a
terrible mistake, and quite possibly a man

who's found the kind of leverage in an old newspaper article he believes will guarantee my silence.

Rather than spending the evening alone, I decide to head into town and grab something to eat at the Miss Eden Falls Diner. Sitting alone might prove uncomfortable for some. Not me. Whether it's a movie theater or table for one I really don't care, so long as I bring along some reading material to fill the time and make me look like I have a purpose. Normally I'd grab a scientific journal, but my subscriptions have lapsed and I can't afford to renew them. This forces me to dig out an old magazine from the waiting room—*Field & Stream*. Hey, the alternative was *Ladies' Home Journal*.

If I'm being honest, Doris's recommendation to act like a stranger has me worried. It makes me wonder exactly what and how much Bobby Cobb shared with his receptionist and his community. Cobb's spin on our estrangement probably included something about me abandoning him in his hour of need, spurning every attempt he made to reach out to me. If the pet owners of Eden Falls have already bought into their beloved Doc's side of the story, there will be no uptick in business, no bonanza of cash, no good faith payment, and my prospects for selling Bedside Manor are doomed. Trying to pass for a stranger might be my best chance to turn a profit and run, but it won't fly. So let's just say I'm headed to the diner out of curiosity with a hint of nostalgia, to see if any of the patrons recognize me as the momma's boy who went there for lunch with her every Sunday.

When I flew up here, it was not with the appropriate clothing to fend off the extreme cold. Hardly surprising, since a South Carolina winter is practically a Vermont summer, right? Consequently I'm forced to borrow some of Cobb's clothes, and after all these years, it's a necessity that still makes me feel awkward. When I needed help with homework, felt sick, or got into trouble, I always went to Mom. Kids gravitate to the parent who will always be there, not the one who says, "Catch me when I'm done," or "Busy now, Son." If fatherhood was a class, Cobb's report card might say his attendance was spotty, always sat at the back, never disruptive but easily distracted. You see he'd let me in from time to time, only not enough. That was the most frustrating part, knowing he had so much more to give. Rightly or wrongly, it made his disinterest feel personal. Enough to notice, enough to hurt.

Frieda at my side, nuzzling into my thigh, I stand at the doorway of what was my parents' bedroom for the first time in twenty-five years. A hint of lavender hits my nose, the aerosolized remnants of a hand cream my mother used through the dry winter months. I (we) head to a dresser on my father's side of the bed before my parents started sleeping in separate rooms. There is a series of framed photographs from my childhood set out above the top drawer, and the recollections hit me like flying shrapnel. Mom pushing me on my old swing set, the two of us playing catch with a Wiffle ball in the backyard, and an enlarged candid close-up of her smiling face. I take in Ruth's cheekbones, her nose, the prominent philtrum, that deep vertical indentation above her top lip, and it's like looking at my reflection. But where it counts, where it haunts me, we differ. The photo captures Mom's green eyes with almond flecks. Mine are a forgettable washed-out shade of blue—their shape, the lids, the brows, the lashes, identical to those of the late Bobby Cobb.

There's one photo I've never seen before, me running track at a meet during my freshman year, before I went down south to boarding school. Strange. Mom never used the camera, a Leica M6 Classic that was Cobb's pride and joy, and I don't remember him attending a single sporting event during my entire education.

I open the top drawer, and to the right of a neatly folded collection of flannel shirts, there are dozens of envelopes bound by a thick elastic band. I instantly recognize the handwriting—mine. From the time I went to boarding school, Mom and I would exchange weekly letters. It became a ritual, a tradition. Even at veterinary school I couldn't afford or justify a cell phone, and the phone in my dorm was on the first floor and I lived on the fourth. The guy with the apartment next to the phone hated taking messages, and whenever I called out, there were always other students around, making noise and listening in. Letters proved unhurried, contemplative, and best of all, private. I stopped writing two weeks before finals because Mom insisted I focus on my studies. What would be her last letter to me arrived only a few days before her death.

I close the top drawer, open the one below, and discover Cobb's collection of sweaters. This stuff is going straight to Goodwill as soon as the house is sold. Settling on a thick white woolen number, I pull it over my head and inhale deep. Mothballs, maybe a hint of a fabric softener. No nasal nostalgia. Perhaps that should tell you something right there. I catch myself in a mirror on the other side of the room. Not good. Naked cheeks and chin still come as a shock, there's a stubborn cowlick of hair sprouting from the back of my head, and now I look a bit like the Gorton's Fisherman.

The diner is a fifteen-minute walk from the practice, if that, so rather than drive there in the Silverado and be forced to abandon it in the middle of the road because I can't reverse into a parking space, I make my apologies to Frieda, finish bundling up, and head out on foot.

Ruth Mills and I made this trek to the

diner come rain, sleet, or snow. It became our thing; then again, though it pains me to say it, pretty much all the good stuff growing up was our thing. There was this one time, back when I was seven or eight, that has always stayed with me. At that age Mom and I walked hand in hand, a custom I never questioned until, on this particular Sunday, I spied a couple of classmates off in the distance. For the first time in my little life I felt a twinge of embarrassment being tethered to my mother, a twinge countered by a sense of guilt for wanting to let go. Long before we converged it was Mom who dropped my hand, pulled off her glove, and pretended to bite a painful hangnail. We crossed paths with the two boys, greetings were exchanged, no one giggled, and to my relief, the prospect of ridicule at school was averted. Though it went unsaid, we were careful not to hold hands in public again. I imagine Mom nodded a sad and silent good-bye to the innocence of a son growing up. Thing is, I never got to thank her.

Near the center of town, hidden behind another snowbank monolith, adjacent to the gas pumps, is a pay phone, and standing in front of the phone, under the yellow streetlights, are two figures I recognize, the incomparable Mrs. Silverman and her husky, Kai.

Mrs. Silverman is being swallowed by plumes of her own dragon breath, and on her head she wears a hand-knitted blue pom-pom hat pulled down over her ears. It's Kai who has my attention, though. He's sitting by Mrs. Silverman's side. Still. Not scratching. Of course this could just be the soothing, numbing effect of the bitter cold or, more likely, that dose of steroids Lewis insisted I give him. Even so, I catch myself hoping it's his change of diet beginning to kick in.

"It's going to be a while," says Ethel Silverman, cupping a big black mitten across the mouthpiece as she sees me heading her way, staring with wide-eyed curiosity, refusing to continue her conversation.

"It's okay," I say, "I don't need it." I smile and point across the street toward the diner.

Mrs. Silverman slips in another quarter, still looking as though I might be about to mug her for her change. As I cross the street, from nowhere, a snowplow rattles by, spraying me with frosty slurry. I have time to notice the driver's smile and dust myself off thinking, *what's wrong with this town?*

You know that moment in every good cowboy movie, when our hero wanders into the busy saloon and, in an instant, conversation stops and heads turn and focus on the new stranger in town. Well, as soon as I open the door to the diner this is exactly what happens to me. Either I've already been labeled as the discredited son of Robert Cobb or cast as the no-good drifter, here to cause trouble. As I hesitate, looking for a sign to tell me whether or not I should seat myself or wait to be seated, I realize that one particular set of eyes is boring a hole straight through to the back of my head. I try not to meet them, but the uniform makes me take notice. I am face-to-face with a police officer. I've never been good at remembering people's names, but for better or for worse, I have a gift for remembering faces. And right now, I know I'm face-to-face with the bully who taunted me during my school days in Vermont.

I look away. The diner is packed and steamy, the air moist with the grease of fried fat. The cop has obviously been paying attention to *The Godfather* and *The Sopranos*. He is seated in a booth with a clear view of everyone who comes in through the front door. As I step into the spotlight of intense and silent scrutiny I feel the familiar tingle at the back of my head and scratch away.

The place is just as I remember it: single room, a little bigger than a railway lunch car, mosaic linoleum, gingham curtains, Formica counters, stools, and a bar on one side of the room, series of two- and four-man booths on the other. The booths have wooden seats, no cushions, uncomfortable like church pews. My mom used to tell me this was to make you eat fast and move on so they could turn over the tables. Two short-order cooks man the grills, and I spy one waitress, way down at the other end of the restaurant. I want her to see me and bail me out, but she seems intent on writing down an order. All I can do is smile and hope the locals understand I come in peace, hurrying over to the only empty booth available, the one directly behind the police officer. I make a point of saying "good evening" to him as I walk past. He follows me with his eyes but makes no re-ply. I take off my coat, hang it up on the dull brass coat hanger at my booth, and shuffle across the seat to rest my elbows on the red-checkered tablecloth.

Though the cop has his back to me, I can see that his proportions are un-changed from his persecution days as a scary senior, when I was a fearful fresh-man. Same defensive end shoulders and ropey triangular neck muscles that tether an oversize head. But time has taken its toll. Tight curly black locks have been re-placed by a bullet head with a reflective glare that resembles one of those tacky garden orbs. The bully has become a slave to vanity. Nothing can disguise the dark shadow of pattern baldness he is probably shaving twice a day.

"Can I get you something to drink?" I look up to see my waitress standing over me, and I jump, rocking back in my booth seat.

"Um . . . oh, yes . . . what was that?"

It's her eyes—one a perfect blue, the other a perfect brown. Not partial but com-plete heterochromia. Fascinating. The condition can be either genetic or acquired. It's extremely rare in people, though, interestingly, nearly 8 percent of water buffaloes have some form of heterochromia.

She wipes down the table and pours ice water into a glass, setting it down next to the collection of condiments and ketchup. "Just so you know, we don't serve alcohol on the premises but we are BYOB."

Complete heterochromia is all about how much melanin pigment you either have or lack in your iris.

"You okay?"

She's speaking to me.

"Yes . . . sorry . . . that's okay, I'm on call." I make it sound as though this is all she needs to know and I can't tell whether she's confused or convinced I'm a troublemaker. I press on. "Any chance of getting a coffee?"

"Of course," she says, looking relieved, "give me a few minutes and I'll make a fresh pot. Here's the menu while you're waiting, and our blue plate specials are on the board."

She points toward a large whiteboard next to where the cooks are busy grilling and flipping. "Be right back." She flashes me a smile, and I like the way she pauses long enough for me to register its sincerity before rushing off.

I watch her go, accosted by another patron at another table before she gets very far. She's attractive, probably in her mid thirties, with thick auburn hair twisted into a braid running an impressive length down her back. She seems to be working the tables alone, and she doesn't wear a name tag. I guess when you're serving the same bunch of regulars every night everybody knows your name.

"Hey, Chief." A stooped old man with a cotton-candy gray beard, on his way out of the diner, has dropped in on the police officer. "When you goin' to get round to having another word with that limey, Greer? Goddamn dog of his was at it again, barking his head off first thing this mornin'. Worse than any cockerel."

"Look, Sam," said the officer, his voice silky smooth and surprisingly calm, "I spoke to Mr. Greer a couple of days ago. He says he's sorry, but he's a heavy sleeper."

"Drunk is what he is," says Sam, twisting his corrugated cardboard face, seething at this Mr. Greer's audacity. "The damn dog

wants someone to get him some breakfast and all his master ever does is sleep
until noon."

"Chief" sighs, leans back, and spreads
his hands wide, palms up. "What more can
I do? Give him a wake-up call? Insist he
get Toby debarked?"

Sam edges away from the table with a
huff.

"Might not be a bad idea," he says, pulling a pipe out of the breast pocket of his
plaid lumberjack shirt and rooting around
in his painter's pants for the pouch of to-
bacco. "Then again, rat bait might not be
such a bad idea, either." And with that Sam
shuffles toward the front door, shaking his
head the whole way.

I check out the slightly sticky laminated
card that serves as a menu. It's standard
diner fare—burgers, club sandwiches,
all-day breakfast, the only form of sea-
food being the ubiquitous clam *chowda*
and tuna melt.

"Here's your coffee," says a voice in my
right ear. The waitress places the steaming mug before me. "Cream?"

"Thanks."

She pours. "Have you decided?"

The acquired form of complete heterochromia can be secondary to trauma, inflammation, and tumors.

Notebook and pencil in hand, she's ready to take my order. Or maybe my gaping fish mouth distracts her.

"No, sorry, what was the special?" From where I sit I'm having a hard time reading what's on the whiteboard.

"Let me see." She looks up at the ceiling for a few seconds. "On Tuesday night, chef offers slices of hardy hand-crafted, grass-fed beef, seasoned with savory vegetables and spices, served over garlic-infused and pureed Yukon Golds, with a sauce of delicately thickened pan juices." She regards me, poised to write, maintaining an air of seriousness and patient anticipation. She really is very pretty. I can feel my eyebrows knitting, my cheeks inexplicably flushing as I try to work out what she said.

"Did you just describe mashed potatoes, meat loaf, and gravy?"

She shrugs, conceding a hint of a smile.

"Sounds good." Before I can ask her name, the Chief twists around in his seat and calls, "Hey, Amy, get another slice while you're up?"

Amy nods as she scribbles and backs away. She's back a couple of minutes later, and when she slides a second piece of pie across the table toward the Chief he appears to catch her by the wrist because she startles as he leans in closer. "Think about it," he says, trying to whisper, but he raises his voice to repeat himself when Amy pulls away. "It's just dinner. It's two old friends catching up. Simple as that. Nothing heavy."

"Really, Matt," she says, her words dripping with sarcasm. "Nothing cute, nothing fancy? You'll play it straight down the line?"

Strange turn of phrase I think. Where have I heard that before? I try to focus on a bottle of ketchup and its fascinating list of ingredients as I listen in.

"First of all, we were never 'friends.'" Amy pulls out the quotation fingers, though based on the daggers she's sending the Chief's way they are totally unnecessary. "And second of all, you're not exactly known among the eligible and not-so-eligible ladies in town for 'nothing heavy.'"

Second time around I thought the quotation fingers packed quite a punch.

Chief Matt is positively squirming in his

seat, angling forward, patting down the air between them for Amy to lower her voice as he shakes his head and tries to whisper, "With respect, that's a goddamn lie and you know it."

This time Amy leans in, flicks a stray strand of hair behind her ear, and places her lips close to his ear. "With considerably less respect, no, it isn't."

And with that she takes a step back and points a finger at me. "Your dinner's coming right up." And then she heads toward the counter to place my order.

I watch her flit across the room. I'm mesmerized, like I spotted a woodland fairy. What's wrong with me? I don't have time for this, so why do I have the inclination? The fact that Chief Matt is enamored of Amy should be reason enough for me to keep my distance. He won't remember me—how many bullies remain haunted by their victims?—but, if I were to mention the R-rated movie *Scarface* (something he boasted watching while my friends and I were still watching the likes of *Bambi*) and the fact that, in school, every time he pitched a dodgeball into my face, he would scream, "Say hello to my little friend," there's a chance I might jolt his memory. Best not go there.

I pull out my worn copy of *Field & Stream*, flick through the first few pages, and remember my cell phone. For the record, I am not, and never will be, addicted to inane telecommunication. I don't have a contact list. I proudly possess a phone regarded as stupid and not smart. You won't find me logging on to Facebook, trying to convince so-called friends that I am leading a better life than they are, and I am not one of the masses that whips out a phone as soon as the airplane touches down because somewhere in the world someone needs to know I have landed safely. I'm simply checking to see that I've still got bars in case I get paged.

I am aware of an occasional glance, a square chin nudged in my direction, but it's impossible to tell whether it's born of recognition and contempt or nosiness and novelty. The concept of having to justify my past to a bunch of strangers fills me with dread. Or maybe, given my current location, I'm more afraid of the past insisting I justify my actions to myself.

Amy appears, steaming plate in hand.

"One meat loaf with mashed potatoes and gravy."

"Thank you." Ordinarily I would leave it at that, but I discover my mind and mouth slyly adding, "Nothing cute, nothing fancy this time?" It's the weird phrase she used earlier. I remembered. It's a quote from a Dirty Harry movie.

She considers me, not sure whether I'm toying with her, and we both notice how Chief Matt's fork has stopped midway to his mouth. He's obviously listening. Amy concedes a laugh and a little shake of her head. "Enjoy your meal."

I watch her go, as does Chief Matt, and for a dreamy second or two, I recognize the fact that I too might be interested in getting to know the feisty Ms. Amy. The unexpected buzz in my pants takes me by surprise. It takes a second to realize it's actually the vibrating pager in my pocket going off.

I read the digital display, fumble for my cell phone, and dial the number. I should ask for a doggie bag, get back to the clinic, and at least have access to some textbooks, given the high probability of being asked about something I have either forgotten or know nothing about. I need not have worried.

"Who's this?" says a female voice I instantly recognize.

"Good evening, Mrs. Silverman, this is Dr. Mills."

"What are you doin' calling me?"

"You called me, or should I say, you paged me."

"See, I wanted to leave a message on the machine for Doris."

If I shuffle across the seat to the window I can see Ethel and her dog, still standing at the pay phone. "I can take a message," I say.

A pause. I see Ethel dithering. "You sure?"

"Of course."

"See, I want her to order me some more of that food you gave me for Kai. Now I'm not saying it's working or anything, but I am saying he will eat it. At least he did this evening. And there's no point in trying it if you lot run out."

I bite my lower lip to keep the smile inside. "Don't worry, Mrs. Silverman, I'll make sure we order in enough for the next few weeks, enough to find out whether it works or not."

"Well just you be sure to do that," she says, and before I can add another word, she hangs up.

Outside the window I can see a young husky making a yellow connect-the-dots drawing in the snow before his owner drags him off down the street. Inside the diner people are chatting, enjoying their food. On the wall next to me there's a framed black-and-white photo of the Three Stooges and a sunlight-weathered poster for Moxie Cream Soda.

Mom refused to have soda in the house, but here in this diner she'd weaken and treat me to a Moxie.

Knife and fork in hand, I tuck in.

"Room for dessert?" asks Amy, picking up my empty plate.

I meet her eyes. Actually that's not quite right. My gaze fixes on her left eye and then moves to her right.

"We do great pies. Boston cream, chocolate cream, coconut cream, lemon meringue, apple."

I should be going, but some part of my brain is reaching out to another part, making connections, willing me to find reasons to stick around.

"Maybe another time," I say, silencing the fickle chatter inside my head. "I really should be going." The berserk snowplow barrels past the window, spraying up another wall of slush. "That guy's nuts. Who is he?"

"Oh, that's Skippy," says Amy. "Skippy De Tora. Usually rides around with his cat on his lap."

"His cat?"

She nods. "The Chairman," she says, barely pausing to add, "Chairman Meow."

We look at one another and let our eyebrows do the talking. I end up staring a little too long.

"What?" asks Amy, but in a gentle, curious way.

"Sorry . . . it's just your eyes . . . they're really . . ." She's waiting, and as I try to find the right word the noise around us seems to recede. "Unusual. They're really unusual."

If I didn't know better I'd say her features switched from momentary concern

to something approaching relief, even pleasure, as though Amy actually approved of
me avoiding a compliment.

"Thanks," she says, adding, "I guess."

"Presumably you were born with two
blue eyes and, in early childhood, one
turned brown. No history of trauma to the
eye?"

"That's right. So you know as much
about humans as you do animals, Doc?"

At first I'm confused until I realize that
she must know that I am the new veterinarian in town. Of course she does, this is
Eden Falls.

"What," she says, "you thought I thought
you were a lobster fisherman?"

Amy laughs, tugs on the front of her uniform, reminding me that I'm dressed like
I'm headed for the Atlantic Ocean. I grimace and pull the itchy woolen collar away
from my neck. Chief Matt is leaning into
the low backrest of the booth. He's been
playing with his second slice of pie, biding
his time, listening in to what the stranger is
saying that *his* girl is finding so funny.

"Anyway, here's the bill."

I pull out cash and hand it over.

"You need change?"

"No, that's for you," I say, realizing too late that a tip of close to 50 percent is far more than I can afford and embarrassingly conspicuous for a local diner.

"Thanks," she says, stuffing the bills into her breast pocket. "Welcome to Eden Falls. And please, do come again."

I watch her glide away to another table. *Was that the promise of another big tip speaking or does she genuinely want to see me again?* A sensible inner monologue is quick to point out that romance will not pay my credit card debt, stave off eviction from my rented apartment in Charleston, or generate the cash I need to appease the money-hungry Mr. Critchley by week's end. Besides, I haven't been out on a date for years let alone engaged in anything approaching a romantic entanglement. Way too awkward.

Extricating myself from the booth, I walk straight past the Chief. I can see his reflection in the glass of the diner's front door. He's watching Amy, who looks up to see me go.

The world outside sucks the air from my lungs, the cold feasting on my nose, ears, and cheeks after the genial glow of the diner. *Winter wonderland. More like polar purgatory!* I cross the street and my pager goes off for a second time. I thought Lewis said he forgets he's even on call.

I'm past the pay phone—no Ethel Silverman. I dial the number on my cell.

"Hi, this is Dr. Mills, someone paged me."

"Doc, it's me." It's a woman and she's clearly on edge. "Denise, remember. Tina, my cat, she's like, in labor. I think she needs a C-section."

I hear the plea for help and I hope I kept the four-letter expletive on the inside of my head, but I'm not sure.

"Where are you?"

"I'm driving over to your place. I'm like, five minutes away."

This time I'm certain the curse gets away from me. "Sorry about that. Look . . . um . . . don't worry. I'll be waiting for you. Denise?" Denise is no longer on the line.

I check my wristwatch, it's just after nine. Crap. This is not happening. Doc Lewis is still at least an hour away. Jogging back to the clinic, opting for the superior traction of the plowed street over the glassy sidewalk, I'm beginning to pant when a couple of headlights appear from somewhere behind me, lighting up my path. I stick out an arm to wave them past and the snow suddenly turns a brilliant blue. There's a *whoop-whoop* sound from a siren, and over my shoulder I see a police vehicle.

The driver's-side window powers down. "Everything okay?"

Chief Matt actually sounds genuinely concerned. "You look like you're in a hurry to get somewhere."

"I'm trying to get back to the clinic. I have a client with an emergency waiting for me."

The cop studies me. It's pitch-black out, but I feel like a skunk wandering around in the daytime and he's trying to figure out whether I'm rabid or not.

"Hop in," he says. "I'll give you a ride."

I thank him, come around to the passenger side, and a thought crosses my mind. Just like Amy, he never asked who I was, which suggests he already knows.

"Thanks," I say again. "Appreciate it. I'm Cyrus, Cyrus Mills."

I offer my hand and we shake. No two ways about it, the man who teased and taunted me through some of my most formative years has turned into a handsome devil, like a model that stepped off the cover of a romance novel, like Fabio only balding. With the interior light on and not yet faded away, the Chief takes a closer look, far more than I might expect with a casual how-do-you-do. If he's going to recognize me, now's his chance.

"Matt Devito. Have we met?"

Say hello to my little friend.

"Don't think so. Not unless you've been to South Carolina."

Matt Devito has to think about this, as if he's wondering whether he might have been on a road trip and maybe we bumped into one another at Shoney's or Popeye's. He shakes off the notion, waits for me to belt up, and guns it. I'm reckoning this ride will take ninety seconds, if that.

"Must be strange for you, moving this far north? All the snow, the cold?"

"Yes." I think he's hoping for more, but I'm playing hard to get.

"Doc Lewis has been talking about finding just the right person to replace Doc Cobb. You think you're the one?"

Another one who said "Doc Cobb," not

"your father." I feign deliberation, trying to buy some time. "Maybe."

I catch him nodding to himself. "Won't be easy to fit in. This is a small town. Everybody knows everybody."

He makes this synopsis of life in Eden Falls feel slightly menacing, like I'm trying to join an exclusive club and there's really no chance that I'll be accepted, so I shouldn't even bother. I wonder if this is really his way of warning me off Amy.

We turn into the practice's parking lot.

"Appreciate it," I say, getting out and feeling the same sense of relief I felt in high school when I got to keep my lunch money or avoided a swirly.

"Be seeing you," says Devito, but it sounds more like, *I'll be keeping my eye on you.*

"Right," I say, and before I can close the door, we both catch sight of Denise extricating herself from her VW.

"Ah, I see the very pregnant Ms. Laroche needs your help." Devito leans my way. "Don't expect to be paid." He fixes me with arching dark eyebrows, as though I should consider myself warned, before wheel-spinning out of the lot. I'm left standing in a cloud of oily blue smog.

"Sorry," says Denise as I approach. "I didn't know what else to do."

"You did the right thing," I say, reaching for Tina and taking Denise by the elbow. "Let's get inside and have a look at her."

In the examination room I spread a clean towel on the table and place Tina down on top of it. The cat is trembling and weak, happy to let her head fall flat.

"She's exhausted," I say.

Denise appears too afraid to speak. I will myself to reach out and squeeze her shoulder. I couldn't feel more awkward, but I'm sure this is what Lewis would do.

"I need to find out what's going on inside her."

Denise nods and makes a hollow sucking sound within her mouth as she ravages a piece of pink gum between her molars. "I didn't leave it too late, did I?"

I don't have an answer so I just reach for a sterile pair of gloves and what seems to be the obligatory tube of K-Y. Denise cradles Tina's head as I lift up the cat's tail and carefully insert a lubricated pinky finger into

a tight birth canal. Instantly, I make a startling discovery—claws. Tiny, soft, and perfectly formed claws. Gently I push a little
farther, feeling an ankle and a knee.

"She's breached," I say.

"What d'you mean?"

"I mean the kitten's coming out backward."

"Is that bad?"

I shake my head. "No. It's common for
kittens and puppies to come out back end
first." Thankfully I read the entire chapter
on small animal birthing disorders while
no one showed up for appointments.

"So don't you have to cut her open and,
like, pull the kitten out or something?"

Denise notices me glancing at my wristwatch. It's not even nine fifteen.

"In theory, yes."

I watch the expression on Denise's face
ratchet up from concern to distress. I'm
guessing she was hoping for a more confident, decisive answer. The thing is the
literature on this subject is perfectly clear—
*Obstruction of the birth canal, regardless
of cause, is an indication for cesarean
section*—but I dare not anesthetize this

cat let alone put scalpel to skin. Just because I know all there is to know about a recipe, doesn't mean it will turn out like it was cooked by Martha Stewart. And that stupid idiom, *See one, do one, teach one,* is about as useful as snapping my fingers and shouting *Hey Presto.* I'm a doctor with zero surgical dexterity and no previous experience.

"Don't," screams Denise. "Please, please don't look afraid."

I guess I wasn't doing such a great job of hiding my fear. It's not her panic that gets to me but the disappointment broadcast from eyes embellished by black eyeliner. And unlike so many other difficult times in my life there's the certainty that this time I cannot turn my back or wriggle out of this one. A mixture of guilt and shame threatens to overwhelm me, and it seems as though the best, the only thing I can do is to come clean.

"I've never done anything like this," I admit.

Though I didn't think it possible, Denise's expression amps up to bewilderment.

"Shut up," she shouts. "You're, like . . .

old. How can Tina be the first pregnant cat you've ever seen?"

"I'm saying I've never delivered kittens myself. In fact, I've never seen it done." Then, purely to provide clarification, I add, "But I have read about it."

Tina's eyes are closed. Denise continues to stroke her cat's head with bitten and cuticle-chewed fingers, the pace more frantic than soothing. For a while we say nothing, our collective silence interrupted by the rhythmic smack of gum. I can smell something fruity, maybe watermelon.

"Okay," she says, as though a period of rumination has helped her come to a decision. "Then we're still good, right? I mean you're still up for this?"

I peer into a young face full of artificial holes pierced with shiny metal, but what I see is a kid smart enough to recognize pity as wasted energy. I reckon this girl with no horizon lives in a permanent state of worry, yet she does so with a stubborn conviction that everything will eventually be okay. When was the last time her life went according to plan? What she's really saying is, *You're all Tina and I have got, so step up.*

"You ever seen *Gone With the Wind*?" I ask.

"No. What kind of music do they play?"

I'll pretend she didn't say that. "It's a movie, actually, and in it there's a line: *You cannot be brave without being scared.*"

From the puzzled expression on Denise's face, I'm guessing she didn't get it.

"In answer to your question, sure, I'm still up for this." I say this not because I want to, but because we both know I have no choice.

Denise digs deep and makes me feel buoyed by her gritty smile.

I grab a urinary catheter, a long, soft, red rubber tube that would normally be threaded into the bladder to divert urine out of the body. In this instance, I'm insert-ing it into the birth canal and using it to in-ject boatloads of lubricant around the back legs of the kitten. The concept is simple, like extricating the kid who gets his head stuck between metal railings. With every-thing slippery and slick there's less chance our little furry friend will get hooked up. The trouble is I still need Mom to help out with a grunt and a push, and judging by the way Tina's head has flopped into Denise's hand, I'm pretty sure this little cat is going to need much more than words of encouragement to bear down.

"I'll give her a shot. See if that helps."

I consider oxytocin, the hormone that increases the frequency of uterine contractions, but if the fetus is truly obstructed, oxytocin is absolutely contraindicated because it risks tearing the uterus. Instead I opt for an injection of calcium gluconate. It's probably less effective, but it might help with the force of uterine contractions and it's a whole lot safer. I keep my pathetic, ulterior motive to myself: a basic need to feel like I'm actually doing something.

For the next few minutes I keep busy, placing an intravenous catheter, giving Tina fluids, monitoring her pulses and her breathing. The whole time Denise offers a whispered abiding promise that we will not let Tina down.

"It's not working. How much longer are you gonna wait?"

Once again, I heed Lewis's sage advice on how best to handle the pet owners of Eden Falls.

"You're right. I thought the calcium shot might have kicked in by now, but Tina's giving us nothing." Again I check my watch. Damn, still not nine thirty.

"She's getting so weak, I can tell, she's. . . ."

And that's it. That's all she's got. Denise has reached the breaking point. The fight has ebbed from her voice. She's done pretending to cope, trying to be strong, make believing everything's going to be okay. I look on as the hard glass exterior of this young girl shatters and the tears come.

At point-blank range, the expectant grief of this expectant mother slices through my defenses. For the better part of my life, when someone cries for help, I've been the guy who dials 911. Here and now, Denise and Tina need me to be the guy who doesn't think, who simply acts, who tears off his jacket and runs into the burning building.

"Let me have one more try," I say, putting on a new pair of gloves. "If this doesn't work, I'll perform a C-section."

The dangers of trying to pull a newborn kitten out of the birth canal had been highlighted in Lewis's textbook, as though one reader had learned the hard way, having gone too far. Fetal limbs are too fragile to handle anything more than the gentlest form of traction. Pull too hard and the kitten will tear apart. Or the mom.

I look to the heavens as I sense the fourth and pinky finger of my right hand separating oh so slightly and between them I can feel two feet, two ankles, and two knees. This is new. Tina must have pushed because her kitten has slid about another centimeter or two into the birth canal. I glance over at Tina's pointy little face and see her eyes are shut tight. I pray she's still in this.

"Come on, Tina, come on sweetheart, just a little more."

I begin to air my inner monologue.

Traction is only advised if the veterinarian can position his fingertips around the fetus's shoulders or hips.

Denise leans into the table, her face in Tina's face. "Please, Tina, please," she whispers, big tears dripping onto her cat's whiskers, causing Tina to snuffle and grunt. Believe me, it's hard to tell, but I think something has moved, no, something has definitely moved because right now I can touch something firm and bony. It could be a hip. I give it the tiniest tug imaginable.

And it's like flipping a switch. Tina is back from the dead, raising her head, meowing, pushing with purpose, and I withdraw just in time to catch a lifeless black blob with pink feet.

Denise and I are frozen, unable to move. We look on as maternal instinct kicks in and Tina gets busy with her barbed pink tongue, chewing off membranes, licking life into the kitten. As I register the soft sound of newborn crying I realize that I am actually basking in a state of wonder, amazed that I can still feel amazed by what I am supposed to do for a living. I did nothing, yet the sight of this tiny angry creature tells me that somehow I did enough. In the deep and complicated relationship that exists between this frightened young girl and her best friend, I, a complete stranger, a transient nobody, have somehow inserted myself into this small but precious moment, a moment the three of us will forever share, a moment that against all expectations, I know I'll treasure.

"Oh my God, like, oh my God." For a second I think the old Denise is back and breezy until I notice how she still looks as anxious as before, as though she simply cannot believe that Tina did it, that she avoided the C-section, that it's all over, that Mom and kitten are doing fine.

I reach out to squeeze her hand and realize too late, this is all me, nothing to do with Lewis.

"I know, I know," I say. "It's going to be okay." Although my heart is racing, I'm beaming with genuine delight.

"No," she says, stepping back from the table. "You don't understand."

I look down and see Denise standing in a massive pool of fluid and for a second I'm confused.

Where could that puddle have possibly come from?

"My water's broken," says Denise. "I'm going to have *my* baby . . . now!"

Wednesday

« 9 »

"Well, well, if it isn't the man of the hour," Doris says the moment I set foot in the packed waiting room. Her audience falls silent as I become the subject of their attention, and I'm totally unprepared. It's a little after ten in the morning. I haven't bothered to shower. I haven't bothered to brush my hair. I'm the disheveled schoolboy who's late to class, embarrassed and on the spot.

"These are yours." Doris negotiates her desk to serve me with a wad of messages. There must be a dozen slips of paper. I look up. Every man, woman, dog, cat, and what appears to be an albino rabbit stares in my direction. I blush, keep my head down, and march through to the back.

My mood improves the moment I see Tina the cat and her newborn kitten spooning peacefully in a cage. I take note of a bowl of fresh water, a neatly primped and clean towel for them to lie on, an empty food bowl, and a pleasantly distended kitten belly. Though I feel like I just stepped off a turbulent red-eye, when I take in this scene, something bitter inside me fizzles and dissipates, replaced by a strange but agreeable calmness. It's a relief to know Lewis has looked in on them this morning. I wonder how Denise and her baby boy are doing. I should call the hospital later this morning.

Over in the examination room I can hear a muted spiel. Lewis is at work, exalting the merits of a high-fiber diet. It's his morning for appointments, hence the full waiting room. I've got a dinosaur-size bone to pick with him for leaving me in the lurch last night, and we still haven't discussed the best way to handle the mysterious newspaper article, but as I begin flicking through my messages, resolve gives way to a swell of nausea ripping through my guts.

Based on the many phone calls Doris has already fielded this morning it looks like I'm about to pay a heavy price for delivering Denise's son in the form of unwanted attention.

Someone named Ron from the *Burlington Free Press* called twice, begging for an exclusive interview. A producer from the local NBC affiliate, WPTZ, and a producer from FOX 44 want to run the story on their evening show. There are phone numbers for Vermont Public Radio, AM 620, and The Zone Talk Radio stations. Mrs. Silverman insists I give her a call—Doris bookended *URGENT* with asterisks for a little extra pep. Someone named Dominique called from the Montreal *Gazette*. Denise called to check in on Tina and her kitten and last, but not least, a Mr. Peter Greer called from the *Eden Falls Gazette*. Why does the name Greer sound familiar?

Everybody knows everybody in this town. Perfect. And there was me, worried about an anonymous extortionist, hoping against hope that he or she might want to trade in private. Why not toss in a little unwanted media attention, improve the odds of a viewer, listener, or reader ratting me out to the state veterinary board? Might as well start packing now.

Back out in the waiting room, ignoring the stares, I walk up to the reception desk. Doris has her head buried in paperwork.

"Doris, how many cases does Lewis have left to see?"

A raised ocher-stained index finger launches toward my face, making me wait until Doris slowly angles her head in my direction and meets my eyes.

"Half a dozen," she says, delivering one of her scary smiles.

I dare to lean in a little closer.

"Look, I need to speak to him."

"I don't think that's going to be possible, Dr. Mills. You see he's already behind, and some of these poor people have been waiting for nearly an hour."

Did she just crank up the volume so that everyone could listen in on our conversation? There's only one thing to do. "Since he's so busy I'll help out by seeing a few of his cases myself."

Doris gives me the kind of glare she might reserve for a family member trapped behind the bars of a prison cell as she refuses to pay their bail so that they might learn their lesson.

"That's kind of you, Dr. Mills, but these clients are specifically here to see Dr. Lewis. We don't want to disappoint them now, do we?"

I'm pretty sure that wasn't a compliment. "Just give me the next file, Doris," I say, under my breath. "And could you please *label it* like we discussed yesterday afternoon."

Doris knows what I'm talking about, so why is she shrugging her scrawny shoulders? If people are going to talk, let it be about the way this new vet expects to get paid for every visit.

There's a theatrical moment in which Doris pretends to catch on. She surreptitiously peels off a yellow Post-it note, scribbles something, slaps it on the inside of a file, and hands it over. I see the patient's name on the front.

"Puck," I call. A seriously overweight, panting black Labrador gets to his feet and trots toward me followed by a woman and a man who is carrying the dog's leash. The man is small, not quite as short as Doc Lewis but pretty close. He's wearing a three-piece royal blue pinstripe suit that's a little long in the sleeves, a white button-down shirt, and a striped tie. The snappy ensemble is finished off with an ungainly pair of black snow boots. As he closes the space between us, I can tell his hair is wrong, the dark brown of the periphery an imperfect match to the toupee up top.

The woman in his wake has to be ten years his junior and a good three inches taller. She's wearing sneakers, a designer tracksuit, and her hair is tied up in a ponytail. She looks like she's going to the gym, except for a fresh, thick layer of bright red lipstick. But what strikes me most is the way she stares at me, as though she can hardly contain her amusement. And that's when it hits me. She's the woman I pulled from the snowbank, the one with the black Lab, the eyewitness who saw me out and about with Frieda.

"Um . . . please, this way." I lead them back into the workspace, trying to regroup. "Sorry it's not the exam room, but I thought we could move things along. I'm Dr. Mills."

"Dr. Ken Haggerty, headmaster at Eden Falls Academy." Haggerty makes his job description sound like a title along the lines of secretary of state. And for a man who should know how to schmooze and work a room, his handshake is surprisingly weak.

"This is my wife, Crystal, and more importantly, this is Puck."

"Actually, we've already met." Crystal, steps in close, and, without her husband noticing, winks as she sandwiches her soft hands around mine. "But I do appreciate the formal introduction." I have to pull my hands from hers. "So," she says, "you're the one who delivered that young girl's baby last night."

"That was pretty special of old Lewis," says Haggerty, "new in town and already throwing you right in at the deep end."

I shrug. "Luck of the draw. I took his on-call so he and his wife could catch dinner and a movie."

Both Dr. and Mrs. Haggerty look surprised.

"Not possible," says Haggerty. "Mrs. Lewis has been living in a special-care facility for the past few months. It's my understanding she has very little time left to live. Isn't that right, dear?"

His wife nods.

I don't know what to say. Why would Lewis lie about such a thing?

Crystal Haggerty catches my dismay. "But we're just as happy to see you, aren't we, Ken?"

"Of course. Where's that accent from?"

Will this inquisition ever stop? I hesitate, unsure of how much to share, and I'm reminded of a quote from *Lawrence of Arabia*.

A man who tells lies, like me, merely hides the truth. But a man who tells half lies has forgotten where he put it.

"The Carolinas."

"North or South?" asks Crystal.

I give up. "South. Charleston."

"Really," she says, unduly excited, "I wonder if you know our friends, Martin and Stephanie, breed Tibetan terriers, very big on the Charleston show circuit?"

"No," I say, too quickly. "I never had anything to do with dog shows."

"Oh, I spoke to Stephanie this morning and she could have sworn your name sounded familiar. Where did you practice?"

My moment of vacillation must look suspicious, and I can't say whether Crystal Haggerty is simply curious or letting me know she's done her homework and she's on to me.

Ken comes to my rescue. "Please, if he had said New York would you have asked him if he knew Donald Trump? Can we focus on why we're here?"

I try not to sigh with relief. "Definitely," I say. "So what's up with Puck?" The name is all it takes for this amiable creature to sidle over, tail working overtime, leaning in for a scratch. "Presumably he's named after the character in *A Midsummer Night's Dream*?"

I'm trying out the whole relate-to-your-clients thing. I'm thinking, Ken's a headmaster, an academic type, it's a reasonable question.

"You're joking, right? I mean, look at him. He's black and chunky. He's named after a hockey puck!"

Okay, no more second-guessing the origin of pets' names.

"He's up to his old tricks," says Dr. Haggerty, mussing his dog's head. "Aren't you boy? Throwing up. It happens every so often, puking once or twice a week, but this time it's once or twice a day."

I stare at Puck, doing his impression of

a Roomba vacuum cleaner, working his nose around the smells on the floor. On the surface he appears to be absolutely fine—focused, tail wagging back and forth, not a care in the world.

"What's normally the problem?" I ask.

Haggerty glances over at his wife. "Where to begin. When you look at Puck you can tell he loves to eat. But it's more than that. It's more than a desire for calories or taste. It's about having stuff in his mouth, stuff he can swallow. I'm talking about jumping up on a kitchen counter to steal a loaf of bread."

I'm not impressed.

"I'm talking about a whole loaf of bread still in its plastic wrapper. I'm talking about an entire Thanksgiving turkey still in its aluminum foil."

This time I shrug my shoulders. A dog has over two hundred and twenty million olfactory receptors in its nose. Humans have only five million. If I'm drooling over the smell of a Thanksgiving turkey, I can only imagine what it can do to a dog.

Haggerty is shaking his head. "You don't understand. It wasn't even cooked. It's not about satisfying his hunger, Puck loves the act of making stuff disappear. Leashes, shoes, seat belts, golf balls, bottle caps, if you can think of it, he's swallowed it. And let's not forget his penchant for underwear. Not mine of course, oh no. Puck has a discerning taste, a preference for my wife's extensive lingerie collection. The poor dog has grazed his way through enough thongs and lace panties and stockings to fill a Victoria's Secret catalog twice over."

As her husband talks I cannot help but notice his wife. Crystal is standing behind him, and as he speaks about her frilly undergarments she offers me a single, raised, meticulously plucked eyebrow, her mouth on the verge of a coy smile. I may be wrong, but it's a look I might expect from a woman half her age, an expression that says, "What's a girl to do?" I turn away before I blush, fearing she might lick her top lip with a slick salacious tongue.

"And you think he's gotten into something more serious?"

"That's why we're here," says Haggerty.

I consider asking Mrs. Haggerty if any particular intimate apparel is missing from her notorious collection but think better of it. "And how long has this been going on?"

The headmaster looks at his wife. "Just over a week, wouldn't you say?"

"Possibly," says Crystal. "It could have been longer."

"No," says Haggerty, "it was definitely after I returned from that weekend conference in Atlanta. Before I went away he was absolutely fine."

Haggerty comes back to me, ready for more pertinent questions. Crystal, on the other hand, appears distracted, wrestling with the recollection.

"Has Puck been drooling?" I ask.

"No," says Haggerty.

There's a long awkward pause as I try to dig up questions pertinent to Puck's problem. I don't know what to say next. *Why can't they leave me alone, let me think without the scrutiny?* The silence between us becomes oppressive and embarrassing and eventually I blurt out, "How's his stool?"

"Normal."

Damn. "No blood, mucus, or excessive straining?"

Haggerty tries to consult with his wife, but she's lost to some type of anxious reverie. He shakes his head.

"Eating and drinking fine?"

"Same as always."

Another awkward pause, and then a classic question floats by and I grab it. "And when Puck throws up, what's it look like?"

Haggerty brings a finger and thumb up to his chin, considering how to word his description.

"I would say yellow, no, buttery, viscous with more than a hint of froth."

Crystal is back but agitated. "It's puke, Ken, not a glass of wine."

"I was merely trying to be helpful."

I interject before this escalates. "And it was definitely an active vomiting process. I mean Puck had to work his abdominal muscles to get it out. He doesn't just lower his head and it falls out."

Finally, they are unified in headshakes. I'm pleased. No, I'm more than pleased. For the first time in my brief and real veterinary career I have *verbally* discarded a long list of red herrings and, in doing so, by default, I'm one step closer to a diagnosis. Though Ken and Crystal may not know it, I just ruled out the possibility of passive regurgitation.

"Good," I say. "Then let's take a look."

At this point, I'm thinking I can probably handle a gregarious Lab, so I squat down, and Puck barrels in with his head, tongue flopping side to side, twisting his rump around to flagellate me with his tail.

"I want to know if there's something obvious stuck in his intestines," says Haggerty, as though nothing could be simpler.

Thankfully, Crystal steps forward to distract Puck by scratching his ears as I set about my palpation of the dog's guts. I take my time, front to back, top to bottom, and Puck is wonderfully relaxed and amenable, his slack belly allowing me to appreciate everything. I'm not exactly sure what I'm feeling but he demonstrates no pain, no wince, no nothing.

"I don't feel a thing out of place. No small children or license plates as far as I can tell." My effort at levity receives dead-eyed stares. Best not try that again. I go with another Lewis tactic—stall. "But there are lots of other things that could be causing him to vomit. At the very least we should think about getting some blood work and some X-rays of his abdomen."

"No, no, no," says Haggerty, waving his hand at me. "I'm sure that won't be necessary."

Did I have dollar signs in my eyes? I pick up the file, carefully open it up, and peek at Doris's Post-it note: *$!* What on earth am I supposed to make of that?

"Puck always passes these things, don't you boy? I just wanted to make sure he was all right."

Puck barks once, as if to confirm that his master speaks the truth.

"Look, if things don't sort themselves out over the next few days, I'll bring him back for more tests, okay?"

"I'll be the one bringing him back," says Crystal, "because my husband is forgetting he's going to be out of town this weekend."

I'm not sure whether this information is intended for Dr. Haggerty's benefit, or for mine. "Very good," I say. "But if anything changes for the worse, be sure to contact either myself or Doc Lewis."

Haggerty steps forward and picks up his dog's leash. "It was nice to meet you. We must have you over for dinner one night, mustn't we, Crystal." But before his wife can reply, Haggerty is heading out the door. "I'll go and warm up the car?"

Does he seriously think he can trade a home-cooked meal for services rendered?

"Doris will be happy to take the fee for today's visit," I shout after him. The effect on those in the waiting room is startling, like screaming "I've got a bomb" on a plane. In unison, they stare at me with alarm in their eyes.

"Oh," says Mrs. Haggerty, unable or unwilling to hide her disappointment, "only Dr. Cobb used to let these 'little visits' slide."

My smile must look like a ventriloquist's dummy.

"Well, it was still a pleasure to meet you." She stretches out her hand to shake mine. "If Puck doesn't turn the corner soon I will definitely be in touch."

Making to leave, she catches herself and says, "Tell me, Doctor, do you make house calls?"

"Yes, of course," I reply, feeling the need to add, "though there's an extra charge for the service."

"Of course," she says. "And if you're ever in the area, drop by. The campus is fabulous, even in the winter. It would be my pleasure to show you what's on offer."

I notice a smudge of red lipstick bonded to one of her upper incisors. Is she flirting with me?

"And I'll be sure to get back to my friend, Stephanie. See what she knows about our famous Dr. Mills from Charleston."

"Thank you," I mumble as Mrs. Crystal Haggerty disappears, wondering if I'm destined to become the love slave of this frustrated urban housewife in order to buy her silence.

I'm ready to pry another file from Doris's boney claw. "Who's next and what was with that note?"

"Sorry," says Doris, under her breath. "I thought it was obvious, like a hotel rating system, you know, one star means a dump, five stars means a palace. So, one dollar means a tightwad who never pays on time, and five will mean loaded to the gills with money to blow. D'you want me to write this down for you?"

"No, I get it. I'll just take the next file."

She hands over a folder as thick as the yellow pages phone directory.

"Here, this belongs to Clint, Harry Carp's dog. The fax with her blood results arrived this morning. I thought you might want to give him a call."

Hum, that was a pretty fast turnaround, and Doris is right, I'd forgotten all about poor Clint.

I flick through the file and can't find the new paperwork. "Where is it?"

"Where it always is, out back next to the microscope."

And to think, I almost believed Doris was being helpful.

I discover the fax machine perched on a counter next to a microscope. There's a note on the counter, carefully laminated and securely taped near the microscope: USE OIL FOR HIGH POWER LENS ONLY! Mom's handiwork again, the absence of *please* duly noted. Hard to believe Cobb kept these reminders of my mother around, but I'm glad he did. They feel like an oasis in a desert of discord, a touchstone to order and discipline.

Lying in the fax machine's tray I find a single sheet of paper, the blood results for an older model mixed-breed dog named Clint Carp. The data is divided into columns: a long list of everything that's been tested, their absolute values, and the upper and lower limits of a normal range for each value. It's a hieroglyphic mix of numbers and enzymes and ions and cell types but, with a vivid recollection of the dog's owner, Harry, I feel compelled to take my time and work on the translation.

Neutrophilic leukocytosis

Hidden in the secret language on the page, all I can say for sure is that Clint has a mild increase in the number of some of her white blood cells. There are too many to blame it on the stress of having your blood drawn by a clumsy novice. There are too few to conclude that Clint is battling some sort of an infection. In short, Clint's blood work results are totally nonspecific and inconclusive.

I find Harry's number in the file and dial. He picks up after the tenth ring. I introduce myself, give him a chance to catch his breath, and tell him about the blood results.

"Could it be cancer?"

"Maybe, but not necessarily," I say. "Neutrophils are a specific lineage of white blood cells, indicative of . . ." My words trail off as I catch myself. For me, there's always been security, a comforting precision, to be found in medical jargon, but right now, for the first time in my career, I appreciate how it's the last thing Harry needs to hear. Having met him, knowing exactly where he is standing in his home, pained expression on his face, odd little creature by his side, I'm struck by a sudden urge to give this dying old man something more meaningful than dumbing down the details. No hedging, no waffling, just a simple "yes" or "no" answer. Harry's quavering voice makes something inside me loosen and break free, something totally irrational and, quite possibly, reckless.

"No," I hear myself say, with absolutely no scientific justification whatsoever. "No, Harry, Clint does not have cancer."

What's come over me? Can this be a lie if there's no malicious intent? But I'm giving him an answer where one does not exist.

A sigh of relief whistles down the phone line, and I have to say, it makes my distortion of the truth much more palatable. There's no point in trying to sort out Clint's illness with her owner dying of worry. If I'm wrong, and, to be honest, I still may be, I'll have to face the music when the time comes.

"That's good to know, but what else can it be?"

That wasn't much of a reprieve.

"Sorry, Harry, I'm still not sure. How's she doing today?"

Another sigh, and I pick up on the subtle distinction between relief and disappointment.

"Same as before. Nibbling at her food, but she's drinking fine."

Ah, the frustration of "ain't doin' right."

"I'll ask Doc Lewis if he can drop by and take a look at her," I say. "Better still, you might want to bring her here to Bedside Manor."

There's a silence on the line. "I'll see if I can get a ride. To be honest, I feel a whole lot better knowing she doesn't have cancer. Thanks, Doc."

Somehow I can't bring myself to say, *me too*.

10

The waiting room is down to its last two cases: a guy in an army surplus camouflage jacket clutching his albino rabbit and a middle-aged woman sitting next to a younger man with a fancy cat carrier.

I approach Her Majesty and whisper, "Who's next?"

Doris says nothing but slides the file (another monster) across the counter toward me, a yellow fingernail tapping a yellow Post-it note on the cover. I look to see what she's pointing to: $$$$$$.

"Six," I mouth, conscious of my own wide-eyed excitement. *Cha-ching!*

Her nod is almost imperceptible as she peels off the note and scrunches it inside her palm.

"Chelsea," I call, twirling around as the young man and the woman get to their feet. I doubt he's made it into his thirties. I doubt she's still in her fifties. *Has to be mother and son.* "I can't tell you how sorry I am to keep you waiting Ms. . . ."

"Weidmeyer, Virginia Weidmeyer, but please, call me Ginny." She reaches forward to shake my hand. "And this is Steven."

Steven gives me a snappy little chin jerk, which, to my way of thinking, only serves to exaggerate the age difference between them. Thank goodness he spared me the "wassup." He wears a long, matte black leather coat over a denim shirt, blue jeans with creases, and shiny cowboy boots. Perhaps he thought the dead cow afforded his Canadian tuxedo a touch of class. I find the look a little contrived, as if he hopes people will ask whether he is on his way to or from a *Matrix* convention.

"Very nice to meet you both, I'm Doctor—"

"I know who you are, Cyrus," says Ginny. "Your father was a dear friend. I'm so sorry."

I've stopped breathing. There might be

drool hanging from the corner of my mouth. This woman must know all about me and my estrangement from Cobb yet she's not spitting in my face or lunging for my jugular.

"Thank you," I manage to mumble, though it feels all wrong. I affect a tickle in my throat. *Get back on track*. "So, this must be Chelsea."

Ginny gasps, lays a splayed palm across her chest, as if she's committed a mortal sin. "Forgive me, yes, this is the love of my life, Chelsea."

Steven raises the carrier in his hand in the manner of someone raising a toast with a glass full of beer. The feline must be in hiding at the back.

"Ginny, back so soon?"

Lewis is guiding his second-to-last clients in the direction of Doris—good man. He and Ginny exchange a peck as Steven looks on.

"Wanted Chelsea to meet her new vet."

"Well then, you'd best take my exam room. I'm sure Malcolm and Mr. Snuffles will be more than happy to hop on back, right Malcolm?"

"Actually, Lewis, I was hoping we might have a quick word in—"

"No time, Dr. Mills. These patients have been patient for far too long. Please." He holds the examination door open, gestures for us to enter, and it seems we have no choice.

Steven deposits the carrier on the floor, takes a seat, and starts messing with his watch. I'm not sure whether he wants me to get a move on or to notice it's a TAG Heuer. Ginny stands by the exam table.

"I should explain the situation," she says. "We're longtime clients of your father."

I try not to wince.

"He's been treating her kidney disease forever. Isn't that right, baby? Steven, be a love. Chelsea needs to say hello to the nice doctor."

On a sigh Steven gets out of his chair, squats down, pops the latch on the little plastic gate, and reaches a hand inside. There's an ungodly growl, an otherworldly hiss, and Steven quickly changes his mind, lifting up the back end of the carrier, angling it upward, attempting to "pour" the cat onto the floor. Chelsea may not have great kidneys, but with her crib tilted at ninety degrees, she clearly retains the power to defy gravity.

"Not like that. Here, let me."

If these two are an item, this scolding sounds totally wrong. Steven shrugs his shoulders, mumbles something about not being much of a cat person, and returns to his seat, unfazed. He seems quite content to look on, stroking his neat goatee like he's checking that it's still there.

Ginny picks up the carrier, places it on the examination table, and this time there are no complaints as she extracts an orange, flat-faced, long-haired cat. My mind should be brainstorming feline kidney disease but it's hit the "pause" button. I've gone totally blank on Chelsea's breed.

"We're hoping you share the same treatment philosophy as your father."

Is she asking me a question? And how do I stop her from using that word?

"Weekly examinations. Regular checkups on her urine. Careful monitoring for dehydration."

Persian. The name of the breed is Persian. Originated in Iran. Known for polycystic kidney disease, an inherited disorder. These particular cats are born with abnormal kidneys, but most don't show clinical signs until three to ten years of age.

It takes me a while to realize Ginny's staring at me, as though I might have succumbed to a narcoleptic event. Was I talking to myself again? "Sorry, yes," I say. "Certainly. Happy to." I run a hand over Chelsea's back and feel the greasy, clumpy fur and boney skeleton of a creature fighting a chronic, relentless disease.

"I'm sure you've heard this before, Doctor, but Chelsea is the best cat in the world. Sorry, I should have asked if you prefer Dr. Mills, or can I call you Cyrus?"

Is this a test? Is she actually questioning my family loyalty?

"Um . . . Cyrus . . . and I don't doubt it . . . about her being the best cat in the world."

"There's nothing I wouldn't do for her. Nothing. Isn't that right, Steven?"

Steven's not listening, still playing with his watch, and once again Ginny waits for a response from me. What does she want me to say? Something philosophical? Something reassuring? I tip my head back, open my mouth, and inhale, desperate to impart some sort of personal, eloquent wisdom. But I've got nothing. Seconds pass, trapped in mute moronic limbo, trustworthy veterinarian transformed into village idiot. In the end I do the only thing that comes to mind. I pick up Chelsea and hug her to my chest.

To my amazement Ginny beams, as though this is exactly what she'd hoped for, and joins me, running her hand down her beloved cat's body. Botox may have limited her ability to express alarm, and yes, she's a little too tight in the wrong places, but her lips can still tremble. This is no act.

Then I notice the left hand that strokes the cat, not the wrinkles—the part of the aging process her cosmetic surgeon cannot hide—but the enormous sparkling rock on the fourth finger. "That's a beautiful ring."

At this Steven is all ears, rocking in his seat, and making a show of interlocking his fingers in his lap. He seems to be accustomed to taking the credit.

"Thank you," says Ginny. "Three carats."

"Three point two," Steven says. "Picked it up in New York. Friend in Midtown gave me a deal. Before Vermont I lived in Manhattan."

"I beg your pardon, three point two."

She overplays the demure shoulder shrug. "Steven surprised me with it, what, couple of months ago. Feels funny, being a fiancée at my age."

This comment actually gets Steven on his feet, placing an arm around Ginny's hip and giving her a disconcerting pat on her derriere. "You're as old as you feel, right, Doc?"

Ginny offers him a playful punch on the arm, and Steven feigns mock pain. Chelsea and I look on. I believe we are unified in our revulsion.

"So," I say, eager to move on. "Chelsea gets her blood tested, urine tested, anything else?"

"X-rays. Doc Cobb was worried about kidney stones."

Most common types of stone: cystine, oxalate, urate, and struvite. "Really. When was the last time she had an X-ray?"

Ginny consults with her boy toy.

"Couple of weeks before he died," says Steven.

Ginny seems to concur. "She won't sit still. I always have to hold her."

I've noticed a couple of wide shelves in the work area, home to large manila envelopes, presumably the clinic's collection of pet X-rays. This feels like an opportunity to finally catch Lewis. "Mind if I track them down? Give me an idea of what's going on."

"Be our guest," says Steven. "Take your time." He winks at me. I don't want to imagine what he hopes to get up to in my absence.

Lewis, grappling with a fluffy white object, seems to be making a conscious effort not to catch my eye as I rifle the shelf of X-rays and find the appropriate folder. It's thick and heavy and the films date back over many months. No question, Ginny Weidmeyer is worried about Chelsea, but, more importantly for Bedside Manor, she's game to spend some serious money on her cat. I wonder if I can continue to make that happen before the end of the week?

There's a viewing box on the wall. I switch it on and begin looking at films in chronological order. It's been a while since I tried to read an X-ray and, unlike Lewis's previous synopsis, it's nothing like riding a bike.

When I put up the final image, taken eleven days before the death of Robert Cobb, I see it, a tiny kidney stone.

I could take a little more time, review a medical textbook, get my questions and facts straight before I go back in, but already my eyes have focused on a totally different area of the X-ray film. I can make out a series of small bones that should not be there—human bones, Ginny's hand, exposed to radiation from restraining her fidgety cat. And the ring, the diamond in its gold setting, is totally white and opaque on the film. How can that be?

Once again another stupid factoid has lodged in my mind: diamond is a cubic lattice structure of one atom, carbon. Diamond will not show up on an X-ray. I should see a black, empty setting. But Ginny's three-carat—sorry, three-point-two-carat—rock is white and opaque. Either Steven was duped when he purchased the ring or, unwittingly, this little cat with a kidney stone has just unmasked lover-boy Steven as a fraud.

No wonder Lewis's appointments last so long. Will the man ever stop talking? I've been finished with Ginny for nearly twenty minutes. I promised to review Chelsea's entire record and evaluate "Dr. Cobb's" treatment plan (I hope she noticed how I referred to him) regarding the kidney stone, before getting back to her. Naturally I said nothing about the fake engagement ring. Intriguing as it is, it's none of my business.

The chime of the shopkeeper's doorbell

is my cue to pounce. "Finally. Can we talk?" I gesture for Lewis to join me in the work area rather than add, "in private," in front of Doris.

"Didn't believe it 'til I came in this morning." A jovial Lewis strolls past me, and I close the door behind him. Why is he acting chipper and congratulatory? And that crimson bow tie with white polka dots is not helping matters. He nods at the cage that's home to Tina and her kitten. "Only way to pry that young girl off her cat was if she had her baby. And that means the rumors about the gifted Dr. Mills must be true."

He steps in and puts an arm around my shoulder like a proud parent, obviously unable to read my irritation. After a restless two hours of sleep, I had stumbled downstairs, intending to tell Lewis about the mysterious newspaper article and confront him over leaving me in the lurch last night. This development with the media has changed my focus. Where to begin?

"Take a look at these."

Lewis pauses as I pass what feels like a handful of warrants for my arrest, regarding me with more optimism than concern, a convivial "how bad could it possibly be" expression. Then he begins to read, and the more he reads, the more his blithe confidence melts away. With it goes my need to terrorize him for the truth about his ailing wife.

"What are we going to do?" I ask. "The last thing I need are reporters asking questions about a veterinarian who thinks he's an obstetrician. If they're curious, they'll dig, and if they dig, they'll find my suspended license and as soon as they do, it's over. If I can't work, I can't turn this practice around, and if I can't sell it as a going concern, I can't get back."

Suddenly Lewis seems filled with sadness, and I can't tell whether it is aimed at me or leaking from him. "Get back to what?"

A minute ago I might have jumped all over him with an emphatic "the private and dispassionate life of a veterinary pathologist, of course." But sensing this change in him, I soften my reply to something I hope he will appreciate. "What I do best."

Lewis keeps his head down, lips pursed, and nods. Was it something he read or something I said?

"You never came right out and said you wanted to sell the practice. I had hoped you were making a new start for yourself. I mean you've only just got here."

I frown. "It's not as though I have a choice. I'm out of money. I've got bills to pay, serious legal fees, and no one was going to hire me without a license to practice. Bedside Manor found me, and for that I will be eternally grateful, but it was always a means to an end. Thing is, if I don't make a significant first payment in three days' time the bank will step in and I'll lose everything."

"How much are we talking?"

I tell him the dollar amount. Lewis appears stunned, as if I as good as handed him his pink slip. Critchley's opening fee should be labeled "heartbreaking disbelief," not good faith.

"When were you thinking of trying to sell?" Lewis asks.

"Ideally within the month."

"Seriously. Less than a month?" For a moment I lose him as the thoughts behind his eyes pull him away from me. I don't know where they take him, but judging from the speed of his transition into the distress written across his face, the destination is painful. When the Lewis I know comes back, he says, "Let me ask you something: last night, when you delivered the kitten, when you delivered the baby, how did it make you feel?"

"Who told you what happened?"

Lewis locates the message from Ethel Silverman and makes it flutter between his fingers like a patriot welcoming home the troops. "Her daughter-in-law works ob-gyn at University Hospital."

I shake my head. Who needs the Internet when you've got Ethel Silverman to turn the town's petty gossip viral?

"And don't worry. I already called Ethel. Kai's fine. And Denise and her baby are doing fine. Ethel just wanted the details of what happened here last night. If nothing else, Mrs. Silverman prefers her tattling to be current and accurate." He waits a beat. "So, tell the truth, how did it make you feel?"

My right hand begins reaching for that imaginary itch at the back of my head. It was a long night. After driving Denise and her son to the hospital in the VW (she was right, it took over an hour to get there, and The Bug's useless in the snow) and fending off disapproving looks from nurses convinced I was the child's illegitimate father, I had to wait for a shift change to hitch an ambulance ride back to Eden Falls.

"If I pretend not to feel like crap and ignore this unwanted attention then . . . sure . . . there was a measure of satisfaction in the process."

Lewis snatches at my restraint. "A measure? Admit it, it felt pretty damned good, right?"

"If you say so."

"Like nothing you've ever experienced looking down a microscope?"

I see where he's going with this. "Different is all. There's plenty of satisfying thrills in pathology."

"Really?" He does a little cant thing with his head. "Since when did pathology make you forget to breathe? Since when did pathology get your heart bursting in your chest?"

My moment of hesitation is proof enough, and he celebrates with an enormous grin. I can't get mad at him. Whatever was lurking in his ominous daydream can stay there for now. First things first.

"What are we going to do about the media?" I use the word *we* without thinking, but Lewis latches onto it as if he's grateful, like there's still hope.

He thumbs through the messages one more time. "You can't hide from this. Saying 'no comment' will only fire up their curiosity, especially on a slow news day. But there may be a way to minimize the damage while maximizing an opportunity to improve business."

I'm not with him.

"Peter Greer. Englishman, nice guy, editor in chief for the *Eden Falls Gazette*. He's been a Bedside Manor client for years. Has a Jack Russell terrier, Toby. We'll tell the other reporters we're going to give our hometown columnist the exclusive. They want their scoop, they're going to have to quote Greer."

"Why choose him?"

"Simple," says Lewis, "Greer's proven himself loyal to the practice and he knows what it's like to be an outsider trying to catch a break in a small town. He'll be receptive. He'll spin the story in our favor. Just focus on the events of last night and make it clear you're hoping to get some good publicity for the practice. Remember, this is the *Eden Falls Gazette*. It's not an interview with *Vanity Fair*. And he's not going to alienate you, not after what you did for Denise Laroche."

I'm not convinced. "You really believe this guy's our best option?"

"This way the story might stay local. Think about it, how many folks actually read the *Gazette*? You call Greer and I'll call Denise and tell her there'll be no charges for last night so long as she refuses to speak to any reporters."

"What? Which bit of 'we need money' did you not hear?"

"You got a cheaper way to buy her silence? Didn't think so. Doris can fend off the rest of this lot in her sleep. After all, articulation to the point of rudeness is Doris's specialty."

I wanted to ask about Mrs. Lewis, about Ginny Weidmeyer's relationship with Cobb, and whether I should be worried about the potentially meddlesome Crystal Haggerty, but Lewis is already headed for the reception desk, triumphantly waving my paper slips over his head.

*   *   *

Peter Greer could not have been nicer during our phone conversation. What's with a plummy English accent—it makes everything you say sound so weighty and indefatigable. Apparently it was "absolutely splendid" of me to give him an exclusive, he assured me that he was not a hack overeager to use the word *hero,* and, if I could "pop-in" around seven this evening for an interview that would be "smashing."

I hang up and think about last night and what Lewis said. The thing is, my experience with Denise and Tina was exhausting, terrifying, humbling, and, wait for it, simply wonderful. It was the rush of what was possible. It was the novelty of actually being thanked, not so much in words, but in a moment of tacit understanding. In my years as a veterinary pathologist I've always felt as though I was late to the party. Last night, for the first time, as a real veterinarian, I was finally its life and soul.

And let's not forget the other big event from last night, my encounter with Amy, the waitress at the diner. I'm not quite sure what happened there, but I instantly felt like a teenage boy with a summer camp crush.

Ridiculous. It's not as though it can go any-where. When I head back to Charleston, what am I going to do, exchange friendship bracelets? Promise to write every day?

"Dr. Mills?" It's Doris. "I put this together for you. It's the bad debt."

Doris hands over a piece of paper with a handwritten list of clients and the amount of money each individual owes. There are about thirty names, and as I requested, she's made two columns: those who can pay, but don't (the Haggertys make this row), and those who can't afford to pay, but try their best (Denise Laroche makes this row). Everybody knows everybody in this town and, I'm guessing, few more so than Doris. Why not exploit her bitterness and innate nosiness?

"Good work, Doris. Not as bad as I thought."

"That's for last month, December. I'll start on the rest of last year tomorrow."

"Whoa! That's bad." And then my inner monologue slips out from under my breath. "What was he thinking?"

Doris looks as though she is dying to give me her opinion and damn the conse-quences, but she puffs up and reins in her tongue, the smart schoolgirl who always knows the answer, forced to give the other kids a chance. "I'll be at lunch."

"Before you leave, I wonder if you could do one more thing for me?"

She waits, increases the frequency of her blinks.

"I need you to call our telephone provider and ask them to hook us up with wireless Internet access. See if they've got any deals." Preferably a package that's free for the first month.

"Hold on, hold on."

Doris scurries over to her desk, scrambles for a piece of paper, and scratches out a note, her lips mouthing the words "wireless Internet" like she's learning a foreign language. Then she digs out an antiquated piece of secretarial equipment, her Rolodex. Squinting at a card, she picks up the phone and dials a number. Maybe I should be grateful she didn't step outside and send a message via carrier pigeon.

Further updates to the twenty-first century will have to wait till another day. It's time to hunt for information about feline kidney disease, all the stuff I never needed until now, like how to treat, how to monitor, and how to recognize that a cat can be suffering, enduring a sad existence, even if it doesn't appear to be in pain. Fifty minutes pass before I have the confidence to call Ginny Weidmeyer, and even then I've got the appropriate pages open and to hand.

"You didn't have to get back to me so soon."

"Not a problem. I strive to be timely and organized." Part of me hopes she'll notice how this raison d'être clearly distinguishes me from Cobb. How many times would I be trying to tell Cobb something about my school day, only to watch his eyes glaze over before he said, "Sorry, Son. Forget to submit a blood sample" or "Forgot to call a client." Cobb thrived on chaos, and for a kid competing with these more important priorities for his attention, this felt a lot like rejection.

"You know," says Ginny, "there were a couple of things I forgot to tell you."

I brace myself, half-expecting her to go off on me. Or maybe she knows the rock is a fake and I'm about to find out that Steven is actually a hired gigolo.

"Chelsea's diet: she's on special food to

reduce the risk of crystals in her urine. You think she should stay on it?"

"Um, definitely. Assuming she's eating it."

"Steven says she is. He feeds her first thing in the morning, before he brings me my cappuccino. He's such a love."

Ginny Weidmeyer has it bad. And her affection for Steven threatens to trigger my vomiting control center.

"Very good," she says. "Now the second point concerns you."

"It does."

"Yes. Both Steven and I got a good feeling about you this morning. And I can tell Chelsea likes you too."

I hear a little tremble creeping into her words.

"I want you to know that if, at any time, you think Chelsea needs a . . ."

The line goes silent, as though she can't bring herself to finish the sentence. There's a rustle, a sniff, and I imagine her wafting away the emotional vapors.

"Sorry about that. What I mean is, if at any time you think Chelsea needs a kidney transplant, please, please, do not hesitate to refer me. It doesn't matter where in the world. It doesn't matter how much it costs. My trust fund for my cat might not be quite as big as Leona Helmsley's for her dog but let's just say money will never limit Chelsea's health care."

Because I think of myself as a scientist, I prefer the concept of "eureka" to "light-bulb" moments. Regardless, this is a significant revelation. "Trouble" Helmsley had a $12 million trust fund. "Not quite" could still mean pretty big. Now it all makes perfect sense—Steven must be a gold digger, fooling Ginny with an engagement ring made of cheap cubic zirconium.

"Of course," I say, "but let's hope it never comes to that. I have plenty more homework to do on Chelsea's case."

"Thank you so much, Cyrus. We're so thrilled you've found your way back to our little corner of the world."

Another five minutes of banal chitchat and I eventually hang up, but Ginny's compliment lingers like a take-away message. And for a moment, the constant awkwardness and prickly unease I have felt since returning to Bedside Manor disappears, replaced by a buoyant easy calm I have not felt since before my mother died.

11

There's a bark, the sound of knuckles rapping on a door, and my golden pillow vanishes, causing my head to thud into the seat cushion. I swing my feet off the couch and stand up, trying to get my bearings. The curtains are open, but it's dark outside, and there's a wad of canine hair plastered to my left cheek. I wander in the direction of another knock and another bark and find Lewis standing at the top of the stairs.

"Time is it?" I ask, squinting into the landing light while Frieda delivers another overblown greeting.

"Just after five."

I yawn. "Guess I needed to catch up after last night." Sensing a reprimand, I add, "Don't worry, I'm going to visit her owner before my interview with Mr. Greer."

Lewis manages to look at me as though he's wavering on this proposal. "Actually, I wondered what might happen if you claimed to have found her. Deliver a baby. Discover a missing dog. You'd be a local media sensation. Caseload would triple overnight."

Is he being serious? "You seem to be forgetting the man who brought her in paid me to kill this dog."

"Point taken. Best sort it out tonight. Don't want to find an angry mob in the waiting room wielding pitchforks and torches." He scratches along Frieda's back. "You got a second?"

Frieda is so enamored of Lewis I have to peel her off him and slip her behind the door. My mentor gestures for me to follow him downstairs, across the work area, the waiting room, and out through the chiming front entrance.

"Look up there," says Lewis, standing in a swirl of moth-size snowflakes, head craned back. "I forgot to tell you, if you don't get the snow off the roof tonight, especially over the front door, you'll have the making of an ice dam by morning. This way."

Brushing past me, he heads to the far end of the waiting room. There's another door marked PRIVATE, and we enter what used to be a storage room in the days when Bedside Manor could still afford to purchase medical supplies and pet food. The room's practically empty, but its proximity to the waiting room gives me an idea.

"You know it wouldn't take much to convert this into a second exam room."

Lewis comes to a halt, like he's set off an alarm exiting a department store. He wheels around to face me. "Now you're talking."

I say nothing. He's clearly mistaken an idea to generate more income as a long-term commitment. "Where are you taking me?"

"You haven't explored this part of the house?"

"Why would I? It always spooked me when I was a kid."

Lewis worries his chipped upper incisor

with his lower lip but doesn't answer, as though I'm meant to notice his intentional silence. He turns, slides back a heavy brass bolt, pulls open a door, flips a switch, and at the bottom of a narrow and steep wooden staircase a fluorescent strip light flickers, hums, and pops into life. By the third step down I'm assaulted by the organic aroma of a moldy fieldstone basement.

I join him at the bottom. To my right, in the shadows, I make out an ancient oil heat furnace and a sump pump (probably for those rare times in this part of the world where water takes on a liquid state). Lewis heads left into the shadows, swatting at a string dangling from the ceiling that turns on a bare electric bulb.

"What's this?" In part I'm asking about an extensive collection of woodworking tools—an enormous workbench, a band saw, a miter saw, and enough sanders, chisels, clamps, and jigs to start a furniture store.

"Bobby Cobb got into working wood," says Lewis. "Chairs, desks, refurbishing antiques. He was good. Made me a nice birdhouse one time."

But what really catches my eye, what I'm really referring to, is everything else. There's a timeworn armchair, an electric space heater, a dorm refrigerator, and a coffeemaker. A solitary white mug perches on the workbench, the dry, shiny brown remnant of Cobb's last drink down here clinging to the bottom of the ceramic.

"I know I've seen that roof rake somewhere," says Lewis, rooting around in my peripheral vision. He'll get no help from me because I'm too busy comprehending what lies against the wall abutting the bench. Adjacent to a Peg-Board tool organizer there's a large corkboard overrun by a collage of photographs. Lewis mumbles something but the photos reach out and suck me in. Once again, they are new to me. Me as a kid with a broken arm, pouting as I display my cast. Me as a crying toddler, holding a stuffed rabbit missing an ear, no doubt chewed off by a dog. Me on my mother's lap, showing off a gap-toothed grin, brandishing an ice cream like I'm the Statue of Liberty. My eyes glide on but I drift back to this last photo. Blindly, the sticky little fingers of my free hand reach upward to caress my mom's cheek, to ensure our connection. And I can tell my mom is basking in the moment, sticky fingers and all. This is the Ruth Mills I loved—mother first, letting down her guard and succumbing to our emotional bond. Thanks to her, the boy in the photo appears happy and secure. Today, a disquieted forty-year-old man must admit how this picture only affirms a state of mind, a lapsed awareness of just how much I've lost.

My eyes hopscotch across the rest of the collage. Each picture is either of me, or of my mother and me. None of Bobby Cobb. Inevitably I'm drawn to the perfect square of brown cork in the dead center of the compilation. It seems strange, this halo of family memories with nothing at its core. Had Bobby Cobb run out of photos, or was there a single photo missing? I take another step closer to make a more careful inspection. In each of the four corners of the empty center square I can make out a distinct and tiny hole where a pin had punctured the cork.

I glance over at Lewis, and there's a moment, a half second, when I catch him looking at me before he turns away.

Is this hunt for a roof rake a bluff? Is this really about me finding these photos?

"Here we go," says Lewis, reaching behind an orderly row of old paint cans to unearth a series of interlocking, one-inch diameter aluminum poles, together with a broad aluminum blade. "Fit these together and you've got yourself a good twenty feet. More than enough to reach your roof."

"What do you know about these?" I jerk my chin toward the board.

Lewis puts down the rake and joins me, scanning the collage as though he'd never noticed it before.

"Looks like you and Ruth, back in the day." And then, on an exhalation, he adds, "You still miss her."

I could say, *I try not to because it hurts too much*, but I prefer to think he's made a statement, not asked a question. I wait a beat. "And this?" I gesture to the chair. "Not exactly the coziest corner of Bedside Manor."

Lewis turns to me, maintaining the same level of scrutiny as he did for the photos.

"Bobby told me this was the only part of the house without memories. That's why he liked to come down here. A place to call his own."

I can't help myself.

"You knew him better than anyone. The two of you never got to talking over a bottle of Jack?"

"That ended a long time ago." Lewis breaches my personal space, making sure his message is clear.

"Really?"

Lewis keeps going. "Definitely. Swore he took his last drink way before your mother died. Developed a wicked sweet tooth though. Always sucking on a peppermint, and he'd gladly drive an hour in a snowstorm to get an ice cream sundae and a decent coffee."

This is news to me, Cobb realizing too late he had a drinking problem. Not that he was ever a mean drunk. More accurate to say alcohol sustained his isolation. I let it go. "There's a picture, in his bedroom, me running track. I only went to this high school freshman year and I don't remember seeing him at a single meet."

Lewis's lips move, but the intensity in his stare doesn't let up. "Just 'cause you didn't see him, doesn't mean he wasn't there."

I let this sink in. "Did he ever talk about me?"

Lewis cracks a wary half-smile. "Only all the time."

I let out a forced laugh. "Couldn't have been pretty."

"He never said a bad word about you." Lewis is dead serious, and in contrast to my uneasy levity, his words hit me like a two-by-four. I feel the tension tighten around us.

"That's hard to believe."

"You don't have to take my word for it," he says, as though I'm about to find out from another source. Then I remember my encounter with Ginny Weidmeyer. Perhaps I already did.

"But I want your word for it. I want to hear your thoughts, to know whether you think I misjudged him, whether you think I was wrong doing what I did?" Even as this hunger for answers gets away from me, I wonder if I've made a mistake.

Lewis maintains his composure. Maybe the old man has rehearsed for this moment.

"On the surface Bobby Cobb was as carefree, as affable a man as you will ever meet. Compassionate, great with the animals, and blessed with a knack for noting the minutiae in people's lives. Didn't matter who you were, he somehow knew to ask if your grandmother was feeling better, if the plumber fixed your pipes, if you ended up buying that new truck. Some might say it was a gift, the way he made you feel special, made you feel like he cared. But I think it was a trick, because what he was really doing was keeping the focus away from himself. I feel like Bobby Cobb made a huge mistake in not letting people into his life. Including you. He placed a premium on his privacy, pretty much to the point of self-inflicted exile." Lewis hesitates. "Now who does that sound like?"

I should be outraged by this comparison, but I bite my tongue. I can tell Lewis isn't waiting for an answer, he's just waiting, letting me know it's okay to open up. I don't know what it is about him but I feel my defenses begin to slip.

"There was this one time, fall, senior year at boarding school, and I was in AP biology, which I loved, mainly because of my teacher, Ms. Collingwood. I'd see her walking the campus every evening with her yellow Lab, Darwin, and one night she asked me about her dog's skin rash. She said she knew my father was a vet and maybe I'd seen something like it before. She seemed surprised that I didn't have a clue, that I couldn't offer any kind of suggestion. How could I? Cobb never let me hang out in his appointments. I felt embarrassed. No, I felt exposed. Best I could do was promise to find out. So I called home. Naturally he was busy, so I left messages, and when Cobb finally got back to me it was the middle of the night. It was the only time I called him out on feeling second best to his patients and his work. And worst of all, I was totally calm. I reckon Cobb could have brushed off anger, but I wanted to hurt him. Sometimes evidence-based criticism is the best way to leave a mark.

"A few days later I received a letter. It was an apology, of sorts, but it was overshadowed by the answer to my question about the dog's skin rash. There was a list of more questions, suggestions on tests to perform, possible results and diagnoses these results might generate. This unseen dog had become another of his patients, and once again Cobb was throwing himself into Darwin's problem in a way he never threw himself into me. In the time it took to read this letter I left behind resentment and jealousy and settled on something just as painful. Disappointment."

Lewis waits a moment, making sure I'm done. "So you didn't really get angry at him until . . . until your mother's death."

I look away, concede a nod but nothing more. Definitely time for a change of subject. "Did he confide in Doris? She seems . . ."

"What?"

"Well . . . enamored."

"Doris may have worshipped your father, but as far as I know there was never another woman in his life after Ruth."

I can believe that. The Doc Cobb I knew was way too busy with work to go chasing after women.

"If he did share secrets about me, with Doris, they weren't pleasant. She already got in a dig about me not being at my mother's funeral."

"Have you been to her grave?"

"No."

Too late I realize I should have said "not yet."

"It's a beautiful spot," he says and grabs me by the upper arms. "You need to go."

How strange, this funny little man with his bow ties and his ridiculous head of steely hair, and a grip tight enough to squeeze muscle like he wants to throttle me. He looks up, unblinking, trying to peek inside, as though he might find what's missing and make a grab for it.

"You need to go." There's a biting sincerity in his voice. This is not a casual suggestion. But then again, it's not an order. It feels heartfelt, wrapped in wisdom, and its novelty pierces me. If I had to guess, this must be the kind of friendly advice you get from a concerned father figure.

I'm gawking, and he's kind enough to bail me out. "Doris will warm to you," he says, "it's just going to take some . . ." Lewis stops short, knowing he's made a mistake, knowing time is precisely what he doesn't have.

I close my eyes and wince with guilt for wanting to sell up and run back to Charleston. On the inside of my lids my mind projects a black-and-white image, Humphrey Bogart as Rick in *Casablanca*. *You'll regret it. Maybe not today. Maybe not tomorrow, but soon and for the rest of your life.*

Softly, I dare to ask, "Why didn't you tell me about Mrs. Lewis?"

Lewis weakens his grip, finds his trademark smile, and for me, this only makes matters worse.

"You've got more than enough on your plate."

"The fresh sheets on my bed, the prepared food in the fridge, the haircut, the night out."

"Guilty. Though I meant no harm by it."

"But why?"

"Bobby took me on to help keep the practice going, so there was something left to pass on to you. But I had my own motives. My wife's dying, Cyrus. Over the past few years I've blown through our savings, including the money from the sale of my practice in Patton. She loves the place she's in right now. Loves the nurses. It's ridiculously expensive, but thanks to Bedside Manor, or should I say, thanks to you, it's covered."

I flash back to my visit from the detestable Mr. Critchley. *Your health insurance costs are ridiculous.*

"Last thing I wanted to do was to add my wife's name to your list of problems. We'll be fine. If she needs to be moved to a Medicaid facility then we'll deal with it, if and when that happens."

No self-pity, no hostility, just the way it is. Then he finishes me off with "you need to focus on what's right for you."

It's too much. Clearly Lewis's plate is heaped pretty high. No way I can burden him with my anonymous news article. I take a step back, study the floor, and score a line in the sawdust with my shoe. Desperate to make this stop, I begin to babble. "I've got Doris working on the bad debt. I reckon she'd know which clients are stalling, hoping we'll go out of business before we send them to collections."

Lewis recognizes the shift in me, knows we're back on safer territory, but he still seems pleased, as though he got a lot further than he expected. "Good, but right now I'd try to make the most of your interview with Peter Greer. Be honest about the way the practice is struggling. Oh, and be careful around his dog."

"What's wrong with his dog?"

"He's fine. Bit like the Guardian of Hades

but otherwise fine. Focus on Greer. He'll help you out." He pauses. "If that's what you really want?"

Lewis has got to me, and I feel an overwhelming need to clarify my situation. "This thing about making money," I say, "it's only so I can sell the practice and pay my bills. It's not as though I'm hoping to live the high life."

"Of course," says Lewis. "Why do you think I believe so completely in your innocence over losing your license? The man who's prepared to lose everything is the man who's telling the truth. Besides, I bet the concept of money never once crossed your mind when you were delivering that kitten. Why would it? Doesn't matter who it is or what it is, providing care and the act of caring is an emotion, and emotions can only be given away. Never bought. What you discovered last night is pretty much priceless."

He's killing me. Time to shut him down. "So what's with the headmaster's wife, Crystal Haggerty?"

Lewis deliberates. "She's . . . gregarious."

"That's the best you've got."

"What were you hoping for?"

"I don't know, promiscuous, immoral, sly. She claims to have friends in Charleston, says she's going to have them look me up."

"I wouldn't worry. Crystal Haggerty is all bluff and bluster. She's bored and lonely, what with her husband always out of town at some conference or other. Yes, she likes to flirt and she's used to getting her way, but she's no femme fatale. Maybe your southern charisma will make her pay her bills on time."

I ignore that one and make a show of checking my watch. "I have to be going if I'm going to sort out Frieda before I meet with Greer."

"Of course. Here you go." He hands over the collection of poles and the blade.

"Thanks," I say and, though I'm referring to our conversation and him bringing me down here, I still add, "for the roof rake."

"You're welcome." Lewis stares into me, cracks a smile, and I know he understands.

« **12** »

In the absence of Google I make do with a telephone directory and a tattered road map to find my way to the home of Mr. and Mrs. Brendon Small. There's nothing fancy here—a cul-de-sac of ranch-style homes, chain-link rather than picket fences, remnants of busy multicolored Christmas lights, competitive snowmen on the front yards, and bad-insulation icicles hanging off gutters like crystal stalactites. I park the truck at the bottom of their driveway. I could blame my lack of a reverse gear but I'd be lying. Truth is, I'm prepared for a quick get-away.

The driveway is a neat rectangle of dry asphalt. Too neat. There is not a patch of residual snow anywhere, and the driveway is lined with precise, Grand Canyon snow walls carved by an experienced snowblower. Clearly the work of a man with far too much free time on his hands.

I take a deep breath and drop down from the truck, marching with purpose. The cold makes my eyes cry tears that instantly dry stiff on my cheeks. *Focus on the mission: return the dog, make sure she's going to be safe, confirm Small is behind the newspaper article, and brace for the possibility of confrontation.*

Standing on a pineapple welcome mat, I ring the doorbell. Only now, at this very second, do I ask myself, *What am I going to do if Brendon Small doesn't answer the—*

"Can I help you?"

I recognize the woman as the one putting up posters, of course. I take in the Red Sox sweatshirt, kind eyes, pixie nose, and short auburn hair with gray feathering in the middle of her center parting.

"Um . . . hello . . . good evening . . . I'm Cyrus Mills, Dr. Cyrus Mills. I work at the animal clinic in town. Bedside Manor. You may have heard of it."

"Yes." And then, as though my presence at this point makes perfect sense, she screams, "Oh my God, you found Frieda?"

Her excitement takes me by surprise.

"Um . . . no. No, I didn't find Frieda." Suddenly I become conscious of not lying to her, of being factual and accurate about what I say, as though not perjuring myself any further might eventually count in my favor. Technically speaking I didn't *find* Frieda. Frieda was *delivered* to me. But as I try to rationalize my misguided logic I see Anne Small jump to the only other conclusion possible. This is her worst-case scenario.

She staggers, dips a little at the knees, and clasps a hand to her mouth. Her sharp intake of air makes it sound as though she is being smothered.

"Mommy?" Emily is everything I imagined from our phone call—bright blue saucers for eyes, red apple cheeks, and long blond hair (though no symmetrical pigtails). From nowhere she appears at her mother's side, and I'm not sure whether she's been listening to our conversation.

Not that it matters. What frightens her mother must be bad, and Emily responds with a trembling lower lip and a tear tumbling over a lower lid, her long blond lashes unable to keep it from falling. For a second, I remember being Emily's age, just home from school, and Bobby Cobb looking up from his microscope saying, "Run this up to your mother, Son," as he hands me a slide. Thrilled to be given this responsibility I carried it in my palm like a baby bird but at the top of the stairs I tripped, the slide shattering on the hardwood floor. When I looked up, through tears of frustration, I saw my mother standing over me, sharing the exact same expression of unconditional love now written on the face of Anne Small.

"Is . . . is Frieda dead?" asks Mrs. Small, putting her arm around Emily.

"No," I say in a somewhat appalled tone before I can remind myself that I am not supposed to know whether their dog is dead or alive. "I mean, I don't know. I just wanted to offer my support. I saw the posters around town. I thought it might help if I put one up in the practice."

My words seem to rescue Anne, release

her from her dread. "I'm so sorry. Please, do come in. It's okay, honey. Mommy made a mistake. The doctor only wants to help us find Frieda. Isn't that nice of him?"

Emily wipes away her tears with the back of her hand as I step across the threshold and find myself standing in a small foyer. There's a den to my right, kitchen, dining room, and stairway to my left. The little girl looks up at the man who frightened her mommy. Her fear has twisted into a frown of distrust. I wonder if she has recognized my accent from our phone call.

"My husband says something's not been right with Frieda for weeks. And we've been meaning to take her to a vet. Never thought I'd be dropping off a missing poster instead. Bedside Manor, right?"

I nod.

"I was there the other day. A woman took it, promised to put it up for me. I guess you've got a wall where you can hang pictures of lost dogs or dogs in need of a home."

For a second, I wonder how Bobby Cobb, the Patron Saint of Lost Dogs, would have handled this particular situation.

Then, in my mind's eye, I see Doris, fabricating a smile before crushing the poster of Frieda in her quick talons as soon as Anne and Emily were out of sight. *If you don't support this practice then this practice won't support you.*

"You think she's okay?" Emily asks. Her voice is small and without the confidence she had yesterday. It's been well below zero for days. No way a domesticated animal could survive out there in the wild. The trouble is, if someone took her in, surely they'd call? Still, as Emily waits for my answer, I catch a glimmer of hope flickering in her bright blue eyes.

Look at her. This child is suffering. Put an end to it right now.

I think about turning around, asking the two of them to come with me, to hurry back to Bedside Manor. But what happens next? What will my actions mean for this family? What will my actions mean for their dog? Inside my head I curse the fact that Brendon Small didn't answer the door.

"Nobody has showed up with an injured golden retriever or a sick golden retriever answering to the name of Frieda."

"It's Frieda Fuzzypaws."

"Sorry, Frieda Fuzzypaws. I stand corrected."

Emily's distress is not to be assuaged. "Why can't she find her way home?"

I think about Frieda camped out in front of my refrigerator. I don't know what to say. Argue that canine GPS is a myth? What if she's seen *Lassie* or *The Incredible Journey*?

"What if someone kidnapped her?"

Anne Small dips down at her knees and gently cups her daughter's face in her hands. "No one would do that, sweetheart. She's wearing her collar."

"But what if they did? What if a bad man took her?" Emily begins to sob into her mother's chest and I stand there, useless, praying the floor will open up and suck me down into the darkest, deepest chasm where I belong.

Anne looks up at me and gives me a reassuring smile. "Hey, your show's on."

From over in the den, what appears to be a talking yellow sponge fills a television screen, and like that, Emily seems okay, leaping for the sofa, wrapping herself up in a blanket, happy to be hypnotized and away from this painful reality. On the cushions next to her, I recognize a familiar calling card—the remnants of a golden fleece.

"Let me grab another poster for your practice. I won't be a second." Anne disappears, and with Emily transfixed by a talking invertebrate, I inch my way into the dining room. Two dog bowls lie by the back door of the kitchen—one for food, one for water. Both are full, as if being ready for Frieda's arrival can somehow make it happen. On top of a sideboard are a portable phone and a series of family photos.

Why am I drawn to these glimpses into other people's lives? Is it because I want to see what's missing in my own? I'm struck by a certain consistency to the composition: husband, wife, and child; child not in the middle, but always on one end, next to Mommy, in Mommy's arms, or on Mommy's lap. Though Brendon is not Emily's biological father it's clear the Smalls feel obliged to act like a normal family for at least the split second it takes to say "cheese." If such a photo exists for the Cobbs, then I've never seen it.

Anne Small strides toward me, a hollow baton of rolled-up poster tapping in the palm of her hand.

"Sorry I missed your husband," I say, tipping my chin toward the photographs.

"Yeah, he's out interviewing for a job." We share a frozen moment before she confides, "Third one this month."

"Well . . . that's good," I say, to be saying something.

Mrs. Small's focus settles on her spellbound daughter. "You don't understand," she says as her voice starts to quiver, "I'm a stay-at-home mom. Brendon got laid off eight months ago." She turns to me, unable to conceal the anguish. "We've missed the last two mortgage payments. Last week one of the cars was repossessed. I don't know how long we can hold on to the satellite and the electricity and the phones and . . ."

"It's a tough economy."

The good mother's eyes flick back to Emily, making sure she is not eavesdropping, making sure she is spared the truth.

"He wants to work. He wants to provide. He just needs a chance. It's stressful, you know."

I can only meet her eyes for so long. I'm clenching my fists. She must sense my desire to run.

She forces a laugh that sounds more like a gasp. "Listen to me, talking to a doctor about stress. You know more about it than me. Working long hours. Always on call. Dealing with emotionally distraught owners."

Trapped in shut-up-and-listen mode, I relinquish a stiff smile.

"I imagine your job is pretty recession proof. People will always want to look after their animals."

"Yes, but you'd be surprised," I say, deciding to push my luck. "Sometimes, as much as someone wants to do the right thing, they simply cannot afford it. I imagine it can be a tough choice, whether to treat a sick animal or put food on the table or a roof over your head."

"Oh, no. There's nothing to think about. As bad as things are right now, I could never imagine any scenario in which I would deny our Frieda veterinary care."

I feel like the best man who discovers the groom is cheating on his bride on the day before their wedding.

"Those people"—she spits out the word—"should not have a pet. Not ever. And they are certainly not the sort of people

I want to be associated with. I mean what kind of a person would do that?"

I try to swallow, but there's no saliva in my mouth.

"Any chance of a glass of water?"

"Sure."

I follow Mrs. Small into the kitchen, but a new awareness of my surroundings stops me in my tracks.

"Nice floors," I say, as though in a trance.

"Thank you. They're reclaimed pine. We had them done last year. Back when life was good and the living was easy."

I hear a cabinet open and imagine her reaching inside for a glass. Whatever she just said passed straight through me. I'm not looking and I'm not listening because right now I'm distracted, busy working out how this situation came to be, piecing together the real reason behind my fateful meeting with Brendon and Frieda. It was the glossy, bowling alley sheen of the hardwood floor that did it (you really thought I was making polite conversation), drawing the eye to a solitary discolored area, an obvious patch where a dog with a chronic urinary tract problem might dull the patina. And the location, right in front of the fridge, made perfect sense—proven to be Frieda's favorite spot in the house.

I watch with openmouthed fascination as Anne Small fills my glass with water from a dispenser built into the door of a refrigerator peppered with crayon drawings of a magical golden dog. And I keep my eye on the dispenser, ignoring the drink that slides across a butcher-block counter toward me.

"Everything okay?"

I take it all in—the floor, the dispenser, the location. I bounce a clenched fist on my lower lip. *It makes perfect sense.*

"Sorry?"

"I asked if everything was okay," says Mrs. Small. "Looked like I'd lost you for a moment there."

I pick up the glass and knock back its contents like a shot of tequila.

"Yes. Thank you."

Knowing that everything will be okay, so long as I can convince Brendon Small that he's been wrong, in more ways than one.

Standing on Mr. Greer's front porch, hand poised over the door knocker, the infinite rural silence is spoilt only by the metallic tinkle of the truck's cooling muffler, until Toby the terrier senses a breach in security. His bark is so piercing, so merciless, I take a step backward, and as I do, I notice the shadowy figure of a neighbor across the street, sweeping back a curtain, rapping on the window and shouting obscenities as if I were the source of the disturbance.

"Ah, Dr. Mills, Peter Greer, an absolute pleasure to meet you. Do come in."

My head is angled upward, since Greer has to be six four or six five, a three-hundred-pound bear in his late fifties for whom his crushing handshake might feel like a polite squeeze. If he's trying to keep the mood homey and casual in his slippers and heavy woolen cardigan, it's not working because, of all things, I'm hooked on his haircut, which is decidedly less laid-back than his outfit. Though the color is still more black than gray, the cut is trendy and foppish, necessitating an occasional sweeping hand gesture to pull it back from his forehead, and this, together with his plummy English accent, makes me feel as though he prefers to flaunt an aura of dashing flamboyance.

"And this is my coconspirator, Toby." The

terrier's shrill soprano downgrades to a grumbling baritone as Greer bends down low to scoop him up, affording me an unwelcome and unexpected glimpse of his silky red boxers.

"Your neighbor seems a little upset," I say, stepping inside.

"Sam from across the street?" Greer closes the door. "He's fine. His own bark is far worse than his bite. This way."

Sam. The old man from the diner with the cotton candy beard, complaining to Chief Matt about Toby's barking. Now I remember.

"I hope this won't take too long," I say as I'm led into a sitting room. "I have a patient to check in on."

"Of course you do."

Do I detect a hint of insincerity?

"Please, have a seat. Help yourself to the nuts and I'll grab us both a drink. I'm trying out a new Malbec. Sound good?"

"Not for me, thanks." If ever I need to be sharp and focused, now is the time.

"Oh, I absolutely insist."

And before I can reply, I'm left alone to explore. I do my best to ignore another copy of Frieda's "Missing" poster on Greer's cluttered desk and instead investigate a mantelpiece over a brick fireplace, which is bookended by a collection of photos and engraved plaques with a common theme: golf. The language is foreign to me (Canadian foursome, Texas scramble) but one name, Greer's partner and fellow runner-up in the club's mixed doubles tournament, I recognize: Virginia Weidmeyer. I pick up the plaque, and suddenly, from somewhere behind me, I hear a malevolent snarl. Toby must have crept into the room with the preternatural stealth of a ninja assassin. I remember Lewis's warning about this hairy banshee and brace for the sensation of hungry fangs sinking deep into my ankles.

"Here we go," says Greer, breezing into the room with an uncorked bottle of red wine and two large glasses in hand. "Ah, you noticed the trophy collection. You play?"

"No. Never." I look down at Toby, who now sits politely by his master's side. He's a handsome little fellow—white and tan, shorthaired, stocky and attentive to what is going on—but as soon as I make direct eye contact he emits a throaty grumble.

"Ginny's a client of mine," I say, flashing Greer the plaque.

"Of course. Chelsea. Hardly seen hide nor hair of Ginny since that mooch, what's his name . . . Steven, whisked her away. What on earth is she thinking? This stranger appears out of thin air at one of our member guest cocktail parties and no one has a clue who invited him and before the evening's over they're leaving together. You've met Ginny. Wonderful woman, cracking short game. Even if she is a tad past her sell-by date she's still a smashing bit of crumpet. Am I right?"

I work to remain expressionless.

"And I've never once seen that man out on the course. As far as I can tell he's a different kind of *playa* altogether," Greer says, adding appropriate air quotes.

I replace the plaque and notice a photo of an attractive woman standing in front of the Eiffel Tower.

"My late wife, Susan. I bounced around this country, drifting from one dying newspaper to another, until she finally insisted on coming home to Vermont. We'd only been back three months when she was killed in a car crash."

He grimaces at the recollection, but pushes on. Very British. Very stiff upper lip. His posh accent makes the word *crash* sound more like *crèche.*

"That was five years ago, and now look at me, editor in chief of the *Gazette*. Turns out this place suits me. You subscribe?"

"Not at the moment," I say, feeling the need to add, "but I'm sure I will."

I'm rewarded with a hearty slap on the back. Why is everyone in this town so physical?

"Please, don't wait on ceremony." Greer gestures to a love seat and a plush oversize chair positioned around a low glass coffee table on which sits a yellow legal pad, a pen, and an enormous bowl full of macadamia nuts. The love seat is covered in fine white hairs, so I choose the chair.

Greer sits opposite, pours two generous glasses of wine. "Cheers. Here's mud in your eye."

I scramble to sit forward, raise my glass, and take the smallest sip.

"Before we get started, I want you to know I was an enormous fan of your father's."

Here we go again. Exposed, inextricably

linked, and not a subject of contempt. Is this why Lewis said Greer would spin the story in our favor? Maybe this interview will be more about publicity than journalism. And, if Lewis was right and Cobb never bad-mouthed me, then what did Cobb tell people about my absence from my mother's funeral?

"Robert was always attentive to Toby's anal sex problem."

There's no hiding the shock written on my face. "I beg your pardon."

"Anal sex," he repeats.

He must see that I'm flabbergasted.

"You know, the two sex, around his anus, the ones that fill up with a foul, odiferous fluid that needs to be emptied once a month."

I calmly nod, as though I had understood all along. His posh English accent has translated *sacs* into *sex*.

"Right," I say, "of course." I look over at Toby roosting on his master's right shoulder, and the terrier tries to smile. That is, if wrinkling his nose to expose his canines counts.

Greer reaches for pad and pen. "So, I imagine the gossip mongers have most of the details down pat. You deliver a kitten, owner gets nervous, goes into labor, and you deliver a healthy baby boy." He waits for a response, a *that's about it, right?* expression on his face. "I'm assuming you weren't moved to tears or said something affecting or profound?"

I think about this. "No."

"Didn't think so," he says, far too quickly for my liking. "You think your success with a cat and a human proves your versatility? I've heard it said that it's harder to become a veterinarian than it is to become an MD. True?"

Is he trying to put words in my mouth?

"I wouldn't know. I've never been an MD."

Greer takes another gulp of his wine.

"How about this: your job is far more difficult because your patients won't tell you where it hurts and you have to deal with a variety of different species and not just one."

I try to lean forward in my chair, but almost nothing happens. I'm sitting in an upholstered Venus flytrap.

"Mr. Greer."

"Peter."

"Peter, I . . . appreciate the compliment, but please, don't pass me off as a wannabe obstetrician. I did what anyone would have done in my situation."

Greer grabs a nut. "Let's come at this from a different angle. What do you think you bring to Eden Falls? What makes you a better veterinarian than old Doc Cobb?"

"I doubt anyone could be a better veterinarian."

I could pretend I was sucking up, but the words are out before I can think, and I'm surprised by how easy they are to say.

Greer smiles, as though that was the right answer.

"How do you feel about . . . something like . . . Doc Mills may be the new, younger face of Bedside Manor but he'll be maintaining the same Doc Cobb excellence in veterinary care that the pet owners of Eden Falls have come to know and love."

"Sounds great. In fact," I say, taking this as my cue, "I'd really appreciate anything you can do in this article that will improve business." Sensing the value in showing deference to the local legend himself, I go so far as to add, "It's hard enough filling Cobb's shoes, let alone being an outsider."

Greer tips his head back and raises his glass. "Absolutely. Be my pleasure." The rest of Greer's red wine vanishes down his gullet and he reaches for the bottle. He tops me off even though I've barely touched a drop. "You know, when I first came to town, I made a big effort to connect with the community. It might be helpful for you to offer some sort of outreach to the pet owners of Eden Falls."

This sounds worrisome. "I'm not sure what you mean."

"You know, something to kick-start interest in you and the practice."

"I thought that's what you might do with this article."

"Of course, old boy, but words on paper don't necessarily translate into traffic through your waiting room. Have you thought about sponsoring a Little League baseball team?"

"Can I be honest?" I ask.

Greer puts his pen down, eases back in the love seat. There's a blur of motion and white light and Toby is curled up in his lap, managing to look angelic.

"I'm not sure the business will be able to survive until the spring." *We might not survive past the end of the week.*

Greer sucks down a sharp intake of breath, closely followed by another mouthful of Malbec. "I see. Then we're going to have to get a bit more aggressive. How are you at public speaking?"

I'm speechless. I hope this is all the answer he needs.

"Hum. That's too bad. I'm sure you'd find a receptive audience at the Knights of Columbus or the Rotary Club."

Greer jabs a finger at me like he knows the answer in a game of charades. "Open house. Set the place up so that you give guided tours of the facilities, no, better still, a behind-the-scenes tour of what it's really like saving the lives of our beloved pets. Throw in some cheap plonk, microwave a few frozen hors d'oeuvres, and Bob's your uncle. The place will be hopping."

I'm petrified. *To my right you can see our empty medicine cabinets and empty dog runs and straight ahead you'll appreciate our fine collection of antiquated and poorly maintained equipment. Best get an X-ray now while stocks last.*

"What?" he asks.

"No . . . it's not a bad idea . . . it's just that . . ."

Greer sighs, narrows his eyes to slits, and I can't tell whether he's peeved or about to get more probing. "Look, if Bedside Manor really is hanging by its short and curlies, it might be best to tell your story to a paper with a bigger readership."

"No." The speed and volume of my response can only corroborate how much I have to hide. I try to rally. "I'm not one for bragging. Blame my southern sensibilities." And thinking about the safest way to get my message across I add, "If Lewis trusts you, I trust you to help me keep Robert Cobb's Bedside Manor alive." I instantly feel the guilt of leaving out the last five words of this sentence—*so I can sell it.*

I can't tell if Greer knows more than he's letting on or thinks that I do. Let's hope he's not tight with Mr. Critchley from Green State Bank.

"Well, I'm awfully grateful for the exclusive. Give me a day or two and I'm sure I can come up with something brilliant to expand your clientele."

"The sooner the better. Appreciate it," I say, grunting with the effort of evacuating the chair and scrambling to my feet. "Thanks for the wine, but I really should be going."

"Ah, that's too bad. Perhaps another time."

"Definitely," I say, watching as Greer pats his thigh and Cujo junior leaps into his arms.

"Now, if you could be the one to find that missing retriever," he says, glancing at the poster on his desk as we walk by, "you'd be all set, as they like to say in these parts."

"Frieda Fuzzypaws," I read, as if for the first time, wondering what Greer can tell me about Brendon Small.

"You must have seen the posters?"

"Yes. Did the dog run off?"

"So I was told. Daughter's all upset."

"It's a kid's dog?"

"Present from her late father. Died a few years back. There's a stepfather in the picture now. Nice enough chap. Been out of work for a while though. I heard rumors of the bank foreclosing on their house."

Nice enough chap. Nice enough to threaten blackmail to buy my silence over Frieda?

"It's dreadful," says Greer. "Hard to imagine any dog could survive outdoors on nights like these."

We've made it to his front door.

"Have to ask before I let you go, you rather I not mention your relationship with your father?"

My immediate *For god's sake, no*, reaction contorts my face.

"Whatever you think to boost business."

Greer seems pleased, but whether he's pleased with my answer or the effect his question has had on me, I cannot tell.

"Very good. And don't worry, mum's the word on getting fired from your last job in Charleston."

« **13** »

It's a totally different diner this evening
with the exception of the one constant I
was hoping for. The rush is over and the
place lacks the clamor of competing con-
versations and the collision of chopping
cutlery, but I spy Amy, wiping down the far-
thest table. To my delight, she smiles as
soon as she sees me.

I pretty much have my choice of where
to sit. Two older gentlemen, who are tuck-
ing into slices of lemon meringue pie, with
what's left of a six-pack on the table between them, occupy one booth, and a

redheaded man has his back to me, elbows on the bar, chatting to the solitary cook between aggressive bites of his burger. Nevertheless, I'm drawn to the same seat I occupied last night.

"Here you go, cream no sugar, right?"

Before I've had a chance to sit down, Amy slides a fresh cup of coffee across the table.

"On the house," she whispers.

I must look confused.

"What? Don't tell me you want decaf."

"No. That's great. But you didn't have to . . ."

She makes sure her back is to the cook and brings an index finger up to her lips.

"What can I get you?"

I pick up the menu and try to read. She's right beside me, her multicolored eyes watching my every move. All I see are words and numbers.

"Any chance of a cooked breakfast?"

I look up and dare to take her in. She's exactly the same, and so is her effect on me.

"Of course. The works?"

I manage to nod.

"We don't got no grits, mind," she says

in a passable southern accent. There's that smile again, and before I can answer she's gone. I watch as she gives the cook my order and the redheaded man turns to check me out. He's eyeballing me like I just asked for prime rib, but I'm distracted by the marking on his face. It's more port wine mask than port wine stain. Nevus flammeus, a vascular malformation of the skin. Present at birth, persistent through life.

I'd almost chickened out on a return trip to the diner after Greer's revelation about investigating my background. He swore he simply typed my name into a search engine and up popped the *Post and Courier* article on my eviction from McCall and Rand Pharmaceuticals. The bit in flashing neon lights about a suspended license went unmentioned, but he calmed me with assurances that folks from Eden Falls don't stalk newcomers online. I drove away believing Greer was not the kind of guy who would stuff a printed version in an envelope and hand deliver it to Bedside Manor. At least I think I did.

One of the beer drinkers lets out a raucous belly laugh, and now I wish I'd drained my glass of wine with Greer. If I'm going to be irrational and irresponsible enough to try to talk to Amy I'm going to need all the help I can get. I don't do "cool." Never have. I've spent the better part of my adult life avoiding this kind of situation, and on those rare occasions where I've weakened, I work hard to keep the conversation on any topic except me. It's like driving at night and always using your high beams—when you dazzle and blind it's difficult for others to see what really lies behind the light. Okay, maybe not dazzle.

"Here you go. Let me know if you need anything else."

A steaming plate of scrambled eggs, grilled bacon, sausages, and hash browns slides in front of me, together with four slices of whole wheat toast.

Amy disappears before I can thank her. Damn. I should have had something ready to say. Disappointed, I unfurl my paper napkin, grab my cutlery, and with the first slice of sausage on its way to my mouth, she's suddenly back, sliding into the seat on the other side of the booth.

"I have to ask . . ."

My fork hovers in the gap between plate and open mouth. Amy places the fingers of both hands on the edge of the table (she bites her fingernails), leans forward, and says, "I heard the rumor."

She knows. She knows about the way things ended up between my father and me.

"And what I want to know is," she pauses, and seemingly deliberating over every word, asks, "were you scared?"

Scared. Scared to abandon the only relative I had left in the world. Scared to come back here. Scared to try my hand at a new job. Scared to practice without a license.

Thankfully, whichever way I interpret the question, the answer is always the same. "Yes," I say. "Of course."

Amy bows her head, but I make out the slightest upturn of her lips. She gets to her feet and double pats the table. "Enjoy your meal."

"Why do you ask?" This time I catch her before she goes.

She meets my eyes, and they seem so serious. "'Every man has his fault, and honesty is his.'"

In the pause of my trying to decipher what she said, she's off and busy again, refilling an aluminum canister with fresh paper napkins. She doesn't return to my table until I've finished eating.

"I thought you might have come back sooner."

"Really? Don't tell me you're one of those people who actually likes their waitress to wait until they have a mouth full of food before she asks, *Is everything okay? Come on, this is a diner."*

Her words buffet me like a squall.

"What you said earlier, was that from a movie?"

"Shakespeare," she says. *"Timon of Athens,* if you really want to know. One of his more obscure plays. What, you don't think a waitress can be educated?"

I don't think she's angry. I think she's trying to tease me.

"No, no, no. Just never heard of that one, that's all."

She places her hands on her hips. "And you, an educated man."

Say something. Stop staring.

"You really should order some pie tonight," she says, saving me from myself. "The lemon meringue is fantastic." And then, "Maybe I'll bring two forks."

"Please," I say, with the conviction of a

shy boy, and pray she doesn't interpret it as a lack of interest. Left alone I have a minute to endure an internal tongue-lashing. What am I going to say? If I have to talk about Shakespeare it's going to be a short conversation.

A thick triangular wedge slides in front of me—sticky yellow on the bottom, crispy white floating on top. Amy sits opposite, hands me a fork, and takes the first bite. "Go on. Try it."

I do as I'm told.

"Really good." I realize too late that I have shown her a half-chewed mouthful of food.

"Did your mother teach you those manners?"

The shock of this question flashes across my face as though she's talking about Ruth. I try to recover with a hand over my mouth and a quick apology. Maybe she didn't notice.

"Funny that you should choose this particular booth two nights in a row."

"Why's that?" I ask, sure to swallow first.

"Because this was Doc Cobb's favorite seat. Nice guy."

I flash my eyebrows and skewer a second fork load. "Beloved, apparently."

She winces. "Hate that word. So over-played. It's almost as bad as *closure* or *empowered*. And don't get me started on *literally* or *like*."

I'm not sure whether to agree or not.

"I did a degree in English literature," she says. "Hence the quote from Shakespeare. I'm trying to finish up a master's degree at UVM. Creative writing . . . So, you ever feel as though you're playing God?"

"Are you always this direct?"

"Would you prefer we talk about your accent, our weather, if you miss wearing your seersucker suits and your penny loafers? I'm sorry, but if something's worth saying, I'll say it. Just the way I am."

For a man who savors privacy and avoids confrontation, both past and present, the discomfort distorting my smile must be obvious.

"You're from South Carolina," Amy says. "Big deal. This is Eden Falls. Take you less than a minute to get your bearings. So let's get to the good stuff. Last night, Denise Laroche, what you did was straight out of an episode of *ER*. I want to know how it made you feel."

Now I get it. The "scared" reference was

about delivering Denise's baby. I jumped to the wrong conclusion, again. I put down my fork. This question I can answer. "Humble. It made me feel humble." But then something dark inside me adds, "Are you disappointed? Would you rather I told you it was no big deal?"

She makes a snapping sound with her mouth, as though the morsel was particularly tart.

"Not at all. Humble is exactly what Cobb would have said. How well did you know him?"

Though I'm tempted to be evasive, her quote about honesty makes me want to come clean. The question is, having started can I stop?

"I'm Bobby Cobb's son."

Everything changed after my mother's death, and this label, *son*, became more bearable than recognizing Cobb as my father. Being his son feels blameless. And suggesting he's my father would give him too much credit, given the way things turned out.

Busy with a tricky bit of the crust, Amy's fork hovers before clattering onto the plate. "You're kidding me. Why didn't you say?

You don't look much like him. Except maybe the eyes."

I want to thank her for the compliment. "I'm told I resemble my late mother."

"Wait a minute. Mills?"

"My mother's maiden name."

Her lips part, and each colored eye sparkles in its own way as she imagines some version of my past. "So, what, you're in the witness protection program?"

I think she's joking but it's not a bad analog —move across the country, change my identity, start life over. With witness protection you're not allowed any contact with your past. Me, I've gone for total immersion in mine.

"I don't remember seeing you at the funeral. Pretty much the whole town turned out for him."

My turn to drop my fork. "I wasn't there. Okay?" No good can come from this but I press on, feeling defensive. "Sometimes it feels like this town is nothing but a shrine to Bobby Cobb. I can almost smell the incense." Pierced by the way Amy recoils, I wait a beat before adding, "Sorry . . . that came out a little . . ."

"Hostile?"

"Angry. I didn't mean to sound so angry."

"Don't worry about it. You only get angry over the things you love, right?"

It's strange (and a little uncomfortable) hearing someone articulate this concept. "Look, he and I were very different. It's just that we fell out some years back."

Amy appears flummoxed, or maybe she's already siding with Cobb. "But he was so popular?"

"Well, yeah, let's just say he wasn't as popular at home."

Her head lists ever so slightly to one side as though, physically and metaphorically, she's starting to see me in a different light.

"He was good with the animals though," I say. "And hey, what's not to like in a man who basically gives away his services for free?"

"You think life's all about making money?"

"If I did, would I be here in Eden Falls?" As soon as I say this I worry that I've offended her. If she's mentally jotting down my answers and keeping tally, I'm not scoring so well. "I don't think your life should be consumed by your work, that's all."

This appears to give her pause.

"Yes, but you've chosen a vocation, right? A calling. The line between the two is bound to blur."

"Maybe. But if you can't see the divide, if you can't strike a balance, someone's going to pay the price."

She puts down her fork. Twelve inches separates her hand from mine. *No jewelry, no wristwatch, no ring.*

"Is that what went wrong between you and him?" she asks, and I wonder if she is doing the same thing, looking at the fourth finger on my left hand—no band, no indentation, no telltale ring of pale skin where the sun never reached. Have I made my estrangement from my father sound like a failed marriage?

"I . . . um . . . I'd rather not . . ."

"It's okay," she says, and we share our first awkward silence.

"So you grew up here? Attend MRH?" she asks.

It takes me a while to remember MRH is Missiquoi Regional High. "Yeah. Just my freshman year. But you're younger than me, so I'm sure our paths never crossed. You lived here your whole life?"

Go back to what works. Use the high beams.

She flinches, as though I hit a nerve. "Why would you think that?"

"I just thought Eden Falls might be home."

"Nah, I'm just back here for a while. I dropped out of school. I still have a few more credits left to take. This waitress thing is fine for right now. They're flexible about my hours, and with people like you around, I make decent tips."

"But you are going to complete your education?"

She bristles, pulls back her hands. "You don't think it's appropriate for a smart woman to work as a waitress?"

"No of course not. I mean, no, I think it's fine. But . . . I think everyone should get a chance to fulfill their potential." Why do I sound so self-important?

"Really. You think I'm a stereotype, an academic dropout forced to choose unskilled labor? You think the only math I can do is calculate fifteen percent? You think I have a kid at home?"

"No, I didn't mean to suggest—"

"Is running Bedside Manor—dreadful name by the way—something you've dreamed of your whole life? This is you fulfilling your potential?"

"I didn't really choose to do this. It's just something I have to do for right now. But I agree with you, about the name."

She straightens and smiles, but it's the smile of a bitter victory. "Something you have to do. Something that feels a bit like a chore, a burden, unpleasant but unavoidable."

"Exactly."

She shakes her head and stands. Given her expression I'm pretty sure I'm in trouble. "It sounds as though we have something in common, but one of us sees the dilemma very differently."

If I could get away with saying nothing I would. "Sees what?" I ask.

"That doing right by someone else, especially someone you love, means having to ditch your pride." She sighs, reaches into her breast pocket, pulls out the bill, and slides it across the table. "Thank you," she says, sounding anything but grateful. "I'll take that when you're ready."

* * *

On the way home I drop by Fancies Convenience Store to pick up a few groceries. First impression: there is nothing particularly fancy about it. It's a converted red barn, rustic, complete with high ceilings and original post-and-beam construction. But I was wrong. Oh, it's no Piggly Wiggly, what with the tight aisles and Lilliputian shopping carts, but for a small town store, Fancies is surprisingly well stocked. It has its own deli, butcher shop, and there's a homemade ice cream counter. Beyond transparent strip curtains lies a chilling treasure trove of beer and wine. I wonder if they have a barista?

The collision of our carts is the stuff of *Ben Hur.*

"Sorry about that."

"Not a problem, Doc." Steven, Ginny Weidmeyer's fiancé, grasps the handlebar of his cart like he's hanging on to a Harley for dear life. I notice a list between his thumb and forefinger and then, like most folks who get to talking in a supermarket, I can't help but peruse the items Steven is about to purchase: a box of Land O' Lakes butter, half a dozen bottles of Grolsch beer, a pint of Cherry Garcia, and a bag of Lavazza espresso. I remember Ginny telling me how Steven always brings her a cappuccino first thing in the morning.

I look up. He appears to have noticed the way curiosity turned into scrutiny. I've got to say something.

"Expensive caffeine habit?"

Steven considers me and forces a polite smile. "Ginny wants to make me tiramisu, whatever that is."

I flash my eyebrows, pretending to draw a blank, when what has really caught my eyes has nothing to do with liquor-soaked ladyfingers and everything to do with Chelsea, the kidney stone cat. Hidden behind a bag of confectioners' sugar and a tub of mascarpone cheese sit several small cans of cat food. These are the antithesis of Chelsea's vital prescription diet. These are the ones you see on the TV ads, served on a silver platter to a fluffy white Dr. No cat by a white-gloved butler.

"How's Chelsea doing?"

"She's absolutely fine," says Steven, with far more animosity than apathy. "Ginny gets all crazy about her. I mean she's old. What does she expect?"

"As I recall Chelsea's ten. Not that old for a cat."

"Not that young either. Ginny tends to lose her perspective. It's like a while back when Chelsea needed her booster vaccinations and she didn't want her to have them. I said, 'What are you worried about, you think Chelsea will go all autistic on you?'"

He cracks up. Waves his list in my face.

"Got to grab some heavy cream. For me, not the cat."

And with that Steven steers around me and heads for a refrigerator full of dairy products.

Unfortunately, with only one cash register open for business, I come in line behind him as he loads up the conveyor belt.

"Need to see some ID," says a pimply young man with lunar landscape cheeks as he sweeps the bar code on the Grolsch beer.

Steven runs a thumb and forefinger down his goatee, the two meeting and tugging on the hairs at the base of his chin, as though the cashier himself might want to think about facial hair as a way to spare the public from the horrors of his acne-scarred features.

"You don't think I look twenty-one?"

"Store policy, sir. Everyone gets carded. Everyone."

Steven looks over his shoulder at me, shakes his head, digs out his wallet from the front pocket of his jeans, and hands over a driver's license. The kid takes it, finishes scanning the cream before inspecting the laminated plastic card like it might be a fake.

"Thanks, Stuart," says the cashier, this time sliding the license across the stationary belt.

Steven snatches it up as if it's the ace he's been waiting for.

"Steven's my middle name," he says to me. "Hated the name Stuart."

I'm pretending to be fascinated by a Brad and Angelina article in *People* magazine. As though I never spied his toxic cat food. As though I couldn't care less about him preferring Steven to Stuart. As though I wasn't quick enough to notice how the man supposedly from Manhattan has a driver's license not from the "Empire State" of New York, but from the "Sunshine State" of Florida.

Thursday

14

Next morning, at nine on the dot, I stroll downstairs to the waiting room and make a peculiar yet gratifying discovery—there's a client waiting to see me. And that's when I notice Doris, my steaming cup of morning cheer, not behind the reception desk but strolling back and forth outside the front door. Unbelievable. She's already on a smoke break. Now I know why she's permanently wearing a ski jacket. It's not that the reception area is too cold for her, it's because she spends more time outside than in, sucking down cigarettes.

I greet the client, assure him I won't be a moment, and head outside.

"Nice job on the roof," says Doris. She winces into a drag, jabbing the glowing end of the cigarette in my direction. Paradoxically she cocks her little finger, like an English lady drinking tea.

I follow the red dot of her laser beam and glance back at the house. *The ice dams.* After my interview with Greer and my disastrous encounter with Amy, I completely forgot about getting rid of the fresh snow with the rake. Thankfully, it looks like Lewis did not.

"You do realize there's a client waiting?"

"Yes, Dr. Mills. You'll notice his file has been waiting for you on top of the reception desk."

I'm not good at glowering but I try my best.

Doris shifts what little weight she possesses from one foot to the other. "The Wi-Fi people said they'd be by this morning." She prefers to say "whiffy" to "Wi-Fi." "And Mrs. Haggerty left a message. Wants you to see Puck again."

I think about this. I can convince myself that blood tests and X-rays on her lingerie-swallowing dog make for good medicine, but if I'm honest, with time running out, I'm desperate enough to perform any kind of money-making diagnostics, even if the woman scares me to death.

"Tell her she should bring him in," I say, without explanation and head back inside. This time I notice Frieda's "Missing" poster. I put it up on Cobb's Wall of Fame. So what if the golden Amelia Earhart is up-stairs dozing in front of my refrigerator.

I pick up the file. Damn, another disap-pointing Post-it note—*$!*

"Mr. Minch."

"That's Dr. Minch."

The man correcting me is a stout fellow who is unwilling to meet my eyes. There's a cheap cardboard cat carrier in his right hand.

I close the door behind us in the exam room. "My apologies, Doctor, what can I do for you?"

Dr. Minch places the carrier on the table between us, wheezing with the exertion. "Neutered male cat. I'm guessing ten or eleven years old, give or take. I adopted him as a stray a few days ago. He has a sarcoma between his shoulder blades."

His synopsis of the creature inside the box is monotone, matter of fact, but he and I both know the word *sarcoma* was slipped in like a secret handshake, enough insider jargon to let me know he's probably not got a PhD in engineering. How long can I last without asking?

"A sarcoma?"

"Correct."

Dr. Minch has little spittle bubbles at the corners of his mouth.

"Is this . . . speculation . . . based on prior experience?"

Something lights up in Minch's piggy eyes. "There's a discreet, firm, nonfluctuant, nonpainful mass, approximately one-by-one centimeter in size, symmetrically aligned between the dorsal spinous processes of the scapulae. Now you tell me, Dr. Mills, what else might it be?"

I'm not loving his condescending tone. He already strikes me as the kind of man who carefully lists his credentials when he sends a friend a birthday card. Nothing will annoy him more than my refusal to inquire about his doctorate. Having said that, Minch's lexicon sounds dangerously familiar.

"May I have a look?"

Minch hesitates, lifts a brow as if to say "you don't believe me," and then, almost begrudgingly, extricates a ginger tom from the carrier.

"Does he have a name?"

"As I mentioned, he's a stray."

I nod, pick the cat up, and inspect under his tail. I will the feline *not* to have a penis, to be female, but Minch is correct, neutered male. I palpate the curious lump between his shoulder blades. The cat couldn't care less. It is exactly as Minch described—no heat, no pain, no redness— just a firm, abnormal lump in a potentially awkward location.

In our game of clinical chess, I decide to draw out his queen.

"You suspect a vaccine-associated sarcoma?"

He offers me a squishy, shar-pei smile and counters with a smug, "Wouldn't you?"

I think about this. Common injection site, and the tumor is thought to be associated with the aluminum adjuvant in rabies and feline leukemia vaccines. Minch's diagnosis appears to be legitimate. "Do you mind if I borrow him for minute?"

Minch huffs, though that may just be the way he breathes, as I pick up the cat and head back to the work area.

"What's happening with Clint?" asks Lewis, his back to me as he stands over the sink, washing up. He's been performing surgery, spaying a cat for one of Doris's friends.

"I'm hoping Harry will bring her in later. Any chance you could feel a lump for me? I think I've got a vaccine-induced sarcoma."

Lewis dries his hands on a paper towel, squeezes the ginger tom's nodule between finger and thumb and, without saying a word, produces a strange-looking hand-held device that he proceeds to pass back and forth over the lump like he's casting a spell. Each pass induces a flashing red light and a high-pitched ping.

"Microchip. Look at it. Your stray has an ID number."

Incredible. How did Lewis know?

"So I'm feeling . . . what . . . scar tissue around the chip?"

"Exactly. Easy mistake. I'll call the recovery service and they'll call the owner. Have the Good Samaritan leave the cat with us. You sort out Frieda?"

"Not exactly. It's complicated."

"Complicated? Really? Do I want to know about your interview with Greer?"

"It went okay. He seems keen to help. Mind if I borrow your scanner thing for a second?"

"Be my guest."

Back in the exam room Dr. Minch stands precisely where I left him, hands clasped together in front of him, offering what I'm sure he considers to be a superior smile, when all I see are slits and folds and creases.

"A little surprised not to see your degree prominently displayed, Dr. Mills."

"Haven't got round to unpacking it yet," I reply, knowing full well that it still sits at the back of my closet in a rented apartment in Charleston, not least because it bears the name Dr. Cyrus Cobb.

Minch concertinas his chin, as though he accepts my excuse. "You concur with my diagnosis?"

Unsmiling, I take the scanner and do Lewis's magic wand trick on the cat purring in my arms. There's a satisfying drama to the sound-and-light special effects. "No, Dr. Minch, I'm afraid you've unearthed a totally benign, totally normal, identification microchip. Thanks to you, I can get this cat back to his rightful owner."

I'm not sure the muscles of Dr. Minch's face are strong enough to distort the over-all ambivalence of his features into visible happiness. My good news is greeted with barely a twitch. He could be upset about giving up his adopted cat, but I doubt it. Whether you're a pet lover or not, thwart-ing cancer is usually cause for celebra-tion. In Minch's case, I think he's unhappy to be proven wrong.

"Very well. Then I'll leave him with you." My reward is a clipped nod, the certainty that this visit is pro bono, and like that, Minch lumbers for the door. I should let him go, but I can't stand the not knowing.

"Dr. Minch. Forgive me for asking, but what's your area of specialization?"

Minch doesn't stop, and for a second I wonder if this is how he's going to punish me. Finally, over his shoulder, he mutters, "Veterinary pathologist. Did the path work for Doc Cobb. Perhaps I'll do the same for you." And then, from the far side of the empty waiting room, the dig he's been hold-ing in reserve, "If you're ever busy enough."

I watch him go, unruffled by the insult but perturbed by the man's choice of career.

"You never said Minch brought the cat in." Lewis comes up behind me. Still holding the cat, I have to take a step back to look him in the eye.

"You know him?"

"Of course," says Lewis. "Excellent pathologist."

"Really. He looks old enough to be retired." And then, remembering whom I'm speaking to, I add, "No offense."

Lewis laughs. "He's only a couple of years older than you. Make you think twice about a doughnut with your coffee."

I don't know what to say, and it has nothing to do with the way obesity can mess with the aging process. It's Minch's personality that I'm struck by. Pompous, snippy, and sour. Would I have even noticed before returning to Eden Falls? Was this a glimpse into my own pathetic future? Am I a double cheeseburger a day shy of becoming another Dr. Minch?

"He didn't appreciate your trick with the scanner."

"No," says Lewis, "sometimes it's hard

to be proven wrong. Especially when it gets rubbed in your face."

I appraise Lewis with a cynical squint to make sure he's still talking about Minch.

"By the way," he says, "the recovery service called right back and gave me the name of the owner. She's very grateful. Hand him over. I'll drop him off on my way to visit Mrs. Lewis. You need anything?"

"No. Thanks. Puck Haggerty's coming back in, so I should check out some stuff on GI disorders."

"Good idea. Keep your focus on the dog and maybe Crystal will stop focusing on you."

Why does Lewis make this sound as though I need "sexual harassment in the workplace" training? I ignore him, disappear into the soothing civility of a textbook, and don't even hear the chime of the shopkeeper's doorbell.

"She's here," says Doris. "Wanted to wait in the exam room."

"Okay. Any other cases coming in that you know of?"

She shakes her head. And then, as I take my first stride toward the room, she adds, "No need to worry about being disturbed."

With my back toward her I allow myself a half-smile. She's good.

Inside my exam room I'm assaulted by an awful new smell—the usual antiseptic overpowered by an intense and sickly, fruity perfume. Like last time, Puck barrels into me, looking for a pat, a scratch, or a wayward T-bone steak. However, it's Crystal Haggerty who has my attention. It's not her hair—coiffed, and down over the shoulders of her white silk shirt, unbuttoned enough to highlight a thick gold chain. It's not her jeans—I'm no fashionista, but they are far too tight and unflattering for her figure, making her ample thighs look distinctly thunderous. No, it's the way she's leaning into the table, cursing, obviously in distress and apparently giving me the finger.

"Goddamn contacts," she screams, and only now do I see the tiny transparent disk on the end of her middle finger. "Feels like there's a rock in my eye. Could you take a look?"

"Oh, I really don't think I should—"

"Please," she begs as a dirty line of

mascara bleeds down her right cheek. "I wouldn't ask if it wasn't so painful."

Sighing my displeasure, I step in close, uncomfortably close, last dance close, in order to inspect her cornea and sclera. "Do you mind if I lift up your eyelid?"

"Not at all," says Crystal Haggerty, the element of fear and discomfort suddenly gone.

Even without a penlight I can appreciate how her conjunctiva is genuinely inflamed. "Is this redness new?"

"No idea," she says.

"I'm just wondering . . ."

"What?"

"Well," I say, "there's the possibility of an infection."

"What kind of an infection?"

"Oh . . . I don't know . . . something like a virus. Perhaps a herpes virus." If Crystal Haggerty were a cat, feline herpes virus might be the first thing that comes to mind.

Mrs. Haggerty leans back. "Herpes! In my eye! I can assure you I've not been looking for love in the wrong places!"

"No, no, it was . . . just a suggestion. Actually, humans can't catch feline herpes virus, and in the same way, you can't give herpes to your cat. Assuming you have a cat."

Judging by the look of dismay on Mrs. Haggerty's face I should shut up.

"Please." I gesture to her, thinking it might be best to finish my examination. In order to rule out a corneal scratch I have to move in so we are almost cheek to cheek. Slowly I become aware of the way Mrs. Haggerty makes her body interlock with mine.

"Have you been experiencing any dryness?"

I feel her lips brushing against my earlobe as she pauses and then whispers, "Not at this particular moment."

When I finally work out what she's actually referring to I jump backward like I was hit in the chest by a defibrillator. My God, this woman thinks she can act like Kathleen Turner in *Body Heat*, only without the body.

"Lighten up, Dr. Mills," she says, as if insulted. "I'm teasing."

"Right, of course," I stutter.

She bows her head, takes a second, and

then, with chilling detachment, comes back at me with, "But if I'm not, I have a sneaking suspicion you can keep a secret."

"I beg your pardon."

"See I called my friend in Charleston, Stephanie, she of the Tibetan terriers. Which practice did you tell me you worked at?"

"I didn't."

"That's right. Yet Stephanie swore she'd heard of you. Are you famous, Dr. Mills? Or infamous?"

She makes the latter sound far more exciting.

I dither. "Neither."

"Maybe you're being modest?"

I say nothing.

"Either way, I'm still waiting to hear back from her when she's discovered more. You okay? Only you've turned quite pale."

Crystal Haggerty delights in the effect her threat has on my physiology. Thankfully Puck comes to my rescue, inserting himself into the gap between us, his nose in my crotch a welcome alternative to what she might have in store for me.

"I'm fine, Mrs. Haggerty. Now, if you don't mind." I squat down and begin palpating Puck's fat Labrador belly, wondering whether I've finally reached my low point, forced to satiate this woman's sexual advances in order to buy her silence over my suspended license. Am I that desperate, and if so, is it about the money or saving Bedside Manor? "Everything feels fine," I say, standing up, careful to keep the dog between us.

"It's only because he gets excited in here."

I can almost see the wheels turning in Crystal Haggerty's cougar-ous mind as she works on a suggestive addendum like "he's not the only one" or "it must be the company." I cut her off.

"Are there any poisons that you know of on the school premises?"

"Don't think so."

"Is Puck on any other medication?"

"No, nothing."

"Will you let me take some of his blood?"

"Why?"

"Because it will tell us whether he has a metabolic disorder or not."

"You think he does?"

"No idea, ma'am. That's why I want to do the test."

Crystal Haggerty gently traces back and forth across her lips with the very tip of her index finger. "Let's say it comes back normal. Then what?"

"Then Puck has to have a problem with his stomach, his small intestines, or somewhere else in his abdomen."

"I'm telling you, this is about something he shouldn't have eaten. It always is."

Dietary indiscretion. Typical orally fixated Labrador. "When did you last feed him?"

"About half an hour ago. He threw up around eight this morning. I felt bad for him, so I fed him again."

"How much did he eat?"

"About two cups of dry food. You were hungry, weren't you boy?" Puck circles around to Crystal for a scratch, and for a second I'm worried that I've lost my wingman. Fortunately he circles back.

This history of a sizable recent meal is not what I wanted to hear. "I had hoped to take an X-ray of his abdomen, but it's likely to be a waste of time and money with a stomach full of food."

"Do you have a portable X-ray unit?"

Am I overreading an unsaid inference in the question? Does Crystal Haggerty suppose my seduction will be inevitable if I make a house call?

"No, Mrs. Haggerty, I do not."

Then my mind does a funny thing, flashing back to her last visit, to the way she became flustered when her husband suggested Puck's problems started after he returned from a conference.

"Has Puck ever stayed with a friend?"

The question catches her off guard.

"No."

"Have you used a pet sitter?"

"No. Why do you ask?"

"Because I suggest you confer with your husband as to whether any of his undergarments are missing." The fact that this particular line of questioning visibly unsettles Mrs. Haggerty makes me push on. "If you prefer, I can call him?"

She must know far more than she is letting on, however my "touché" moment is interrupted by a commotion in the waiting room, and when I investigate Peter Greer comes at me, carrying a lifeless creature in his arms. "I think he's been poisoned. Is he dying?"

Truth be told, Toby the terrier does look fairly close to death, so much so that I dare reach into the hammock of the editor's big hands and place my thumb and fingers over the dog's heart. The beat is weak and way too fast.

"I found him in the kitchen, out cold by the doggy door. He can't stop trembling."

I turn back to Crystal. Puck sits at her side, calm, almost respectful, as though the Labrador senses there's an animal with a bigger problem than his.

"Sorry, I need to deal with this."

"Of course," says Crystal, waving away the need for an explanation. "I'll be in touch." But as Puck makes to leave, Crystal fails to hide the discomfort, the uneasiness that passes between her and Greer. Their exchange seems overly formal and intentionally distant. What's that about?

Greer follows me into the back, where I set up a makeshift bed on a counter. Toby is barely responsive to my examination. I take his rectal temperature and he doesn't lift a lip, let alone his head.

"One hundred six point two degrees Fahrenheit," I say. Irreversible cell damage starts to occur at 108 degrees Fahrenheit. "He's burning up."

"So he's been poisoned. I knew it. That

old bastard Sam Cartwright's always threatening to kill him."

I reach for an intravenous catheter, a bag of fluids, and an extension set. "We need to get Toby cooled off before jumping to conclusions, Mr. Greer. Here, help me find a decent vein."

Though well intentioned, the big Limey proves to be an inept assistant. The nervous tremble in my hands is barely perceptible compared to the seismic shaking of Greer's. Thankfully, quite possibly for the first time in his life, Toby could not be more malleable, impervious to the curses and rants of his irate master.

"Okay. Now I need you to take a couple of those towels, run them in cold water, wring them dry, and wrap them around his body."

Greer does as he is told while I grab some ice cubes from the refrigerator, put them in a bowl, and run the plastic tubing through them so the fluid entering Toby's blood will be nicely chilled. I think of giving Greer a white wine analogy but decide against it.

Five minutes later I take another temperature. "One hundred four point eight.

Much better. But we're going to have to watch this very closely. Don't want him going the other way and getting too cold."

Greer seems elsewhere. "I knew something was wrong when he didn't bark this morning."

Once again I replay the conversation I overheard on my first night in the diner, Sam saying, "Rat bait might not be such a bad idea." Was that round of barking when I visited Greer last night the final straw? Did Sam drop by this morning with an all-you-can-eat d-CON breakfast special for Toby?

"Toby normally barks in the morning, right?"

"He's like an alarm clock. I can usually turn over, press an imaginary snooze button inside my head, and fall back to sleep but eventually I have to get up and fix his breakfast. The fact that he *wasn't* barking this morning was why I woke up."

I think about how familiar this sounds. "The curious incident of the dog in the night-time."

Greer smiles for the first time, and I notice the cracked remnants of last night's red wine still clinging to his dry lips. "Very good, Dr. Mills. I might have known you'd be a Sherlock Holmes fan."

"Prefer the Sherlock Holmes movies. Especially the ones starring Basil Rathbone. But I did read that one, back when I was a boy." Once again, Ruth Mills trying to nurture a deductive mind.

"Then you'll remember how the dog knew the killer. That was why he didn't bark. That was why Holmes found it curious. And that's what makes no sense."

"Not sure I'm with you."

"Because Toby knows Sam Cartwright well enough to bark and bite and maim."

Now I see it. If Toby lunged at the old man's jugular, it's likely he did so screaming a battle cry. Then again, at Greer's house, I also witnessed the terrier's silent stealth. I'm not sure this observation, this absence of barking, is relevant, so I put it aside for now.

"When was the last time you saw Toby acting fine?"

"Bedtime. I must have passed out around midnight."

That was well after I left and plenty of time for Greer to gather more incriminating evidence from my past. "Look, leave him with me. I'll cool him off, and as soon as he comes round I'll make him vomit to empty his stomach. See if he's eaten something he shouldn't. Anything changes I'll call. On your cell?"

Greer nods, and together we get Toby settled in one of the dog runs. I lead the reporter out to the waiting room, and once again it's far from empty. For starters, Doris is actually behind her desk and a stern-looking Chief Matt Devito is striding toward me. However, it's the couple—a woman and a dog—over the Chief's shoulder that claims most of my attention because they make no sense being together. Clint is lying on the floor, her head outstretched, resting on her crossed paws, eyes closed. And to my amazement, on the end of her leash, sitting in a chair, is, of all people, Amy.

15

Amy's hair is all wrong and all right at the same time. No longer constrained by the requisites of food hygiene, she wears it down, perfectly framing her face.

"Dr. Mills." The Chief offers me his hand to shake. Looks like the dodgeball bully still hasn't recognized me. "Mr. Greer tells me his dog's been poisoned."

I turn to the reporter.

"I called the Chief on the way over. I had to. One can't go trying to kill other people's dogs."

Though I feel Doris's raptor eyes on me,

I'm acutely aware that Amy appears to be hanging on what I am about to say.

"I don't know that the dog's been poisoned. Not yet."

Greer snorts. "Can't you do some sort of test?"

"A toxicology screen." Devito takes care to insert the phrase as a formal, almost professional, clarification, and I begin to wonder if the Chief wants to impress a certain member of the audience. Amy's in my line of sight, not his, and he doesn't notice as she rolls her eyeballs and shakes her head, unimpressed by his enduring appreciation of *CSI* and *Law & Order* reruns.

"I could," I say, though in truth, I don't know the answer. "But for now, I believe our focus should be on saving the dog's life, not trying to blame someone for trying to take it."

Amy looks directly at me, makes me suffer for at least five seconds, and then, just when I've given up, she concedes the faintest of smiles.

"We'll see which way the clinical signs progress. Everything will depend on how Toby responds to my treatment over the next few hours." I look at Greer. "Check out your basement, backyard, garage, under your kitchen sink, anywhere Toby might have gotten into something he shouldn't. If you come up empty-handed, and everything begins to trend to rat poisoning, only then would I start pointing fingers."

Devito looks like I have pulled the rug out from under him, thwarting his big investigation. Greer's distinctive bushy brows oscillate above his bloodshot eyes somewhere between objection and compliance.

"Now, if you don't mind, I should be attending to my patient."

Greer sides with this concession, shakes my hand, and insists I call if there are any developments.

The Chief leans in, his breath minty fresh. I wouldn't expect anything less.

"All the same, I think I'll have a chat with Sam." And then, raising a solitary eyebrow, he adds, "See if he cracks."

I wonder how often Chief Matt yearns to say "freeze" or "cover me, I'm going in," only to be deprived by the law-abiding affability of his jurisdiction. Who am I to deny him the thrill of an interrogation?

Offering him a weak smile of encouragement, I notice Amy getting to her feet as, reluctantly, so does Clint. The Chief catches my eye, glances at Amy, and turns back to me. "Keep me posted."

This comes out as an order. I nod accordingly, wait a beat until he heads for the door, and take a step toward Amy and Clint. "I barely recognized you."

Amy feigns shock. "With my clothes on you mean."

She says this loud enough to stop Chief Matt in his tracks as he passes the front desk, loud enough to induce a coughing fit in Doris. My face turns crimson and my ears burst into flames.

"Uh, no . . . not . . ."—heat continues to radiate from my cheeks—"with your hair down." I want to slow down my words and crank up the volume for the benefit of the peanut gallery. "Out of uniform."

She's enjoying this.

"And what are you doing with Harry Carp's dog?"

Amy moves closer, and Doris and the Chief fade away as I take in the symmetry of her face, not counting the color of her eyes. "Harry Carp is my grandfather."

She lets this statement hang there, lets it sink in, knowing how far down this important kernel of information has to go before it settles in the right place. I'm flashing back to last night at the diner, to the way everything came out wrong, arrogant and dismissive, insisting she was wasting her life and her talents when all along she is doing the right thing, doing the hard thing, putting her life on hold for the sake of someone she loves. Now it makes sense. Amy is the one who made the mysterious tire tracks in Harry's driveway. Amy is the one bringing him dinner, the one taking Clint for a walk. Amy is Harry Carp's angel.

"Why didn't you say?"

"Should it have made a difference?"

I don't know whether the question or the look in her eyes stings the most. "No. It shouldn't," I manage, but Amy's feeling generous.

"Look, about last night. Your private life's none of my business. I was just venting." She runs a hand through her hair, locks a loose strand behind her ear. "School's pressuring me about when I'm coming back, going on about taking up valuable space in their course, as if I'm supposed to predict how long my grandfather's got left to live." I can see how the act of saying this out loud upsets her almost to the point of tears. "I was snippy and antagonistic. I took it out on you, and I'm sorry. I'm hoping we can start over. I'm here because Grandpa said you needed to see his dog."

Part of me doesn't want to get off that easy. "I've been trained to make inferences from available information. I sometimes get ahead of myself and jump to conclusions. It's not my best trait."

"Didn't look like you rushed to judgment back then, when Mr. Greer wanted to lynch Sam Cartwright."

I look away, concede a reluctant "I'm trying," and look back, catching Amy's expression, as though the jury's definitely still out on what to make of me.

"Well, Grandpa's usually a good judge of character. Usually. And he seems to like you. God knows why, because as far as I can tell, you still haven't fixed his dog."

Pleading upturned eyes bring me back. "Where are my manners?" I squat down and cradle Clint's head in my hand. It's an effort for Clint to wag her tail from side to side, just once, before she curls inside my open arms and crumples into me as though she is spent. This dog is in serious trouble.

"Let's take her back. Find out what's going on."

What am I thinking, asking Amy to join me? Why not go with a simple "you should leave Clint with me," take her out of the equation, and avoid the possibility of more awkward conversation and uncomfortable introspection? But I can't help myself. I deliberate, weigh the possibilities, and I ask all the same.

We start with Clint's X-rays.

"You usually work alone?"

"Yes," I say, reassuring Clint as she lies on her side. No sedation required. No need for strategically placed sandbags to hold her still. Clint is more than happy to close her eyes and have her picture taken.

I focus the illuminated crosshairs of light on the center of the dog's chest. Lewis went over the basics of how to take an X-ray, but this is still my first time. I want to see what's going on inside Clint's body, not leave her with a permanent Chernobyl glow.

"Please, step back around the corner."

"You think every single girl in this town is pregnant?" Amy hits me with a wide-eyed glare before taking dramatic big steps backward. "I'm kidding."

I depress the button on the handheld controls, hear the *ping,* and step forward to retrieve the unprocessed film. What used to be a half bathroom off the main work area was long ago converted into a compact, lightproof developing room.

"I won't be a minute."

"Can I see how it's done?"

"It's mostly touch. In total darkness."

Amy's shrug tells me she is no less interested, so I switch on the red safe light, the two of us step inside, and as Lewis insisted, I lock the door to prevent anyone bursting in and spoiling the precious film.

I'll be honest. Trapped inside a dusky six-by-four space with this beautiful woman ignites a certain clandestine, almost pubescent excitement in me. This essential darkness works as "mood lighting." It's like a teenage date in a linen closet.

"There can't be any light when I put Clint's film through the processor or when I reload the cartridge."

Amy nods, I hit the switch, and we disappear into the abyss.

For a few seconds I pad and clunk around, getting my bearings.

"Have you always preferred being alone?"

"I like to be independent, autonomous. It suits me."

"I meant being a bachelor. Being single."

I flinch, and the X-ray of Clint's chest slips from my fingers, the sheet of unprocessed film seesawing its way toward the floor in my imagination. I curse.

"Problem?" asks Amy.

"Stay exactly where you are."

I bend at the waist and begin sweeping my hand back and forth until I feel the top of my head brush up against something soft.

"I don't know about South Carolina but I'm pretty sure that constitutes sexual harassment in this state."

"Sorry," I snap. "It's so damned dark in here. I managed to drop the . . ."

"Is this what you are looking for?"

Something flat but flexible brushes against the back of my hand.

"Thank you," I say, taking the film.

"My pleasure," says Amy, her nonchalance belying her amusement.

But now, of course, I am completely out of position. The mental image of the cabinet containing what few remaining sheets of X-ray film the practice possesses, and the mouth to the processor, are no longer where my mind left them before we were plunged into total darkness.

"Did you ever play blind man's bluff as a kid?"

"No," I hiss before crying out as I drive my hip into something sharp.

"Have much luck beating the crap out of a birthday piñata?"

She's obviously enjoying herself.

"Not that I recall." I grimace as the mouth of the lightproof cabinet tries to amputate my fingertips. "Why d'you ask?"

"Oh, no reason."

My mind jumps to *When Harry Met Sally*, Billy Crystal talking to Meg Ryan.

There are two kinds of women: high maintenance and low maintenance.

Which one am I?

You're the worst kind. You're high maintenance but you think you're low maintenance.

It's another sixty seconds before the film has disappeared into the machine and it's okay to switch the red safe light back on again.

But I don't.

I wait and listen to her breathing. I wait and savor her proximity, her presence, and the faintest smell of apples that seems to be coming from her hair.

"Everything okay?"

"Fine. It's processing."

I risk waiting a little longer and reach for the switch.

"So, why is Dr. Cyrus Mills all alone?"

I freeze and the sound of my inhalation, the pause as I hold my breath, fills the tiny room. My index finger hovers. Cloaked in the security of darkness I reply, "I think you get used to being alone, of not needing to share a life, of believing you're not missing out on much. You let the work take over, let it squeeze out all the rest. After a while you forget to think about any other type of future. I guess hope yields to frustration and eventually you become resigned to disappointment."

I catch myself before the silence stretches too far. Can't believe I let that get away from me. "Sorry, that sounded a lot more grim than it was meant to."

I can almost sense her deliberation.

"No girlfriends? No wife?"

"I've known some women in my time," I say, sounding almost offended.

"Really. Pretty women? Sexy women? Strong women?"

"Um . . . maybe."

In the pause I wonder if her rosebud lips are smiling.

"But not the right woman."

I don't answer but flip the switch, hoping the red haze will mask any incriminating discoloration of my cheeks. "Here's the film. Let's take a look."

I gesture for Amy to leave. She unlocks the door, steps into the halogen light of the work area, and I follow, blinking and confused, stumbling into the back of her.

"Ah, there you are, Dr. Mills. Been looking everywhere for you. The whiffy man just finished up. Apparently your cybernet should be good to go."

I think it might be easier to deal with Doris if she would act embarrassed or appalled to see Amy and I stumbling out of the pitch-black X-ray room. Instead she appears indifferent, as though she is used to her boss's inability to keep it in his pants. She scurries off to her desk before I have a chance to explain.

I put up the image on the viewing box and the perils of the dark room fade away, to be replaced by a different quandary, the bright objectivity of confusing shades of gray.

"See anything?" asks Amy.

"I see lots of things."

"Anything abnormal?"

I scrutinize the lungs, the heart, the bones of the spine. "I'm not sure."

The bark, actually more of a yap, comes from the dog run, and we both turn to find Toby standing at the bars, swaying like he's had one too many.

"Like father like son," says Amy, opening the door, bending down and petting Toby's head. Struck by her confidence I join her, my presence inciting a halfhearted grumble.

"Whoa. Someone's feeling better. Could you hang on to him a second while I take his temperature."

Amy holds Toby, and his grumble escalates to a growl until I extract the thermometer.

"Don't think this dog likes you."

"He hates me," I say. "One hundred two point six, almost back to normal. No more ice and cold IV fluids for you."

"Does this mean he wasn't poisoned?"

An experienced veterinarian would probably be able to answer this question. I wonder if Amy can tell.

"Ever read any Conan Doyle?" I ask.

"Of course."

"'Silver Blaze'? The one with the curious incident of the dog in the night-time?"

"Uh-huh," says Amy, as though everyone has at one time or another.

"Well, Greer told me he woke up because Toby did *not* bark."

"How could the dog bark if he was poisoned?"

She has a point. Why am I getting hung up on this stupid failure-to-bark thing? Because, like Lewis said, I may not have been blessed with a sixth sense but there may be an advantage to seeing cases from a different perspective. For the past fourteen years, when some small detail niggled me, the least it deserved was consideration, even if I wasn't smart enough to know where it fit in.

"Do you have to be somewhere?"

She checks her watch. It's nearly eleven.

"I need to pick up a prescription for my grandpa. And I'm working the lunch shift. But I'm okay for a while, why?"

Once again I am making excuses to keep this woman around, hoping that eventually I might say the right thing. "Mr. Greer and your friend the Chief—"

"The Chief's not my friend. We happened to go to the same high school, but, given our age difference, I was probably in kindergarten when he was a freshman."

"My apologies. Mr. Greer and . . . what . . . your . . . vague acquaintance"— Amy gives me an approving nod—"Chief Devito, seem bent on blaming Toby's illness on Sam because Sam vented about silencing the dog once and for all with rat bait."

Amy looks confused. "When?"

"My first night at the diner."

"That's awful."

"I'm pretty sure it was an empty threat. But, given what's happened, I'd like to have proof. I wonder . . . no . . . you've got stuff to do, I can do it."

"What?"

I meet her eyes and find a genuine desire to help. "I think Toby's doing better. I want to prioritize Clint, but I'd hate for Mr. Greer to do something he might regret. If I take another view of Clint's chest and two more views of her abdomen is there any chance you could look something up for me?"

Amy purses her lips, like she's puckering up for a kiss. "You're worried about another awkward moment in the darkroom?"

I don't do witty comebacks.

"Sure," she says. "Point me in the right direction."

Knowing it will take a while to set up the new Wi-Fi on my laptop, I lead her over to the cabinet housing the textbooks and select a few on general and emergency medicine. "I'd look under 'rodenticide poisoning' in the . . ."

She turns me to stone with a look that says, *I think I know how to use an index.*

"You know where to find me," I say, chastened.

Fifteen minutes later, having placed Clint in a nest of freshly laundered towels in the run next to Toby, I begin reviewing her new X-rays. It's rare for me to study these cryptic images of disease. Why bother when you can touch and feel the real thing? Hard as I try, squinting, imagining, willing something to leap out of the shades of gray, I still cannot define the cause of Clint's malaise.

"This might help."

I join Amy where she has laid out three thick books.

"A few of Toby's signs do seem to fit for rat poison. But according to this, he should be much sicker by now."

I inch closer, careful not to make physical contact, my eyes darting over the text, sucking down visible information.

"It's hard to remember all these details, you know."

"Sure it is." She doesn't sound convinced.

I run my fingers down a list of differential diagnoses, other toxins that could be mistaken for rat bait poisoning. And then my finger stops. There, to my surprise, is the answer to why Toby had not barked.

"We need to make Toby vomit," I say sounding ridiculously frantic.

Amy looks confused. "Okay. How do you want to do it?"

Suddenly I have no idea except the certainty that I should. No excuses for not knowing this one and no way to look it up in a textbook with her standing beside me.

"You want to try a little hydrogen peroxide solution?" she asks.

Is this a trap?

"Of course, I just don't know where Doc Cobb kept it."

If she suspects my flawed knowledge of the practical aspects of the job I can't read it in her face as she begins opening cabinets and drawers. And it doesn't help that she finds it before me.

"You got a syringe?"

I head through the back door to the examination room and return with the biggest one I can find.

"Come on, Toby's a terrier not a Great Dane."

Damn, I knew I shouldn't have invited her back here. I say nothing. Use your brain, Cyrus. If the biggest is appropriate for a Dane, then a tiny 3-cc syringe should be about right for a terrier. I go back, grab one, and hand it over. Amy approves and, with confident dexterity, loads it with a small volume of the peroxide solution.

"Here you go." About to give me the syringe, she snatches it back. "You going to tell me why you want to make him throw up?"

"Not yet," I say, taking the syringe as we round on Toby. My attempt to get near his head is greeted with what, for Toby, are tepid, mouthy lunges at my hands.

"Here, let me," says Amy, kneeling down, soothing Satan's sidekick as, with an unnerving ease and a magician's sleight of hand, she has the contents of the syringe unloaded into his lip folds and down his gullet. "Grew up with dogs. Help me up?"

I reach down, grab her hand, pull her to her feet, but she refuses to loosen her grip, inspecting my wrists, my forearm, and finally the front and back of my hand.

"Don't tell me you read palms?" I ask.

"If I did I'd never guess you were a veterinarian."

"Why would you say that?"

"Because your hands are wrong. When did you graduate?"

"Fourteen years ago."

"Plenty of time."

"Plenty of time for what?"

"Plenty of time to get bitten, to get scratched. There's not a scar, not a blemish, not a mark anywhere on your hands or forearms. How can that be, working with animals for fourteen years?"

For a moment, I feel like I have a flock of hummingbirds trapped inside my rib cage. I can't read her features. Disparaging? No, I don't think so. Perhaps I should keep my mouth shut, but there is something about this woman that makes me want to stop running from the past, stop living this facade. "Dead dogs don't bite or scratch."

"I don't follow."

"I'm saying that before I came back to Bedside Manor the only animals I've ever worked on have been dead. Yes, I graduated vet school, I'm a qualified veterinarian, but I trained to be a veterinary pathologist not a general practitioner. As you can tell I skipped the lecture on how to make a corpse puke."

I brace for an acerbic comeback, but Amy surprises me with a look that feels more lenient than judgmental, a look that encourages me to go on. Relief and the weightlessness of a secret shared suffuse me. "It was my mother's fault. She was a perfectionist, and back here in this house she haunts me. I mean that in a good way. Even if I'm not sure what I'm doing I'm always striving for excellence. I hate not knowing enough, not being practical enough. Ruth Mills taught me never to do mediocre."

"And what did your father teach you?"

I am open, ready to vent, but I hold back. "Indirectly, he taught me it was dangerous to get too attached, to care too much."

She tips her head back, narrows those brown and blue eyes, and with just enough humor to give me hope says, "Really? And how's that working for you?"

And that's when Toby comes to my rescue.

"What the . . ."

"Chewed macadamia nuts," I say, squatting down to examine a large pool of vomit at my feet. "They're poisonous to dogs. I noticed them on the list of poisons causing clinical signs similar to rat bait poisoning. Last night, I was over at Greer's house being interviewed about delivering Denise's baby, and he had a big bowl of macadamias sitting out on a coffee table. Now it makes sense. Toby barks every morning because he wants his breakfast."

Amy smiles, catching up.

"And Toby doesn't bark if he's already eaten his breakfast. I like it."

"Exactly."

"That's brilliant."

"Not really."

"No, it is," she says with a sassy smile, "for someone pretending to be a veterinarian."

And that's when Lewis charges into the center of the room and, nearly stepping into the puddle of vomit, cries out, "Tell me that's from the dog and not one of you two."

"And that's when you walked in," I say, joining Lewis on the floor. I insisted he give me a second opinion by examining Clint. It's time for him to share some of my guilt for not discovering what's wrong with the poor dog.

"I'm pleased you've found someone you can open up to," he says, lifting up a lip, pressing his thumb into Clint's upper gum, releasing his thumb, watching as the tissue blanches white and blushes pink.

I wonder if he feels slighted, like I chose Amy over him.

"When's she coming back?"

"Around three," I say. "You think I should have kept quiet?"

Lewis places his fingers on Clint's lower jaw, gently pries open her mouth, and takes a good look at the back of her throat.

"Did you mention the license?"

"Course not," I say, though part of me wishes I'd got that off my chest as well.

"Good. If she's any relative of Harry Carp she's not going to say anything. Like I said, I'm glad to see you let your guard down. You should do it more often. Folks prefer someone who's flawed over someone who needs to be a perfectionist."

"Hey, I opened a crack, if that, with one person, in private. The rest of Eden Falls can take me on face value."

Lewis glances my way, squeezes the lymph nodes around Clint's throat, causing her to swallow. "It's not your fault, the way you come across." Like an experienced chiropractor he begins to manipulate Clint's neck, up and down, side to side, gently flex, gently extend. "Why the long face? You know exactly what I'm talking about . . . aloof. Like Dr. Minch only less round."

"Please," I say, rising to his temerity, "there's a big difference between being antisocial and preferring my privacy."

"It's one thing to be private." The old man acts casual as he slips on his stethoscope. "It's another to be a recluse."

"Just because I don't see the point of inane conversation, doesn't make me a recluse."

"Okay, then answer me this. For the past fourteen years what have you been doing with yourself when you're not at work?"

The fact that I need to think about the answer only adds to my frustration. "I consider myself something of a movie buff." Saying this out loud only affirms my status as a total geek.

"Okay. What else?"

"I read."

"Let me guess. Journals, textbooks."

"I travel."

"Yes, where?"

"All over. Peru. China. Egypt. Iceland."

Lewis raises an index finger, requesting silence as he hangs on the rhythms and breezes inside Clint's chest. He removes the earbuds and slings the scope around his neck.

"Alone?"

"Does it matter? I choose places that interest me, places with unique and different cultures."

"You mean places that don't speak English? Never been tempted to take a cruise, relax at a resort?"

"What's the point of travel if it doesn't broaden your mind?"

"Fair enough. But, what's the point of living if it doesn't broaden your mind?"

With a deft and gentle touch, Lewis eases Clint into a position in which he can rummage the contents of her abdomen, feeling for any peculiarity. The cracking sounds come from Lewis's arthritic knees and ankles.

"How about sports?"

"I run. Try to stay in shape."

Lewis meets my eyes but keeps his hands on the move. "Running, not exactly a team sport."

I've had enough of this. I get to my feet. "What are you trying to say?"

Lewis looks up at me, working that

chipped incisor. "I'm trying to make you see that there's more to life than what you left behind. Oh, I know this practice is in big trouble and I know Eden Falls is a far cry from Charleston, but deep down I also know there's a part of you that's finally coming alive."

I shake my head and grapple with a smile because it still feels like the right thing to do. That's when Clint cries out in pain.

"Easy girl, I'm sorry," says Lewis, meeting her eyes, making sure she understands that he meant no harm. "It's between her shoulder blades. If I press down hard like . . ."

Once more Clint flinches, but this time, taking no chances, she trots off to the other side of the room.

Lewis gestures for me to give him a hand up.

"What do you make of that?" I ask.

"I don't know. I didn't feel anything, and the X-rays look fine. But in a stoic dog like Clint I have to believe we're on to something."

I wipe my palms down my face. "This is so much harder than I remembered."

Lewis interrupts the minor adjustment to his bow tie (today's number is navy-and-white plaid) in order to squeeze my upper arm. "You know, the more you care, the harder it gets."

I'm not impressed. "You steal that one from James Herriot?"

"No," says Lewis. "Dr. Robert Cobb."

I try to defy the old man's eyes for as long as I can, but I have to look away and pull back. I'm afraid of what might happen if he hugs me. Cobb's best friend always seems to get to me. I hate being so vulnerable. No, it's more than that. I hate being so transparent.

"I know what you're up to," I say. Of course Lewis wants me to stay, wants me to believe that Bedside Manor offers a clear path forward. He's ignoring the fact that I was fired from my last job, leaving me jaded enough to think this new grass is a whole lot greener than it really is. "And I don't want you to think I'm not grateful for everything you've done for me."

There's an empty pause in which I should have added, *and my father.*

"You make it sound like I'm wasting my time?"

Though I hear the question, I say nothing, because deep down where it counts I'm not brave enough to say, *no you're not*, out loud.

Suddenly Doris sweeps into the room with tornadic fury. "Sorry to interrupt, Dr. Lewis, but the nursing home called to say you need to get over there right away."

In the split second that follows, I watch as something bends and breaks inside the funny little man with the silk bow ties and it's like a bucket of ice being poured down my back as I realize how trivial my concerns are compared to losing the love of your life.

"And, Dr. Mills, I found another hand-delivered package on the door step."

With some trepidation, Doris hands over an identical manila envelope with my name on the front and no address or stamp.

I take it. Lewis seems to be frozen in place. For a moment, I wonder if he registered the word *another*.

"Go, get out of here, Lewis," I say. "We'll be fine."

It's all he can do to nod his appreciation and shuffle off, as though, finally, seventy-three years have caught up to him.

I wait until I'm alone, an ugly blend of

emotions simmering nicely and coming to the boil. I reckon you can sympathize with the fear, the dread over what new damning evidence lies in my hand. But then, sadly, there's a jealousy, a freshly kindled reminder of the way I never got to say good-bye to the person in the world *I* loved the most, my mother.

I rip the package apart and inside, stapled together, are nine sheets of paper. The title page reads:

The Vermont Statutes
Title 26: Professions and Occupations
Chapter 44: VETERINARY MEDICINE

What should be dry, boring legalese packs a very different gut-lurching punch when a single paragraph is circled in a bold, inky ring of black.

§ 2402. Prohibition; offenses

(a) No person shall:

(1) practice or attempt to practice veterinary medicine or hold himself or herself out as being able to so in this state without first having obtained a license from the board;

Though my hands are trembling, I'm more angry than scared. My extortionist may think he or she is clever, joining the dots, seeing the bigger picture, but there's a difference between upping the ante and crossing the line. Forget about curiosity or amusement. This offense just got an upgrade from trying nuisance to full-scale combat. This is personal, and I will not be intimidated. Though it runs contrary to every fiber of my being, it's time to fight back.

16

Ruth Mills would have been proud of me. Standing next to the microscope where she first introduced me to the delights of cytology and histology I can still hear her mantra: *The answer lies before you, Cyrus. To find it, take in the big picture with a low power lens, see the woods before the trees, survey the entire landscape before you search for your culprit's mug shot. Keep your mind open, weigh all the possibilities, be thorough, consistent, and entirely reproducible.* I may be seething and my stomach may be tied in a gnarly bowline but I'm determined to remain rational (which is not the same as cool), to heed my mother's advice, and get to the bottom of this treachery once and for all.

Cleary some form of coercion is inevitable and must be driven by one or more of three different motives: money, revenge or, most troubling of all, cold-blooded malevolence. Based on Cobb's beloved status in the community I'm inclined to believe the target is me rather than Bedside Manor, and so, if I follow this logic, I can come up with four individuals with reasons ranging from making me squirm to ensuring I spend time in a federal penitentiary.

The first is McCall and Rand Pharmaceuticals. What better way to throw out a wrongful dismissal lawsuit against your company than discovering the plaintiff is practicing veterinary medicine illegally out of state? Though I can't rule this out, this kind of blackmail feels a little heavy-handed for a multibillion-dollar company.

Next up, Peter Greer. Oh, he seemed nice enough, but he's an editor in chief, he's all about selling newspapers. Greer has the incentive and wherewithal to uncover my past, and if he's really a two-faced, ungrateful, stonehearted journalist hoping to trade his silence for money then he's going to be sorely disappointed.

My third suspect has to be Crystal Haggerty. She was here this morning and could have easily dropped off the package, misdirecting me with the story about her inquisitive friend from Charleston. Try as I might to assume that her only motivation must be free veterinary care for life, I fear her desire for leverage might be driven by her desire for sexual favors. Can't she get the hint that I am not the least bit interested? Is this her way of saying, *I'll do whatever it takes to satisfy my lust*?

This leaves me with my pick of the bunch. Brendon Small. Here's a guy who knows he's in the wrong on so many levels. He has to be playing for a Mexican standoff—my silence for his silence—and my showing up at his home last night must have totally rattled his cage. Mom was always a fan of Occam's razor, and I'd bet that the simplest answer is the correct one this time. Brendon Small is behind the packages, and that's why I dial his number.

Anne Small picks up on the third ring, thwarting my momentum. "Ah . . . hello,

Mrs. Small, it's Dr. Mills again . . . did your dog turn up?"

"No." There's a flatness in her voice that tells me she's moved beyond hope, from rescue to recovery.

The phrase "no news is good news" pops into my head but I can't say it. "I wonder if I might have a word with your husband?"

There's silence on the line. "He's out of town at a job fair. He'll be back late tomorrow. Can I ask what it's about?"

I've got nothing.

"Dr. Mills, you still there?"

"Yes. Tell him it's about something I noticed the other night. Something important. He can call me whenever he gets a chance. Sorry to disturb you." My finger is hovering over the end button, but I think about little Emily and stop myself. "Frieda's going to be fine," I say before hanging up.

Two o'clock. Doris, pacing outside, takes her last slow drag and holds it in deep, giving herself enough nicotine to get through the next few minutes as she wipes the snow off her shoes and opens the front door.

"Any news?"

Doris shakes her head. "Looks like you're flying solo." She points at the phone on her desk. "Did you listen to your messages?"

Before I can answer Doris presses a button on an answering machine below a digital number "2."

Message one was received at 1:35 P.M. today.

Dr. Mills, this is Ginny Weidmeyer. Chelsea seems much worse to me today and I'm not sure she's strong enough to come out to your clinic. Could you please make a house call at your earliest convenience? I'll be in for the rest of the day. Thank you.

Doris scratches something on a scrap of paper. "This is her address."

She slides it toward me like a croupier. I make no move to pick it up.

Message two was received at 1:42 P.M. today.

I hate to be a pest, Dr. Mills, a sheepish Crystal Haggerty draws out my name for dramatic effect. *But Puck is still not right. You really must see him in his natural environment. By the way, my friend Stephanie got back to me ... aren't you the dark horse?* And then, emphatically, *I'll expect you no later than five thirty.*

Doris writes another note on a second scrap, slaps it down on the first.

"And these are the directions to the Eden Falls Academy. Assuming you don't already know the way? Don't look so worried," says Doris. "If anyone shows up while you're out, I'll tell them you'll be right back. That should keep them in their seats, don't you think?"

I can ignore the innuendo, the professional emasculation, but the pleasure she derives, the wickedness worming its way through the creases of those sticky orange lips, finally makes me snap.

"What is it, Doris? What makes you ride me so hard? What have you wanted to say since the moment you laid eyes on me?"

Doris takes her time, straightens up, waiting for the animosity to rise, spread, and harden her features. "You have no idea what that man did for you. And I don't care what he told folks, because it was a lie and you know it."

"What are you talking about?"

"The funeral, what else? What kind of a

son doesn't show up at his own mother's funeral? I'll tell you what kind . . . the kind who only thinks about himself. And what does Doc Cobb do? He does what he's always done, makes excuses, telling everyone you're doing some sort of volunteer work, somewhere foreign, middle of nowhere, no way to reach you. And everyone believed him, except me, because less than two hours after your mother is lying in her grave, he's back there, talking to you on the phone, and all I can hear are poor Doc Cobb's tears and screams. Don't shake your head at me. I checked the phone records. I saw them with my own eyes. He called your dorm at college. You never went anywhere. You just wanted to be a thousand miles away from the one man in the world who needed you by his side."

In the end I had to walk away, into the work area, preferring the curses of a rabid terrier to the wrath of a rabid receptionist.

People are prepared to baby you 'cause that's what Doc Cobb wanted. Well, I'm telling you, I ain't one of them anymore.

What did she mean by this? And that word *anymore*? Up until now Doris has been babying me?

I should have tried to explain, to tell her that this was how my fourteen-year estrangement began. Though Cobb's failure to share my mother's passing was the final straw, the camel's back had been ready to break for years. For my mother, work became the man's mistress; for me, work became the man's favorite son. With each passing year of my childhood, Cobb became increasingly consumed by his veterinary life, increasingly removed from his family life. Long before boarding school, Mom and I eventually stopped asking if he would join us on our road trips to visit her sister in the Carolinas. Neither of us could bear to hear the same old excuse, *someone's got to stay and man the fort*.

Cobb made that fateful phone call from this very room. Up until then, the distance in our relationship was a letdown, but he was who he was. Bottom line, Cobb simply cared for his patients too much. I learned to acquiesce. What choice did I have? Then came the call that changed everything. By the time I hung up, my desire to renounce my name and never speak to him again was final. Time may have softened the impact and provided some sort of perspective, but with Cobb's passing, any chance for reconciliation disappeared. Doris will always be an unapologetic Cobb groupie. How do I get *my* side of the story across? Here, in this town, my ugly past seems determined to reach out and snag me. I am the man who chose to run, and now I've been wrenched to a dead stop. If I'm being honest, worse than the prying eyes and the slanderous chatter, there's the fear of having to finally face myself and what I have done.

Toby's growl maintains the slow and steady beat of a metronome with every pass in front of his cage as, for the umpteenth time, I read the words from the statutes. *Without first having obtained a license from the board.* I look up and make the mistake of catching the terrier's eye. He stares at me with such evil intent it's like he's pointing a paw in my face before drawing it across his furry throat in the manner of a knife. I guess he's feeling better. Time to give Greer an update and a chance to come clean. I dial his number, but it goes straight to voice mail. Damn. I leave a message that hits the highlights—macadamia nuts, road to recovery, call back later.

With Tina busy breast-feeding her kitten and Clint resting comfortably after I gave her an injection of an antibiotic and an anti-inflammatory (Lewis's "can't hurt" suggestion), I succumb to guilt and a wayward sense of duty by making those annoying house calls, starting with the home of Ginny Weidmeyer.

Even from the bottom of a plowed driveway that has to be a quarter of a mile long, the word *home* feels impotent for this acropolis. Amid acres of reclaimed woodland, open fields roll into a massive frozen lake, with an unencumbered view of a craggy mountain range tossed in for good measure.

I park on the circular driveway. No need for reverse. Check. There's a huge outdoor fountain in the middle, looking like it was stolen from the Piazza Navona. Most striking is the fact that it's still working, babbling away even in this weather. Obviously Ginny would rather pay to heat the steaming water flowing through the mouth of Triton, or

whoever it is, than be deprived of its soothing sounds.

I step down from the truck. To one side
of the main house there's a massive four-
season porch, positioned to take in the
vistas, and on the other, a four-car garage,
outside of which lurks a brand-new black
Range Rover bearing the license plate
ONFYA.

I press the doorbell, and I'm treated to
Mozart's *Eine Kleine Nachtmusik*.

"Dr. Mills, thank you so much for coming out to see us."

Ginny wears a pink polo shirt, skin-
tight riding breeches, and leather riding
boots. I'm sure there's plenty of room for
a barn and indoor arena out back, unless
she's simply playing dress-up for . . . enter the man himself, clad in white bathrobe and flip-flops, clopping across the
marble floor of the foyer. Why do I have
the uncomfortable feeling that he is naked underneath?

"Hey, Doc," says Steven, mussing his
slick wet hair with a towel.

"Please," says Ginny, gesturing for me
to come through. "She's in the great room."

Bag o' tricks in hand, I follow them into

what appears to be a private country club. Besides the vaulted ceilings and the French doors that open onto a bluestone terrace with a covered swimming pool, I see two fireplaces, three antique Persian rugs, and enough sofas, love seats, and armchairs to furnish four good-size living rooms.

"Here's my baby."

Ginny kneels into a sheepskin rug on which Chelsea luxuriates in the golden glow of burning embers.

"What has you worried, Ms. Weidmeyer?"

I want to be empathetic, really I do, but my dispassionate cadence reveals a man with more pressing problems on his mind.

"I've not seen her drink or pee today. And she feels a little dehydrated to me."

I catch the whites of Steven's eyes and the inconspicuous shake of his head.

I join Ginny on the rug, as if the two of us are in prayer, carefully pinch Chelsea's skin around the scruff of her neck, and watch as innate elasticity slowly sucks it back down. Too slowly. I lift the cat's lip, run my finger across the gum line, blanch it out, and time the capillary refill. Three seconds. Too long. Despite my skepticism,

Ginny is correct. Chelsea is becoming clinically dehydrated.

I get to my feet and step away from the heat of the fire. I see the familiar plaques and awards for golf that I saw at Greer's house and, angled toward Chelsea, what appears to be a security camera.

"You worried she might get kidnapped?" There's no humor in my question as I point into the optical eye.

"It's a webcam," says Ginny. "I have four of them set up in her favorite spots around the house, recording her every move. Gives me peace of mind. I can check up on her whenever I'm out and about. What d'you think?"

"She's fine," Steven says, sidling in close to Ginny. Real close.

I guess I'm already on a short fuse. Maybe, since I seem to be going down in flames, I feel like embracing an uncharacteristic, "all guns blazing" attitude. My revulsion at the sight of Steven pressing the palm of one hand across Ginny's buttock, thrumming out a rhythm with his impatient fingers, doesn't help matters. If I have to blame what I am about to say on a single catalyst, I choose the brazen presumption in Steven's flashing eyebrows, as if they broadcast a secret message of: "You and I *are* on the same page, right, Doc?"

"No, she's not fine, Steven, if that really is your name. She's actually five to seven percent dehydrated, hardly ideal for a cat with a kidney stone."

Ginny looks like I may as well have just smacked her across the face. Instantly, the set of Steven's jaw switches up from cordiality to hostility.

For a moment I flounder and clear my throat. "My apologies for my candor, Ms. Weidmeyer, but yesterday evening I bumped into your fiancé at the local convenience store where he was purchasing, among other items, nonprescription cat food. Assuming Chelsea to be your only cat, and that you yourself are not a fan of canned beef and giblets, I have to conclude that the food has been maliciously administered to sabotage your attempts to control her kidney disorder."

"What the hell are you talking about?" Steven is in my face, pupils dilated, no doubt some of that Dutch beer on his breath.

I turn to face Ginny. "Steven is an alias;

his real name's Stuart. According to his driver's license he's from somewhere in Florida, not Manhattan. What you two do together is absolutely none of my business, but what is my business is assuring the well-being of this little cat."

Chelsea raises her head, ever so slightly, as if to request we keep it down, before settling back into her white pelt and closing her eyes.

"You told me yourself, you're not the one getting Chelsea her breakfast in the morning. That's when I suspected she's eating a diet high in salt and protein. Hold back on her access to water and, for a cat with her kidneys, subclinical dehydration quickly sets in."

Ginny still looks more alarmed than interested.

"If you're the one who feeds her in the evening, you've probably noticed how she's hardly touching her food. That's because those high-salt diets are highly addictive, just the way the pet food company designs them."

Ginny's blank stare neither confirms nor denies my supposition.

"Get your stuff and get the hell out of

here," says Steven, shoving a flat hand into my sternum. "How dare you come into our house, making these ridiculous accusations."

The blow makes me grunt. There's not a hint of a quaver to his voice. I'm guessing Steven is quite comfortable with confrontation.

"She needs fifty milliliters of normal saline injected subcutaneously." I direct my treatment instructions to Ginny as the man formerly known as Steven begins dragging me toward the front door. I wonder if he senses that I still have one more bomb to drop from my apocalyptic payload.

"Just you wait 'til I contact the State Board, the Better Business Bureau, the attorney general," he barks, and I feel the spittle land on my left ear. "After I've finished with you, you'll be lucky to get a job as a butcher."

I think about telling him to take a number and get in line but, over my shoulder, marching at double time, I shout, "Have a professional jeweler look at your diamond ring, Ms. Weidmeyer. It's a fake. I noticed it on one of Chelsea's X-rays. Probably cubic zirconium."

With all the efficiency of an experienced bouncer, I'm tossed off their front stoop, forward momentum having fun with minimal friction at my expense as I slip on a patch of black ice and land hard on my coccyx.

I look back to find Steven delivering what I can best describe as a "withering farewell." I'm not talking about the gritted teeth, the jabbing index finger, and the fire in his eyes when he insists, "You're so dead." Instead, I refer to the fact that the man safeguarding the threshold, despite the arctic chill, seems totally unaware that his bathrobe has fallen wide open.

My suspicions were correct.

17

I pull out of Ginny's driveway, punch in the number, and it feels as though I've spent my whole life *not* making this type of phone call. When it came to my mother, I was unable. When it came to my father, I was unwilling. Self-preservation or selfish, I prefer the big decisions in life to impact only one person. Me. Now, thanks to Bedside Manor, I'm bound to a nicotine-addicted receptionist, a terminally ill woman I've never met, a kidnapped golden retriever, and a growing list of people and animals that constantly fill my head with worry and responsibility.

"It's me, how's Mrs. Lewis?"

"She's good, just a second." I hear footsteps and imagine the old man leaving a hospital room to find a corridor where he can speak and not get into trouble with an officious nurse for interfering with the monitors.

"Thanks for checking in. She fainted. Or at least they think she fainted. They didn't want to take a chance, you know?"

Lewis's obvious gratitude leaves me with a heady sense of guilt for bugging him about my problems. "Of course."

"Everything fine on your end?"

"Sure. No problems."

There's a pause. "I'm not deaf, what's going on? And what was that package Doris gave you?"

The guy doesn't miss a trick. I tell him everything and hope it helps justify my run-in with Steven.

"Trust me, it's not Greer."

"How can you be so sure?"

"Why are you ignoring the phrase 'trust me'? How's Toby?"

"From what I can tell, back to his evil self."

"Good. If I were you I'd discharge him

this evening. I guarantee Greer's focus will be on what you've done for his dog."

"But what about Ginny Weidmeyer?"

"Leave Ginny to me. I don't know about this fiancé of hers, but she's a good person. I have a feeling I can talk her down."

Again, there's a clandestine certainty in Lewis's tone.

"You think Brendon Small sent the article?"

"No idea," says Lewis, "but maybe it's no bad thing."

"What? How can you say that?"

Somehow I know Lewis is smiling on the other end of the line. "Because you're actually worried about what you stand to lose and that means you must be starting to care."

He's wrong. "Maybe I just don't like losing is all."

But Lewis has the last word.

"Or maybe you're not the man you used to be."

Eden Falls Academy bears no resemblance to my late Aunt Rachel's private school in Beaufort, South Carolina. For starters, the campus signposts gratuitously steer visitors like me (and, presumably, the parents of prospective pupils) past what looks to be a brand-new Center for the Performing Arts. And for those who find themselves overwhelmed by the size of the nearby sports center, little white hands with pointy fingers are eager to show off the "Olympic pool," "indoor track," an ice hockey rink, and dance studio. Did I mention I passed the school's private ski resort on the way in?

Eventually I locate "The Master's Lodge," though the word *lodge* feels far too crude and earthy for the classic multigabled Colonial the Haggertys call home. I park out front. There's light behind drawn curtains in several rooms.

Maybe Dr. Haggerty is home?

Encouraged by this prospect, I grab my bag, select one of the three possible front doors, march up the salty walkway, and knock. The door yields into my first rap, opens a couple of inches, and Puck comes bounding toward the crack, barking with junkyard ferocity.

"Hello, it's Dr. Mills," I shout, reassuring

the black Lab that I'm friend not foe. "Anybody home?"

I'm standing in a large vestibule featuring a freestanding staircase and an extravagant crystal chandelier. From somewhere on the second floor I hear Crystal shout, "Go on through, Doctor, I'll be with you in a moment."

I feel my earlier optimism waning as Puck adopts the role of butler and leads the way toward the back of the house. He deposits me in an expansive kitchen, trots over to his bed in a little breakfast nook, pads around, and lies down.

Is he weary of yet another gentleman caller?

As I vacillate over the option to bolt, my eyes fall upon what I can only describe as a smoking gun: an uncorked bottle of Veuve Clicquot on ice and two champagne flutes.

Stop jumping to conclusions. Concentrate on the Lab who loves lingerie. "What's happening, Puck?"

I park myself on the floor next to him, struck by the difference in his demeanor. Crystal Haggerty was right. Puck acts like a different dog at home. The cordial and chirpy "Fatador" from my exam room has morphed into a mopey and withdrawn husk of his former self.

Though he's reluctant, I get Puck to his feet so I can examine him properly, and this time I appreciate some significant bloating of his belly, up front where his stomach lies. He actually grunts when I press too hard, which is probably as vocal as this indomitable creature ever gets.

I kneel-walk my way around to Puck's blocky head and get totally suckered into feeling sorry for him. It's the way he stands there, pathetic, jowls hound-dog floppy, eyes sad and waxy, like he's fed up with feeling seasick and why can't we head back to shore?

That's when I register the approach of clicking high heels on hardwood floors, rummage for my stethoscope, shove the buds in my ears, close my eyes, and twist my features into my best imitation of concentration as I listen to Puck's lungs.

In order to sell Bedside Manor I am prepared to endure a certain amount of humiliation, but that does not include spending the rest of tonight locked inside Mrs. Haggerty's love dungeon. I become aware of her presence, very near, almost hovering over me. Head bowed, out of the corner of my left eye, I catch sight of a glossy black stiletto. If the shoe is a harbinger for what lies above, this isn't good.

Deep breath. Open your eyes and look up.

"Be a love and zip me up?"

From my submissive position, practically genuflecting, I'm forced to take in the view. If she were some twenty years younger and about to visit a Vegas nightclub, then I'm sure she's appropriately dressed. But for Eden Falls? Her black cocktail dress is all about plunging down and rearing up, clearly designed to emphasize an oversize bosom and shapely legs. Did Mrs. Haggerty select this particular outfit to intimidate me? Should I defuse the situation, nip any sexual tension in the bud, suggest she rethink the sheer black nylons failing to disguise the cottage cheese cellulite of her thighs?

I scramble to my feet as she twirls around, theatrically, clearly with the goal of inviting compliments. As it is I'm unable to speak. For some reason I had assumed that when a woman uses the phrase "zip me up," she's looking for help sealing the awkward last six inches at the top of a dress. Silly me. When Crystal Haggerty turns around, the entire length of the zipper lies undone. And what is just barely passing for a dress filleted open, reveals an abundance of skin, lace, and frilly straps.

I feel like Dustin Hoffman to her Anne Bancroft in *The Graduate*.

Do you find me undesirable?

Oh no, Mrs. Robinson, I think you're the most attractive of all my parents' friends.

"Whoa, there, Mrs. Haggerty, this is entirely inappropriate."

She spins back to face me, and I watch as her woozy aura of flirtation and fun melts away, replaced by a slap of humiliation and outrage.

"Don't lecture me on what's entirely inappropriate, Doctor, assuming I should even call you doctor."

I gesture with open palms of surrender. "Please, I have no desire to upset you."

Her laugh is sharp and piercing. "As far as I can tell you have no desire period. My friend Stephanie was right. She read about you in the Charleston papers and not in a good way. Wasn't hard to discover your license is not only from out of state, it's currently suspended." A sly menace slithers into the fine cracks around her eyes and lips. "So, I must assume you're here to see me for reasons other than curing my poor dog."

"You sent the anonymous packages?"

Her knitted brow gives me her answer. Great. So if it wasn't Crystal Haggerty then there's still someone else out there hell-bent on my personal destruction.

Crystal straightens her spine, puffs out her chest, and raises her chin, as though this posturing alone will rejuvenate her confidence and sexuality. "Look," she says, taking a step toward me. "I don't have to be at this charity event for another hour and a half. Think of this as a wellness visit, a way of improving client relations." Another click, another step closer. "What I know about your past is simply . . . an insurance policy. Useful to have, but probably unnecessary."

"Mrs. Haggerty, I will not . . ."

And at that precise moment, Puck, bless his heart, drops his head, stretches out his neck, and yaks up an enormous wad of wet and foamy, discolored fabric. The noise is so gut-wrenching, the smell so fetid, the deposit so bizarre, it instantly shatters what little mood Mrs. Haggerty has so desperately been trying to create.

"What is it?" asks Crystal, with a fresh awareness of the real world, as though she's totally sober after a disappointing night out.

I leap to the dog's side and pat his head to reassure him that it's okay, in fact, it's more than okay. It's perfect. And then I take a closer look at the item that has been hiding in his stomach. "Not sure," I say, grabbing a pair of latex gloves from my bag o' tricks and putting them on. "Do you have a trash bag I can use?"

She clip-clops over to a drawer as I pick at the item like I've discovered a washed-up creature in the surf. It's large and folded on itself, but as I open it up, it quickly becomes apparent that it is, after all, a single, intact, undigested piece of intimate apparel.

"Dear God" is all Crystal Haggerty can manage as she joins me in a silent moment of homage to the ingestive prowess of the Labrador.

"That's one way to put it," I say. "It must have been lodged in Puck's stomach for quite some time. It was only a problem when it blocked the outflow, causing the rest of the stomach contents to come up. Thank goodness he finally managed to get it out."

I can't tell whether she's nauseated, in shock, or panic-stricken. And that's when it hits me. I know exactly where this particular item of underwear came from.

"Red boxer shorts. And no ordinary pair of boxer shorts. Silk, no less." If she detects a smugness to my tone, I really don't care. Like I told Harry Carp, I'm not big on fate or destiny, but if "coincidence is God's way of remaining anonymous," the convenience and harmony of this discovery threatens to make me a believer. "And they're big, very big," I say, letting this fact blossom in our shared silence, along with the unspoken observation that these shorts could in no way fit her puny husband. "And what's this?"

I peel back the elasticized waistband to reveal a label, expecting to find something like Hanes or Fruit of the Loom or Calvin Klein. Instead I read out loud:

"Marks & Spencer. Never heard of that brand before. You?"

"I'll take that," she says, quite forcibly.

"No, I don't think so." I snatch the garbage bag from her hand and deposit my soggy cache and soiled gloves inside. "You don't have to believe me, but they were wrong to take away my license. You see . . . I don't plan to stay in Eden Falls . . . but I imagine you do. My scandal promises to be a flash in the pan compared to yours. So . . . let's just say this is *my* insurance policy."

Though I deliver my reprisal with queasy trepidation I can't tell whether she finds me infuriating or masterful. Eventually she concedes a deep nasal inhalation. "I've changed my mind about this evening. This . . . development, has been a little unsettling. I'm afraid my husband will have to cope on his own."

I try to act understanding, grab everything, and head for the front door, leaving her in the kitchen.

"Just a moment," she cries before I can make my exit.

Half a minute later, Crystal Haggerty joins me in her hallway. She's slipped off her heels and lost so much more than height.

"I'd like to settle up. For everything." She reaches forward and hands me a check. I notice it's from her personal account and it's for far more than the cost of a house call.

"This is way too much, Mrs. Haggerty."

"Not at all. Let me know if it doesn't cover how much we already owe Dr. Cobb."

I take in the check and all its lovely zeros. Hush money. It's not nearly enough to keep Mr. Critchley and Green State Bank off my back, but it's definitely going to make a dent in his first payment.

I study Mrs. Haggerty, who is looking penitent and far more worried about me destroying her life than the other way round. I think back to what Lewis said in the basement, describing her as gregarious rather than immoral. It's risky, it's giving up my advantage, but in the end I trust Lewis. I pocket the check and hand over the garbage bag.

"I'm pretty sure Puck's going to feel a whole lot better. A bland light diet for the next few days will help settle his stomach.

Please tell your husband to stop leaving his boxers lying around. Okay?"

And I can tell her indebted smile isn't holding back the phrase *I will*. Instead, it's stopping her from saying *Thank you*.

The Band-Aid on my index finger is the forget-me-not that makes me smile. My first professional war wound. The old Toby is back, nailed me when I went to take his temperature. Broke the skin, spared the knuckle, but guaranteed to leave a scar. I wonder if Amy will notice? Despite the absence of a whip, wooden stool, and a safari outfit, I manage to coax Toby outside for his evening constitutional (I imagine this is how Greer would describe it) and lure him back into his run with the promise of dinner. Leaving the terrier to chase the metal bowl around the floor, sounding like a cowbell, I fire up my laptop and hook it up to my new Wi-Fi and Google:

"Marks & Spencer label."

"British retailer, Marks & Spencer sells clothes and food, headquartered in London." British, just as I expected. The owner of the stray silk boxer shorts, hastily discarded and presumably consumed by Puck during a steamy rendezvous at the Master's Lodge, has to be none other than the clandestine Don Juan of Eden Falls, Mr. Peter Greer.

Let me be clear: I have no intention of ever using this information. It's none of my business. But Lewis is right; I don't want to lose Bedside Manor. And before you think I've finally cracked and gone all sentimental, this revelation has nothing to do with the emotional upheaval of returning home or preserving my father's legacy. Chances are I'm going to fail, that Mr. Critchley will have his pound of flesh before the weekend's over, and I'm okay with that, so long as I get a fair fight. I've always believed that inevitable failure is the best incentive to succeed. But if Greer thinks he can sell newspapers and gain notoriety for breaking a scandal and exposing an unlicensed veterinarian, then he needs to know that I'm also armed with equally dangerous and incriminating material. It's like Sean Connery says in *The Untouchables*, "They pull a knife, you pull a gun." So what if my gun happens to be a pair of gastric-juice-covered boxers from England?

Amy must have come back while I was out because Clint's run is empty. I check in on Tina, get her fed and watered, change her litter box and towels, and gently pat a satiated kitten tummy. With the damning photocopied articles on the counter next to the phone I make my call. "Hello, Mr. Greer, sorry to be calling so late but I got tied up by a couple of house—"

"How is he?"

"He's great. Just ate dinner."

"Really?"

"Yes. You can swing by and pick him up anytime."

"He's fully recovered?"

"Yes."

"Did he try to bite you?"

"No, he succeeded in biting me. Keep him away from macadamias and he'll be fine. Did you sort things out with your neighbor?"

"I've already instigated a cunning ploy to achieve a lasting peace with Sam. Amazing what a bottle of single malt will do."

Though there is absolutely no hint of deception or relish in his voice, though it speaks volumes about my inability to trust, I still feel the need to dig and prod.

"How's the article coming along?"

"Smashing. I think you will appreciate my surprise."

Surprise.

"It's bold, it's creative, and it's tailor-made to appeal to the pet owners of Eden Falls."

"Mr. Greer, I'll be blunt. I've received a number of . . . correspondence, containing some . . . well . . . details from my past . . . details that suggest someone wants to discredit me. They were sent anonymously but they were meant to send a message."

"And you think I sent them?"

"I'm asking." I'm treated to a hiss of disappointment.

"He said you could be a willful and suspicious bugger."

"Who said?"

"Your father, of course. Last time I saw him, Bobby and I chatted about you and Bedside Manor."

"What about me? What about it?"

Greer laughs, as though once again, my questions prove him right. "He made me promise to help you out, if you ever came back here. Do you really think I would deprive this town of the veterinarian who not only saved my dog's life but also stopped me from making a complete arsehole of myself by wrongly accusing my neighbor? I may be daft but I'm not stupid. And anonymous, not my style. If I dig up a relevant skeleton, you'll be the first to know."

Relevant. What does he mean by *relevant*?

"Mark my words, you're going to look back on what I'm about to set in motion and say 'Greer's a bloody genius, putting this practice back on the map.'"

I don't know what to say.

"You familiar with the SAS, British Special Air Service? Bit like your Navy SEALs?"

"Not really."

"They have a motto—*Qui audet adipiscitur.*"

"Never heard of it."

"It means 'who dares, wins.' Think of it as my inspiration."

Now he's got me seriously worried. "Not sure I'm the daring type," I say, stopping short of admitting, *but I do like to win.* "All the same, thanks, Mr. Greer. I appreciate it. Toby's ready when you are."

"I'm on my way. And it's Peter, dear boy, Peter."

I hang up. Perhaps it would be best to let Crystal Haggerty fill him in on the benefits of going commando.

Friday

« **18** »

What's wrong with me? It's precisely 9:32 in the morning and though I could pretend to be scrutinizing a patient for possible skin cancer, let's call it as it is, I'm sprawled across the couch, content to pet Frieda. As the captain of a sinking ship I should feel trapped but strangely I feel liberated. From the moment I came back to Bedside Manor I've never felt alone. Sure, the captivated creature staring up at me has helped, but there's this awareness of being a small part of something bigger. And though that "bigger" might well be bigger debt or bigger personal degradation, it might be bigger reach.

It might be a sense that compared to where my life has been headed, I'm finally doing something worthwhile.

"Dr. Mills, you planning on working today?" Forget the courtesy of a knock on my door, Doris shouts from the bottom of the stairway. "Two clients are here to see you."

It's tricky extricating myself from the retriever, and my bounty of golden hairs insists on coming with me as I rush downstairs and into the waiting room. I glimpse Doris, already outside, pacing. Who knows where her trail of frosty condensation ends and the toxic fog begins. But the two individuals seated on opposite sides of the room take me completely by surprise.

"I'm not saying he's cured," says Ethel Silverman, actually laying her hand on top of Kai's head. "But I am saying he likes this new diet of yours. Makes him less itchy. Smells a whole lot better as well."

I squat down to rassle with the periwinkle-eyed husky. Funny how I don't hesitate anymore. Kai looks great, those reptilian patches around his ears and muzzle beginning to fade away. Best of all, I can tell how he relishes a physical contact that is so much more than relieving an itch.

"I'll take that as a compliment, Mrs. Silverman."

"Take it any way you want, young man. I'm only here to get more food."

And, as if on cue, Doris is generous enough to give up some of her valuable smoking time by joining us.

"Doris, would you mind grabbing a bag for Mrs. Silverman's dog food? Thank you."

Doris glares at me, as though I ordered her to fetch me a coffee or a birthday present for my wife. The two geriatric ski bunnies huddle, winterized to look like Michelin men, sharing whispered disapproval of a man with the audacity to act like he's cured Ethel's dog. They make for a daunting duo.

I'm hoping to find my reception on the opposite side of the waiting room less hostile. "Denise, how are you? Out of hospital so soon?"

Denise Laroche is considerably less round than I remember. And she looks well, no need for a blood transfusion, thanks to a little restraint with the vampire makeup. In fact, I barely even notice the piercings.

"Doin' great but I hate hospitals. I was like, get me out of here."

"And who's this?"

Beside her, lying in a stroller, snuggled in blankets, I make out the face of her sleeping son.

"This is Michael."

Once again I squat down. I'm conscious of not waking him, and having not washed my hands and, strangely, of how good he smells. "Michael. Good name. He's . . . adorable." For a moment there I had hoped she was going to say, *and this is Cyrus*.

"Yeah. I think so too. But I'm here to pick up Tina and her kitten. And to get him registered as your patient."

The way she says the phrase "your patient" has a strange effect on me. It's part pride and part fear. Until now, every case I've seen has been acquired, originally under the care of Cobb or Lewis. Tina's kitten promises to be the first case generated solely by me.

"Of course. Come on through to the back."

Denise and Michael follow me and, apologizing to Tina, I open her cage and extricate a writhing fur ball. "You want to hold him?"

Denise smiles as I hand him over for her inspection. "Sure," she says. "I just wanted you to know that I'm, like, naming him Cyrus, after you, after what you did for him. For us."

A sentimental wave washes over me, a powerful, ridiculous notion that I am honored to receive such a silly but genuine show of gratitude from a girl who has almost nothing else to give. I become uncomfortably aware of the possibility, however faint, that I might actually shed a tear.

And that's when I realize, while I'm feeling as though I've just been asked to be a godfather, that I've never properly examined her kitten. There was no time during the frenzy of Denise's delivery, and it's never crossed my mind since. So it should come as no surprise when I discover a detail that averts any threat of tears and ensures a blush of embarrassment. Cyrus is a girl.

It wasn't as though I didn't know what I was getting into. Not exactly *High Noon* or *Gunfight at the O.K. Corral,* but one way or another there's going to be confrontation. This certainty is based on the venue where Lewis suggested we meet for coffee. It's late afternoon, and I walk into a flat, two-dimensional world where corpse white snow meets dishwater gray sky. It's visually chilling. Think more haunting than serene. Stubborn cold adds to the foreboding. Dormant trees gather like a crowd of sinister onlookers, and the caw of a distant crow is unnaturally amplified in the hush. It's stark, it's sacred, and it fills me with dread. But then I guess it should because, for the first time in my life, I stand at my mother's graveside.

"Here you go," says Lewis. "Cream, no sugar."

I nod, more grateful for the warmth than the drink itself. "I could think of cozier places to chat."

"Cozier, maybe, but more pertinent, I doubt it."

Lewis watches me, undoubtedly noticing that I've barely glanced at the tombstone.

"Sounds ominous," I say, and I'm not striving for levity. "But I'm used to living a life without looking back, without nostalgia. I'm pretty sure any attempt at a frost-bitten intervention won't make that much difference."

Lewis takes a step closer, sips his drink, and eyes me over the rim.

"The other night, down in the basement, you asked me whether I thought you misjudged your father."

I'm wary of where this is headed. "Yes."

"Well, it all depends on your perspective."

"Perspective? Perspective suggests that there's more than one way to interpret the facts, and the facts about what happened when my mother died are incontrovertible."

Lewis is not smiling. "The thing is, I think there might be three versions of what happened here fourteen years ago."

I laugh and it sounds too jumpy, too defensive. "Three? Where d'you get three? This is all about me not knowing Ruth Mills was dead until *after* she'd been buried. This is all about never getting to hold her one last time, never getting to say good-bye. I don't really care about being branded as the absent son. This was my mother. I never got to lose her. The person I loved most in this world was amputated from my life, and it was Bobby Cobb who cut me out."

I wait a beat, swallow my drink, which is too bitter. Feeling this much is like an awakening and part of me is ready. Part of me wants the walls to come crashing down.

"But, Cyrus, why would Bobby Cobb want to hurt you?"

"Because he could. Because he resented what Mom and I had. Because he'd rather be a veterinarian than a father. I'll never know and I really don't care because whichever way you slice it, what he did was unforgiveable."

The old man's breath lingers, swirling around him like a lazy cloud. My breath looks more like a steam train struggling up a hill.

"It sounds like he punished you, so you punished him right back?"

"Damn right," I say, letting the same Pavlovian anger of that fateful phone call kick in. "How else are you going to respond? I never wanted to see or hear from him again. No phone calls, no letters, nothing. I couldn't stand the thought of being tethered to his last name but I couldn't get a court date until after graduation. Yes, it was Cobb who insisted I go to boarding school, and yes, I know I got a better education because of it, but Ruth was the one who inspired, guided, and yearned for me to be a vet. Taking her maiden name was the least I could do to honor her."

Lewis's lips part enough for me to catch the neat rows of his Scrabble-tile teeth. But he doesn't look pleased. "So when did you acquire Ruth's sense of objectivity and need for deliberation?"

I flash to one of my mom's favorite truisms: *the harder you have to convince yourself, the more you need to listen to your inner doubt.*

"Hey, don't get all preachy on me." My interjection comes out fast and animated and I know I'm hooked. "At least you're getting to be there with your wife at the end. The day Cobb put me in that much pain I earned the right to be reflexive and narrow-minded."

I feel sick. I want to apologize. I want to let him know, it's more than pain. It's guilt.

Lewis waits, choosing his moment, like he needed to read my remorse before moving on. "Bobby told everyone you couldn't be at Ruth's funeral because you were doing volunteer work overseas. He said you were totally unreachable. He said by the time you found out, chances were you wouldn't be able to get back before Ruth was laid to rest. Nothing anyone could do."

I stare down at the snow, trying to focus on the eerie blue glow filling the holes I've made with my boots. "That's what Doris told me, and even she didn't buy it. She said Cobb was covering for me, as if I chose not to be there."

"I'm telling you what he told me, some years back. No reason not to believe him."

"Please, he just wanted to save face. You say your son can't make it, so you avoid the confrontation, the ugly scene in front of friends and clients. Cobb made sure he gave Ruth a sanitized funeral where he was in total control."

Lewis makes to squeeze my arm. "You and I both know Bobby was far from perfect, but . . ."

I shake off his hand. "No, he wasn't, and what kills me is the fact that everyone in this town thinks he was. Everyone."

Lewis is silent, begins to dig around in his coat pocket.

"Far from perfect. Ruth was my mother and Ruth was my father. Bobby Cobb's only child was his work. As far as I'm concerned he made a choice, and in the end, so did I. You don't get to choose your parents. You don't get to choose your childhood. You don't get to choose that moment when your mind realizes that being constantly overlooked feels pretty much the same as being rejected. So when the time comes and you finally get to choose, the path you take is less about what it *is*, and more about what it is *not*."

Lewis pulls out a stick of balm, applies it to his lips. They must be too dry and stiff to worry that cracked incisor. "You asked me if he and I talked. We talked a lot, especially at the end. Believe me, your father knew he let you both down."

I frown, wanting him to know I don't believe him, and Lewis takes a moment, considering how best to prove his point.

"D'you know when Bobby first knew something was wrong with Ruth? When she started to go bald from the chemo. What kind of a husband never notices his wife getting sick, never shares the fear of her diagnosis, or the horror of her treatment until the poor woman's hair falls out in clumps? I'll tell you what kind. The kind whose obsession with work creates a divisive isolation. The kind who finally must face what he has become. When it came to Ruth, Bobby knew there could be no redemption for what he had done."

Hearing this I want to say "nor should there be," but I keep my mouth shut.

"But he never gave up hope that he could somehow turn things around with you. That picture of you running track, the one in his bedroom, that was from way back. It proves he was there, even though you never saw him. Same with your graduation."

"He wasn't at my graduation. I wouldn't let him be there." I want him to hear the desperation more than the outrage. "It was Mom's day. She was the one who made it happen. It was nothing to do with him."

"Look in his office. It's not a great shot, a lot of heads in the way, but I could tell it was you walking across the stage to pick up your degree. He was there."

I flash to the day of my graduation from veterinary school, standing without a family, brandishing my isolation. I didn't want to, but I walked for Mom; no cheers, no whoops, no name calls, just polite applause. Why does this revelation feel more like a betrayal than a display of Cobb's anonymous support? Mom would have given anything to be there. Defeated, but with a sense of obligation, I say, "You said there were three versions."

Lewis nods. "Yours, Bobby Cobb's, and"—Lewis waits a beat—"what I believe to be the truth."

"The truth?" No sarcasm, genuine surprise. Mom comes to me in a slow blink, stern but sympathetic. *When someone tells the truth, someone takes responsibility.* Always her voice in my head.

"It came out right at the end, and I mean the very end, as these things often do, before Bobby asked me to do him one last favor."

"Lewis, please, you mean well, but this is getting to be a little much."

The old man considers me, stern but sympathetic. "I know, but I think you need to hear this."

He may be right but over the last fourteen years I've learned to accept that this particular story doesn't have a happy ending.

"According to Cobb, the truth lies right here. You're looking at her, or at least you should be."

"I'm not with you."

"Ruth Mills. Ruth Mills was the reason things turned out the way they did."

For the first time I take a long hard look at her tombstone. Big mistake. Lewis has obviously dusted off the snow, enough for me to read, chiseled in the granite, LOVING MOTHER OF DR. CYRUS COBB, DVM. Me, wearing his last name, on her tombstone, even before I graduated.

"He told me you visited her a few weeks before her death. He said at that stage she didn't look too bad, all things considered."

I can't even nod.

"The end came real quick, real unexpected. He said hours not days. And this was right when you were starting your finals. All the same, Bobby wanted to pull you out, wanted you home." He's watching my reaction. "It was Ruth who stopped him."

Here's another chance to lash out, but something in the old man's eyes holds me back. It's more than "hear me out," it's "let me in," it's "trust me."

"Sadly, I never got to know Ruth, but if there was anything bad anyone said about your mother it was that she could be incredibly stubborn and pragmatic, sometimes to the point of being a total pain in the ass."

An authentic smile gets away from me.

"Bobby swore she argued that if you couldn't sit those crucial exams, if you were absent, you would fail, and that meant you would fail because of *her*. She'd wanted this for you from the first time you told her 'I want to be a vet.' Everything had been about these exams. She knew you were ready, poised to get it right first time. She couldn't be the one to deprive you over something as inevitable, as predictable, as her own death."

I think about the last letter Mom sent me. I read it as a pep talk before my grueling finals, a fond recollection of every important moment growing up that had brought me to the brink of graduating from veterinary school. Did I get it wrong? Was it really her way of saying good-bye?

"Remember, we're talking about a pathologist here. Death, and things that cause death, was her life's work. That's why she insisted Bobby Cobb promise not to tell you how sick she was until you were all finished. And he did. He reckoned he owed her. Bobby kept his promise, in part because he believed Ruth would hang in there long enough that he could call you and you could get back in time."

I breathe in Lewis's speech bubble, suck down each sentence, deep inside, and slowly the words begin to register and have meaning. That's when my body kicks in, no longer simple "fight or flight," not this time, this is war and jet fuel, and it doesn't come on in increments, it explodes like a shock wave resonating through my gut and my chest. The coffee cup leaves my hand. I feel like I'm either going to be sick or pass out. Lewis is still speaking but I can barely hear let alone comprehend.

"Ruth knew your exam schedule. Bobby called first chance he got, as soon as you were done. Two hours *after* she had been laid to rest."

I come back enough to realize this must have been the phone call Doris said she overheard. My vocal cords feel weak, as though they'll fail me. It's all I can do to ask, "Why didn't he tell me?"

Lewis looks anxious, like this is just as painful for him. "He told me he wanted to be punished. In the sorry aftermath of Ruth's death he felt like he deserved it.

Eventually, over time, he wanted to explain. He reached out—letters, phone calls, he even tried e-mail—but you sealed him off and shut him down so completely he stopped trying. His will was all he had left, his last attempt to let his son know just how sorry he was. He had no expectation of whether you would or could take on Bedside Manor, but if you did, his one hope was for you to finally walk in his shoes, to feel how the work becomes all-consuming, the way you get lost in the lives of the people and the animals who come to depend on you. He wanted you to get it, to understand their fear, to appreciate their joy, to recognize the challenge of balancing a life inside and outside of work."

For a moment there, Lewis seems so very old and fragile, and I realize that here, in this graveyard, he's like a man on thin ice, with not much separating this world from his next.

I'm open-mouth breathing, my lower jaw slung like a hammock rocking side to side. "Why? Why did he need me to do this?"

"Because he wanted you to understand. Because he wanted what we all want when our time comes."

"And what's that?"

Lewis leans in, places both his hands on my upper arms. This time I let him. "A chance to be forgiven."

I wince, lick my lips, and squeeze them together, wringing the blood out of them until the pain makes the scream inside my head go away. It's as though he's wedged a knife in deep, pried me open, and I already know there's nothing good inside worth shucking out. Nothing except shame.

"When you left this town," says Lewis, "you left something of yourself, something essential, behind. Possessing a sharp mind doesn't make you a genius in the same way that possessing a heart doesn't make you compassionate. As far as I can tell you're back, in more ways than one. It's time to reclaim what you lost."

His kindness feels misguided and so much more than I deserve. "You said he asked you to do one last thing."

"That's right," says Lewis, unzipping the front of his coat and fumbling inside. "He wanted something from the basement, from the workshop. He said it was what he wanted to be looking at when he died."

Lewis hands over a Polaroid, and I take it, keeping my eyes on his, catching the way he raises his chin, encouraging me to look, and I don't want to, and I'm afraid to, but slowly I bow my head and take it in, all the way. I notice the four small holes in the white border, precise, neat, one in each corner. The picture from the heart of the collage. I'm sitting on his lap and his arm is out to the side, wrapped around Mom's waist. I'm smiling, my mom is smiling, and though his eyes are almost closed, my dad is smiling too. The three of us are together, a family, trapped in a moment of genuine happiness.

That's as far as I got. And as I knew he would, like he's been from the moment I came back, Lewis is there to catch me, joining me in the snow, holding me so tight as the tears come, letting me let go, and helping me to turn fourteen years of misplaced anger into fourteen years' worth of grief.

All of a sudden I've got work to do. And it's not because I've found a solution to my problems. I wish. In fact I'd be exaggerating if I described it as a plan. It's more of a tactic—risky and irreversible and embarrassing and it could totally backfire, but for the first time in a long time, I'm all in. Dispose of the water wings and send the lifeguard home. Look what proof, objectivity, and deliberation got me. Time to believe in the power of my conviction. Time to let go of the sides and wade out until I'm completely in over my head.

I go down to the basement. Dad's workshop seems different. I dig around and check it out with a fresh eye. There's a half-eaten pack of Oreos in the top shelf of the fridge, unopened quart of vanilla ice cream in the freezer—fine antidotes to the cravings of a sweet tooth. I run my finger-tips over two pieces of wood sitting in a vise, set at a right angle to one another thanks to a perfect dovetail joint. No weep-ing glue, no nails, just precise craftsman-ship. There's a pocket-size, dust-covered transistor radio, sitting on the bench, tele-scopic aerial extended, divining a signal. I'm about to turn it on when I stop myself and try to guess what I'm about to hear. Right now everything is about the truth, however painful, and the truth is I've no idea. I play the odds, guess sports, or talk radio, flick on the power, and once more Bobby Cobb proves how little I knew about the man—I'm listening to a string quartet.

I pull the Polaroid photograph of my fam-ily out of my breast pocket and with great care I insert pins into the existing holes at its corners and restore the centerpiece of the collage. Now I see how it fits, framed by images of a wife and son radiating from its core, drawing the eye to a focal point around which everything else revolves. I step back, take it in, and change my mind, unhooking the entire corkboard from the wall and carefully carry it upstairs.

Next on my "to do" list is a call to my landlord back in Charleston. I need him to get into my studio, raid my closet, and locate a certain framed certificate of graduation. After months of legal wrangling with McCall and Rand Pharmaceuticals, I've become a regular down at the FedEx office, three blocks from my apartment. This particular store closes at five, but if he hurries he can overnight it to Vermont.

Frieda remains parked where I left her, in front of the refrigerator. Given her predilection for this spot, this is where I set up her dog bed.

"Quick walk before supper?"

If it's dark enough for stars it's safe for us to go out, though this venture on the trails can't take long, given the way the cold air burns my lungs with every breath. Frieda stays on leash, trotting to heel, my sentinel. The image of my mother's graveside flashes through my mind and I wonder how many times I will have to replay my conversation with Lewis for it all to feel less raw.

"Why didn't *you* call me?" I had asked Lewis as the two of us kneeled in the snow and I squeezed him tighter and tighter, in a vain effort to break the rhythm of my tears. "Why didn't you tell me what really happened, before he died?"

Lewis broke my grip and pushed me back, wanting to be sure I saw everything in his answer. "If I had, would you have believed me? Would you have come? Before everything you've experienced since you took on Bedside Manor?"

And though I said nothing, we both knew the answer.

"Sorry, Frieda, that's going to have to do it." Quarter of a mile, if that, but Frieda doesn't complain when I about turn. I read the same old contented smile on her face and it softens the pain. Then my inner demons get to work and I'm smiling too. More than anything else, Bobby Cobb wanted to be understood. He wanted to be forgiven. And here I am, back in Eden Falls, trying to do the exact same thing. Time to say good-bye to the man I have been for the last fourteen years. So long as I haven't left it too late.

No doubt Amy will despise the word *epiphany,* but I want her to know what happened today, to know I was so very wrong about Bobby Cobb. It's one thing to misjudge a person, it's another to convict them and refuse them their day in court. I'm not deliberating about talking to Amy, I'm not weighing the pros and cons, I'm just following an innate desire to set the record straight with a woman I barely know. I've never been smitten or besotted, but if I was, Amy might be the first. That's why I want a chance, and for a confident straight shooter like Amy, honesty seems like the best place to start.

Down at the diner, this time actually wanting to slide into my father's favorite booth, I find it occupied by a familiar face—Chief Matt Devito.

"Hey, Doc, take a seat, I've been meaning to drop by and thank you."

"You have?" I say, keeping my coat on for now.

"That thing with Mr. Greer's dog and his neighbor. Could've gotten ugly. Appreciate the way you handled it. Buy you a coffee?"

"Uh . . . sure," I say, my back to the door, scanning the booths and counter. I don't see Amy anywhere.

Devito follows my gaze. "Looking for someone?" He cocks an eyebrow, like he's on to me.

A waitress appears and it's not Amy.

"Can I get a coffee, please, cream no sugar?"

I can't tell whether the woman, in her sixties, hears my request. She gives away nothing—not acknowledgment, not pleasure, not disgust, but just traces her footsteps back the way she came.

"That's Maggie. Bit different from Amy."

I raise my chin, not touching this subject. I want to head back to the practice and call over to Harry Carp's house, but I try to look interested in the rest of the clientele.

"You know," says Devito, half-smiling, jabbing an index finger in my direction, "there's something about you. Just can't put my finger on it."

Say hello to my little friend.

"Really? Tell me, Chief, any luck finding

that missing golden retriever? I've seen the posters everywhere."

My coffee arrives, sloshing over the sides of the mug as Maggie slides it across the table like a barkeep serving a beer. She tosses me a handful of tiny half-and-half containers, and even though Devito's still picking at the remains of his French fries, she whisks away his plate without a word.

"Not yet. But I've had a couple of interesting leads."

The Chief's intonation begs me to ask. "Like what?"

Devito leans back into his pew, checks the coast is clear, leans forward. He really has been watching way too many TV police procedurals. "Being as this is still an ongoing investigation, all I can tell you is I'm interested in talking to a man, about your height, about your age, likes to wear a hat with fur earflaps and might be trying to disguise his victim as a male."

"I see," I say, pouring in three artificial creams. "And how are the family holding up?"

"Devastated. At least the mother and daughter are. Dad seems fine."

"Why's that?" I ask, trying to sound surprised.

"Anne Small was married to a friend of mine, her first husband, Brian. Great guy. Died about two years ago. Sources tell me the replacement is having a hard time adjusting to the fact that the wife came as a package deal with a daughter and a dog."

"What do you mean by hard time?"

The Chief interlaces the fingers of both hands and cups the back of his bald head. "I'm saying he has motive, if it turns out the retriever is more than just missing."

Devito winks, letting me know I heard it here first.

I reach for my coffee but get waylaid by my phone buzzing in my pocket. "Hello," I answer.

"Cyrus."

There's something wrong in her voice. "Amy. You okay?"

The Chief's hands drop to his sides, his ears on high alert, listening in.

"Not really. It's Clint. I think she's dying. Can you see her?"

"Of course, I'll be right over."

I'm on my feet.

"Too late," she says. "We're on our way over to you."

She hangs up.

"I've got to go. Thanks for the coffee."

I shuffle out of the booth, more than enough time for the Chief to fire off a jibe. "Word to the wise, Doc, and that word is *unattainable*." He flashes his brows, creases rippling to the top of his crown. "Pretty sure she plays for the other side, if you catch my drift."

Ordinarily, the old Cyrus would have let this go. But not this time, not after today, not with this woman. I beckon him closer, lean in, and say, "Pretty sure she doesn't."

Be damned with chivalry and southern politeness, I fix him with my best attempt at the smile of a man who can only refute his accusation thanks to carnal knowledge. And judging by Devito's reaction, I think I did okay.

I want to be prepared—IV catheter and fluids to hand, X-ray machine warming up, last set of Clint's X-rays on the viewing box. But what am I preparing for? How can I treat let alone cure what I've failed to diagnose? I replay Amy's words. *I think she's dying*. And that's when I realize it wasn't fear catching in her voice; it was defeat, resignation, the inevitability of failure, *my* failure to save her dying grandfather's dog. Amy's phone call wasn't a cry for help, it was a plea for mercy. Perhaps I should be prepared with a needle and a syringe full of blue juice.

Headlights pull into the parking lot and the surprises keep coming.

"She's in the backseat," shouts Amy. She jumps down from the driver's side of her SUV, glances at me over her shoulder, like she barely knows who I am, and instead of joining me at the rear passenger door, she disappears around the hood, to the opposite side, attending to the other sickly patient in her life, Harry Carp.

"You okay, Grandpa? Take your time. I've got you."

Why am I surprised? He's here to say the good-bye to Clint, when what he most wanted was for her to be there to say good-bye to him.

I open the door to the backseat. Clint is sprawled across a plaid blanket. Her eyes are closed. She's perfectly still. I'm too late. Frigid night air rushes into the truck, diluting the warm air, and I can't see any smoky breath from her nostrils or her mouth. I grab her, and in one frantic and awkward motion, I scoop her into my arms. Stepping back, I keep both eyes on Harry. The pronouncement is forming on my tongue, but then there's a faint whimper from under the blankets, a stirring, and my breath catches in my chest, inducing a reciprocal whimper of my own.

"Sorry to ruin your evening," Harry says. "But she's suffering. Can't have that. Not this dog."

Amy has a firm grasp of Harry's arm, but I still worry about the ice underfoot and him falling and cracking a hip. Leave breaking his heart to me.

We shuffle inside, back to the work area, and I lay Clint and her blanket down on a table.

"Can I get you a chair, Harry?"

Harry frowns, shakes his head. "Thanks, but I need to be here by her side." A liver-spotted hand reaches for the top of Clint's head. The way Clint leans into his familiar touch is subtle, but important in a way I wouldn't have understood just a week ago.

"She won't get up," Amy says. "Won't

eat, won't drink. I tried to help her to her feet, and she moaned in pain. You've got to be able to find what's wrong with her."

It could be criticism. It could be encouragement. I can't read her blue eye or her brown eye so I turn to Harry for guidance.

"Take one last look for me, Doc. But if you can't give me an answer, I'll let her go. You with me?"

I nod, which I think is enough for Harry to know that I understand and respect his decision.

Amy puts her arm around her grandfather. He's watching me and she's watching him and I know I must ignore them and focus on a funny-looking female dog named after a movie star.

Clint's stats are not good. Her pulse is quick and thready, she's dehydrated, her temperature is 103.5°F. She's depressed, reluctant to stand let alone walk, and there it is again, that wince, that moan, when I press down hard on her spine behind her shoulder blades. I revisit her X-rays on the viewing box, once more scrutinizing her spine, her chest.

Nothing.

"What do I know? I know that if I touch

her in a specific location I elicit pain. What sort of pain? Well, what types of pain are there? Gnawing, throbbing, burning, stabbing, pressing, postoperative, colicky, muscle, and . . . referred. Referred."

"You do know we can hear you talking to yourself." Amy sounds genuinely concerned.

"Referred," I repeat, ignoring her. "Referred pain occurs when a painful sensation is felt in a site other than the one where it is actually occurring."

I go back to the X-ray. I stand back. I move close. I squint, tilt my head this way and that.

Maybe.

"I need to take another X-ray of Clint's chest. Amy, can you give me a hand positioning her?"

Carefully, I carry Clint over to the machine, Harry shuffling along at her side, his hand never letting go of her fur. Amy grabs a couple of sandbags, purely to help stretch Clint's front legs forward for her picture. I clear the room (though it's a struggle to pry Harry off his dog, even for a few seconds), snap a shot, and process the image.

"There," I say, pointing to a fuzzy, fluffy patch of whiteness, "that's a little different from last time."

"What is it?" asks Harry.

I'm already on it, pulling out drawers and opening cabinets in the X-ray room. I'm looking for something Bobby Cobb would keep in stock—cheap, practical, and often a remedy in its own right. The fifth chemical element in Group Two of the Periodic Table—barium. "We're about to find out," I say, showing off a gallon container half full of a viscous white liquid.

"What are you going to do with barium?" asks Amy, and I sense she's worried where I'm going with this and thinking this is getting a little desperate. Maybe she's chalking it up to the clinical ramblings of a doctor who can't accept failure.

"I'd like to give Clint a small dose by mouth, let her swallow it down, and take another X-ray."

Where it comes from I don't know— determination, conviction, lack of viable alternatives—but I'm lucid and calm.

Amy takes her time, as though she's reading more into my state of mind than considering what I'm suggesting.

"Grandpa?"

I like the way this is Harry's decision. Harry nods, and I draw up ten milliliters of the liquid barium in a syringe, and that's when another piece of my past catches up to me. I flash to a postmortem examination from my days as a pathology resident, to the lungs of a dog that accidentally inhaled barium and subsequently died of pneumonia.

"You okay?" asks Amy, tuning in to my reverie.

"Sure," I say, positioning Clint so she's sitting upright as I gently open the corner of her lip, creating a pouch near the back of her mouth in which to squirt my chalky medicine.

Barium tastes bitter, and Clint squirms and gags, zombie drool dripping from her lips, but most of it goes down the hatch. Amy and I set up for another X-ray, take the picture, and four minutes later I have the two latest images side by side for comparison, before barium and after barium.

I stand back, but I don't need to deliberate and I don't need to work my imagination. The answer is right there, in front of my eyes, and with it comes a bigger, far more cogent question, one that eclipses any thoughts of celebrating a diagnosis. It begs me to ask whether or not it was there all along, before Clint got so sick, before she began to suffer, before it was too late.

"Well?"

Did I underread the original films? Did I fail to take in the big picture? Is Clint another milestone in a life being defined by an endless series of mistakes?

"Dr. Mills?"

This time it's Harry, and I want to tell him but I also want to be sure.

"Amy, you bring home a meal for Harry most nights, right?"

"What's that got to do with . . . ?"

"Yes, she does," says Harry.

"Bear with me a moment," I plead. "And, Harry, you told me you 'sometimes' feed Clint table scraps, yes, though I think you meant to say 'always,' right?"

Harry nods, though he looks lost. I turn to Amy. "What do you bring him from the diner?"

"Whatever's on special."

"And does that vary?"

"On a daily basis, sure, but it's pretty much the same week to week."

"So what was it today?"

"Spaghetti and meatballs."

"And yesterday?"

"Chicken parmesan."

"And the day before?"

"Lasagna."

I gesture for her to keep going.

"Chicken marsala. Pork."

Pork. "What sort of pork?"

"Pork chops. Why?"

I take a deep inhalation, but it's one of pain, not relief. Taking a step closer to the X-rays, I tap what was once a white fluffy cloud, that now, stripped of its cloak of invisibility thanks to a thin layer of barium, has been unmasked as a half-chewed piece of bone.

"Clint has a piece of pork chop lodged at the bottom of her esophagus. It's stuck just in front of the opening to her stomach. Maybe it's mainly gristle or cartilage, because I don't see it properly on the plain X-ray, but the barium doesn't lie. That's why she has pain behind her shoulders. That's why she was having a hard time eating and drinking."

Harry's moving beyond the diagnosis,

tuning in to the fact that I'm not pleased with what I've discovered. "Is this bad?"

"Potentially, yes."

"Potentially?" snaps Amy. "What does *potentially* mean?"

Harry pats her arm, like he's used to reining her in. I try to swallow. My mouth is dry gulch.

"If the bone or cartilage or whatever has been stuck in the same spot for the past few days, it could have caused pressure necrosis on the mucosa of the . . ." I stop myself and start over. "A rotting piece of wedged pork chop could have worn a hole in the esophagus, the tube from the mouth to the stomach, allowing saliva and ingested food and bacteria free access to the inside of Clint's chest."

Harry and Amy stare at the X-rays, as though they might discover the answer for themselves.

"Can you see a leak?" asks Amy.

"No, but it still might be there. We didn't use enough barium to know for sure."

"What can we do?" asks Harry, brushing past me to hug Clint around her neck, to put his face in hers, to whisper in her ear. I don't want to eavesdrop but I can't help but hear the strangled words "I'm so sorry. I'm so sorry."

Amy and I glance at one another, powerless to stem Harry's tears.

Not so long ago, I would have dismissed Harry's connection to Clint as irrelevant to my diagnosis and superfluous to my cure. But here and now, embedded in this crisis, I can't ignore the tremor in Harry's grip and the insistent rhythm of Clint's beating tail. If this is the end, then this must be a dog with no regrets, no wish for anything different in her life. And as these two best friends look into each other's eyes, I am convinced that Harry and Clint know more about giving than most.

Is this what Lewis meant? Is this what I left behind? Empathy?

"You didn't answer me," says Harry, ignoring the tears and mucus and fur plastered across his face.

"What?"

"I asked about what we could do."

"Right. Well, it's not coming out through her mouth," I say. "Way too risky trying to grab it and yank it backward. Something's going to rip or tear. I can call around and try to find a surgeon who's prepared to open her chest, take it out that way, but I'm guessing it will have to wait until tomorrow."

"She won't last until tomorrow. She's ready to leave me. I can see it in her eyes."

"Then, I'm sorry to say, there's not much else I can do."

Amy steps closer to me. "That's it. You're giving up."

I look over at Harry. His eyes are pinched shut, but they're still leaking tears. I lower my voice. "First do no harm, you know?"

Her heterochromic eyes come into some kind of focus on mine, penetrating and resolute. "'Strong reasons make strong actions.'"

She pauses, maybe for effect. Truth is she didn't need to say a word. What lies behind her stare says it all. It's the push I need.

"Shakespeare?"

She nods. "*King John*."

No time to comment on her impressive knowledge of the more obscure works of the Bard. "It might be possible to push the bone into the stomach."

Her eyes narrow, chin tilting up and to the right.

"But it'll still be stuck inside her," she says. "How long before it gets hung up on another part of her guts?"

I shrug. "Stomach acid and digestive enzymes should be able to break it down. I'm more worried about what will happen if I try to make it move."

"A tear?" Amy whispers.

I nod.

"Fatal?"

"If untreated, yes."

She straightens up, looks over at Harry and Clint. "Give me a moment."

I watch her go to Harry, fishing for tissues in her coat pocket, easing him away from his dog, enough to wipe down his raw cheeks and silver-stubbled chin. They talk quietly for a few minutes, fear and trust and pain and love bouncing back and forth between them until they embrace in a hug that has Harry crying again.

"We want you to try," Amy says. She strokes a finger below her right eyelid, the brown one, before I can say for sure that a single tear got away from her.

I come over to Harry, and do something rash, something I would never ordinarily do. I reach out, place my hands on both his shoulders, and squeeze. When Lewis held me at my mother's graveside, he couldn't stop the pain, but what he could do was make a physical contact that let me know his intent to try. After what happened today, it's dangerous for me to look too long into the old man's milky blues, so I'm quick to pull back.

"I need something long enough to get down there."

"What are we talking?" Amy asks.

I come around to the front of the table, touch the tip of Clint's dry nose with one index finger and, like a tailor measuring for a suit, stretch my other index finger down to the back of her rib cage.

"Couple of feet. And I need something perfectly smooth, no rough edges, something round, tubular but not too big in diameter."

"What about a length of garden hose?" Harry asks.

"Probably not stiff enough. I need something more rigid."

"What about a broom handle?" Amy asks.

And for some reason, the cogs interdigitate, the wheels turn, and something inside my head falls into place. "Hang on a minute." I disappear through the waiting room, the unused storage room, and go down to the basement. I need the roof rake, or should I say, I need one of the individual tubular aluminum segments that make up the roof rake.

Lewis has put it back where he found it. I grab a segment, a hacksaw hanging over the workbench (just in case it's too long) and yes, I glance over at that empty space where the collage of photos used to hang. It's enough to imagine the only smile my father left behind, the one I get to keep, the one with his eyes half closed, the one that makes me think to ask, *what would you do, Dad?*

I make a silent promise to hang it some-place where I can seek his advice on a regular basis. Force him to be there for the tough calls, the difficult cases. What would he make of Clint? I've got nothing, but for today I'm going to believe that he'd want me to have a go.

"I think this might work," I say, handing a segment to Amy for her inspection. "Light, strong, nice diameter. Put some strips of white tape over the cut end and make sure there's no sharp edges."

I realize too late that I've given an order, as if I'm her boss and Amy's a fully trained veterinary technician. I'm relieved when she goes along with it. "Harry, I need your help placing a catheter. Okay?"

Harry nods, and it strikes me that I should have done this sooner, started Clint on fluids, got Harry involved and distracted and doing something physical to help his best friend. It's also better to be working with him and not Amy, so I don't have to feel her scrutiny as my hands shake, blowing a vein in Clint's right foreleg before I manage to get it in on the left.

"This do?"

Amy hands me the tube and I check her work, the way she's cushioned the end that must coax the bone into Clint's stomach. "Feels good. Here, hold this bag as high as you can and squeeze it as hard as you can."

I pass her a liter bag of warm fluids that's hooked up and running into Clint's vein. I want to get it into Clint's circulation as fast as possible. "Okay. She's pretty out of it, but I'm sure she's going to fight this tube going down. I'm going to give her a little something to keep her calm."

I find the drawer containing the anesthetic agents—what little we have left—
and pull out a small bottle of what looks
like milk. I read the drug dosage information written on the label, guesstimate Clint's
weight, and draw up the appropriate volume in a syringe.

"What's that?" asks Amy.

"Propofol."

Nothing registers on Harry's face, but
Amy's eyebrows are up like hackles. "Pro-
pofol. Isn't that the stuff that killed Michael
Jackson?"

There's not much that gets past Amy.
"Look, I don't want her to struggle or panic.
I'm going to titrate it very carefully."

I say this casually, with certainty, like a
doctor in control, even though Amy has
unsettled me. I don't know if I'm actually
prepared for what I'm about to do. I'm not
sure I will ever be. I pull over our antiquated
anesthetic machine with its supply of oxygen and grab a selection of tubes to place
in Clint's airway if she decides to stop
breathing for herself. There are probably a
dozen other things I should be doing, and
the fact that this is the only preparation
that comes to mind does little to improve

my confidence. "Right then, you want to stay, Harry, or you want to take a seat in the waiting room?"

Harry shakes his head and hugs Clint a little tighter.

"That's fine, but maybe you can pat her back end. Amy, I need you to hold her head up, neck outstretched as far as you can go, giving me a straight shot down her throat."

Amy does as she is told and I inject a small amount of milky liquid into the catheter in her vein, wait ten seconds, and see how Clint relaxes into Amy's grip. I press a finger down on what's left of Clint's rock-chewed incisors and appreciate the slack jaw of a semiconscious dog.

Pulling Clint's tongue toward me I push the aluminum tube dripping with K-Y jelly into the back of her throat, gently advancing it down and down. It keeps going and Clint's not swallowing or fighting and her color looks fine, and Amy's eyes begin to widen, as though I'm performing some bizarre sword-swallowing trick with her grandfather's dog and suddenly, I stop.

"I think I'm there," I say, sniffing the open end of the tube in my hand. I inhale deeply, drawing in the fetid air of rotten tissue that tells me I'm in the right place. I wince.

"Now what?" asks Harry, his head turned away, his arms clutching Clint around her hips as though he thinks she might be about to buck and leap off the table.

I'm not listening. I'm feeling. I have no point of reference for what I'm about to do but I close my eyes and see a shard of pork chop bumping up against the end of my aluminum tube. I poke it, feel its resistance, and know I can't coax it, can't simply persuade it to let go and drop into the stomach, so I push, I push hard, harder than I ever imagined possible.

I wonder if Harry notices the way Clint has come around enough to squirm, to fight whatever it is I'm doing to her. I wonder if Amy thinks she hears the rip, the bone driven into Clint's chest, bouncing off the inside of the dog's rib cage, a fermenting broth of bacteria basting her heart and lungs. The thing is, they don't feel what I feel, a distinctive pop, and then Clint letting go with a moan of relief as the resistance disappears, the bone pushed on and into her stomach.

I have the tube out of her throat in seconds. "I think I did it. I felt it go."

Amy's expression tells me she doesn't know whether I'm talking about a tear in the esophagus or the bone being pushed into the stomach.

Harry hears none of this ambiguity. He's up and coming toward me, the look on his face already telling me his version. "She's all set, right?"

"Maybe . . . I don't know. We should take another X-ray to make sure I didn't cause any damage."

"I thought you said you might not find a leak even if there is one," says Amy.

"I did, but I was talking about the liquid barium. Now I'm talking about air. If there's a tear, air will get through where the bone used to be. We should see it on the X-ray."

Harry can't believe it, can't believe it's not over, that there's still another hurdle to jump. He reaches out to the exam table for support.

"Give me a hand." Once more Amy helps me to position Clint and once more I run the film. Clint seems to be hanging in there, not better, not worse, but who knows what gore exists deep inside. It's got to be the longest four minutes of my life. I can't imagine how long it feels for Harry.

When the film finally falls from the processor, I don't want to touch it. It's like the letter from the college of your dreams—acceptance or rejection—about to change your life either way, and though you want to rip it open you're hanging on to this moment, this now, because it might be the only hope you have left.

I pick up the film, clear a space on the viewing box, and Amy slides in on my right, Harry actually leaving Clint's side to hover on my left. The three of us share the silence as I put the image up on the screen.

No one speaks. If they're looking at me, I don't notice because tunnel vision makes everything fade to black except the shades of gray inside Clint's chest. Overall impressions distort into details, what I can't see more important than what I can. I can't see black striations, black commas, black pockets, black bubbles, or black lines. But beyond this moment, and most important of all, my mind's eye does not see an old man sitting next to an empty dog bed where his best friend used to lie.

"Looks good," I say, as though that's it, no big deal, just another day at the office when what I really feel is the crash, the aftermath of adrenaline being turned off, the switch thrown. And for the second time today I want to drop to my knees.

Harry's on me like a long-lost relative, hugging me to him. My arms are trapped by my side and his tears run down my neck. I'm looking over at Amy. She hesitates, takes me in as I'm being bear-hugged to death by her grandfather, and an understated delight begins to shape her lips. I don't know how best to describe it.

Harry releases his grip and moves past me, back to Clint. He's in her face. "You're going to be fine, my love. I might never forgive myself, but you're going to be fine."

I join him. "I'm going to continue her on fluids, start some antibiotics, antacids, and give her something for the pain."

Harry looks up at me, and I can tell there's no point in me trying to warn him that we need to keep a close eye on her for the next couple of days.

"Doc, tell me, what can I do to thank you?"

I look down at him, clinging to his dog,

relief written across his face, and I think to myself, *you just did, this moment, this scene, this memory, it's all the thanks I will ever need.*

Then, as I sense Amy closing in behind me, a reckless idea begins to evolve and I find myself cupping a hand to Harry's ear.

"You could convince your granddaughter to come out to dinner with me."

Saturday

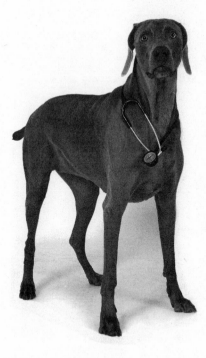

« 20 »

D-day has finally arrived, and in my world the *D* could stand for *dreaded, debt-ridden,* or *doom*, take your pick. Somehow, by close of business, Bedside Manor needs to have generated enough income in my first week on the job to fend off the money-grubbing Mr. Critchley and his repo men from Green State Bank. And by my reckoning, despite the hush money from Crystal Haggerty, we're still not even close.

Not that I've given up. I've managed to establish a new line of credit with our medical supply company. I've signed a new maintenance contract for the X-ray and the anesthetic equipment. I've convinced the medical waste facility to give us a second chance. Doris swears she's making headway with the bad debt, doing what she does best—badgering. I've got three estimates pending from contractors to convert the supply room into a second exam room. I've got Clint curled in my lap, her tail keeping a beat as she devours a slurry of liquidized dog food as if it were filet mignon. And, last but not least, I've got a seven-thirty dinner reservation for two at the Inn at Falls View Farm.

To be honest, this positive attitude has nothing to do with dreamy notions of a financial miracle in my future or Critchley saying, "Hey, no worries, you can slide another week." It's driven by Lewis, and the way he seemed irrationally undaunted by the prospect of failing to make our good faith payment or taking on more credit when I discussed my plans with him this morning. "Doris tells me I'm busy, booked solid, so do what you need to do, but make sure you're around to see your cases later this afternoon."

He had folded his arms across his chest

and delivered a stiff downward nod, like a father who insists his son get home before curfew. I didn't question the demand or his confidence in our future beyond close of business today. I assured him I'd be there. Even if I still feared the waiting room would remain as empty as always whenever it was my turn to be on duty.

By three o'clock, convinced I'm on a roll, I take a shot at redemption. I drive out to the home of Ginny Weidmeyer. And don't think this new outward vitality makes my fears and foibles any less. I'm still bracing for the call from the Vermont State Veterinary Board and still haven't heard any word from Brendon Small regarding Frieda. If the last twenty-four hours have taught me anything, it's the realization that "out of sight, out of mind" is a Band-Aid on a wound that needs to be stitched up. I was the veterinary pathologist who embraced an isolation that deadened his pain. But the past is a bully who always circles back, picking away at the weakness of an easy mark. Eventually you can't ignore it, leaving you with two options—run away, or face it head-on. Facing Ginny Weidmeyer is the right thing to do, and besides, I need all the practice I can get learning to say "I'm sorry."

Lewis told me he left several messages with Ginny but she hadn't called him back, and as I reach the ornate fountain outside the mansion I see it's no longer running, Triton's gaping maw is now dripping with icicles. The black Range Rover with the ONFYA license plate is gone.

Have Ginny, Chelsea, and Steven absconded to St. Barts? Leave the un-pleasantries to the lawyers?

I ring the doorbell. *Eine Kleine Nacht-musik* has been replaced by the opening bars of Beethoven's Fifth.

The door opens and there's Ginny— immaculate makeup, cashmere sweater, cheerful silk scarf around her neck—with Chelsea in her arms.

"Ms. Weidmeyer, you're here . . . sorry . . . I thought you might be . . . I should have called, but I wanted to tell you in per-son how very sorry I am about what . . ."

Ginny raises a hand, stopping me in my tracks, but it comes over as a polite re-quest. "Come in, Cyrus. I need to show you something."

Her use of my first name is not lost on

me, neither is the sadness in her voice as she leads me to a different sofa in front of a different fireplace in her country club of a living room.

"Sit down and take a look at this." She pats a cushion next to her. I do as I'm told as she opens the lid on a laptop, angling the screen my way. The screen is divided into four images of high-definition, surveillance camera footage. There's the white rug in front of a fireplace, the bottom of a king-size bed, an aerial view of a room full of saddles and bridles, and a tiled floor featuring food and water bowls.

"These are the four most likely places to find Chelsea at any given time. When I'm out, all I have to do is check my cell phone. Usually I just use real time, but I went back to see what had been recorded." She presses a button on the keypad. "The screen in the bottom right-hand corner."

A digital clock and calendar tells me it's from two mornings ago. There's a hand picking up a bowl and returning it to the floor a few seconds later piled high with brown, meaty mounds of canned cat food. Chelsea pounces as soon as it hits the floor.

"Doesn't look much like dry prescription cat food, does it?" She closes the lid, places the laptop off to one side, and turns to me. Ginny holds Chelsea like a mother cradles a child, the cat facing the other way, resting her furry chin on Ginny's shoulder. I think of the pictures in the collage, of Ruth carrying me, so instinctive for a mother, so strange for a cat, and yet Chelsea seems to have come to appreciate the security of this embrace, come to love it even. She purrs into the palm of Ginny's left hand, and I realize it's missing. The engagement ring is gone.

Ginny notices me noticing. "Do you think it's possible to fall in love at any age?" She wiggles the naked ring finger. "Believe me, I know jewelry and I know a fake when I see one. I had hoped he wanted to impress me but couldn't afford to do it." She takes her time, and we both know she needs to get this out. "I've never thought of myself as a . . . cougar. Steven happened to be a younger man, a little lost, in need of direction, but full of big ideas and on his way up. He was always so appreciative, always armed with a compliment, and it's invigorating, to know someone finds me attractive at my age." She laughs. "I confess, I loved being the subject of gossip, I loved being defiant, chasing the forbidden fruit. It was infectious, intoxicating. It felt like I was recapturing my youth, like getting a second wind."

For a second I see her lost in the high, but it's brief. "The trouble with being seduced is you no longer see what's in front of your eyes. When you get addicted, you begin to enable. You convince yourself that your friends are wrong and you're right because they don't know him like you do. Sometimes you'll believe anything not to be alone."

She smiles, lips closed, a joyless smile of a woman grateful to be heard. "You made me see what was right in front of me, Cyrus, and you saw the truth because you weren't thinking of me." She reaches forward to pat my forearm. "You stuck your nose in and your neck out and you had everything to lose, but you kept going for the sake of Chelsea's health. You know your father begged me to be supportive if you came back, supportive and . . . tolerant. He needn't have worried. You did exactly what he would have done, you focused on what matters most, and I will never forget that."

I feel a strange and paradoxical, but gratifying thrill at being compared to Bobby Cobb. I know that Ginny means it as the best of compliments, and I decide that yes, it is just that.

I came here prepared for a tongue-lashing. Did I ever misjudge how today's conversation with Ginny would turn out? Of course she never answered Lewis's call. She's heartbroken and hiding from the world. And yet here she is, practically thanking me for being rude enough to end her engagement.

I want to ask her what happened to Steven and why he had it in for Chelsea. Maybe he resented the competition for Ginny's affection. More likely he had his eye on the money sidelined for Chelsea's long-term health care, which would have cut into his own inheritance.

"Here," I say, arms outstretched, "let me have a look at her. See how she's doing."

I decline the offer of coffee and for ten more minutes I try to examine Chelsea as she crawls around my neck and shoulders, a squirming furry boa, loving the attention and feeling good. Ginny did a fine job with the subcutaneous fluids. Chelsea's normal hydration is fully restored.

The two of them escort me to the front door. "If you're having trouble getting her to eat her special diet, give me a call and I'll see if we can change the brand or the flavors. Improve what's on the menu."

"Thanks. And thanks for stopping by. We'll see you later."

I catch this last remark as I'm halfway to the truck. Was that simply a throwaway line, a variation on "have a nice day"? To my surprise, in spite of the cold, they're still standing at the door, waiting to see me off.

I wave another good-bye, climb into the cab, turn the engine over, find first gear, and that's when I discover I'm stuck. Oh, the engine's whining and the wheels are spinning but forward movement requires traction, which is problematic for a vehicle with bald tires wedged within a series of deep icy ruts akin to chiseled blocks of granite.

I get out to inspect the problem, see the front door close, and a minute later Ginny has joined me. She's in a winter coat and gloves, and she's brought a bag of ice melt.

"If you switch back and forth between forward and reverse, you can usually rock your way out."

"I'd try, but I've got no reverse. It doesn't work."

Ginny looks at me, unflustered, in control, sleeves rolled up like Rosie the Riveter. "Put it in neutral and we'll see if we can do it with muscle."

I do as I'm told, ready to steer and push from the driver's side while Ginny comes around on the open passenger side. She calls "one, two, three" across the front seats and together we push, the wheels rolling up the side of their icy chocks. Ginny screams to push harder. I grunt and drive and then there's a moment when I know we've hit the point of no return and the wheels are going to climb up and over and out.

Ginny's smiling and this time there's teeth and gums and satisfaction. "Sometimes there's no going backward." She closes the passenger-side door and taps the hood twice before heading back to the house.

I'm at the end of the long driveway when

I wonder whether she was referring to her own future or whether she was using the truck as a cheap and clumsy metaphor for my past.

My cell phone rings.

"Where are you?"

It's Doris. Nice introduction—obviously she's still in bad-debt mode.

"Coming back from Ginny Weidmeyer's."

"Good. Cause there's someone in your exam room."

"I've got a client already?" I check my watch. It's just after four. Evening appointments don't start until four thirty, if they start at all.

"Said it was important. Needs to speak to you in private."

Finally. It must be Brendon Small. "Excellent. Have him stay put. I'll be right there."

"Is he still in there?" I ask.

Doris considers me from behind her desk.

"Does *he* have a name?"

Will she ever stop narrowing her eyes and easing her head away from me whenever I ask her a question?

"Refused to give it. Said this is a private not a professional matter."

Then another peril slams an open palm against my forehead. What if it's Steven the gold digger, back to make good on his promise, *you're so dead*? I scan the parking lot, looking for a black Range Rover with a vanity plate. I don't see it.

"Okay, Doris, please pay attention to what I have to say."

"Why are you whispering?"

"If you hear the sound of two men coming to blows from behind that door I need you to dial 911. Am I clear?"

Her eyes roll upward. Her nod of understanding is more like the wobble of a bobble-head toy. I pivot, pad toward the exam room, hover for a second, and realize that I've never been in a minor altercation, let alone a fistfight. When I was physically escorted off the premises at McCall and Rand, caught up in my most animated, most agitated state, it was still little more than a heated oral exchange. Experience at getting hot under the collar won't be much use when I need a right hook to the temple.

I open the examination room door and step into the ring.

"You've got a nerve."

He's all teeth and sneering lips, already moving in, and I turn my back on him to make sure the door is shut. There's a rush of relief at who it is and I can feel the breathlessness, the flutter inside my chest starting to subside, but I don't want to let it go. So I focus on what matters: an innocent golden retriever, on Anne and Emily and what they've been through. I welcome the angry buzz rebounding in my veins and turn to face Brendon Small.

"I could say the same about you."

He's in jeans and an open navy blue parka and he's slapping a woolen hat in the palm of his hand as if it's a billy club. There's a mixture of emotions written across his face, and I can't tell which one is winning, anger or angst.

"I wouldn't be here if you could take a hint. Where do you get off, calling my house, hassling my wife in my own kitchen?"

I've thought a lot about this exchange and I'm feeling armed and dangerous.

"Where do *you* get off sending me

anonymous threats?" There's a flicker of amusement in his eyes, an ugly upward curl to the corner of his mouth, enough to confirm his guilt. "Where do you get off insisting I destroy a dog without your wife's knowledge, behind her back and, more importantly, behind your daughter's back?"

"Stepdaughter." He spits out the word like he wants to make sure I appreciate how this doe-eyed little girl is not of his seed.

"There was nothing wrong with Frieda. She may have been old (I rehearsed using the past tense) but her bladder was in perfect working order. Yes, there's a stain on the kitchen floor, right in front of the refrigerator, and this may have been her favorite spot to hang out, but you and I know exactly what happened the morning after you brought her here to be put to sleep."

"What are you talking about?"

"I'm betting you're the first one up at your house. Feed the dog, let her outside, bring the wife a coffee."

Brendon Small says nothing.

"Every morning you'd find that puddle in front of the fridge and you'd scold that dog, maybe you'd hit her . . ."

"I never hit her."

". . . and you'd wipe up the mess and swear you were going to get rid of her once and for all. And then, after a long day, another job rejection, and a skin-full of consolatory beers, you finally snapped and brought her to me. I like to think a part of you struggled with what you asked me to do. But maybe I'm being too kind. Next morning you woke up, went downstairs, and couldn't believe your eyes. That puddle of clear liquid you consistently blamed on Frieda was still there, exact same spot in front of the fridge, even though Frieda was gone. That's when you realized what you had done. Killed an innocent dog because the faucet on your water dispenser was broken. You and Anne and Emily probably use it enough during the day that the leak doesn't overflow, but for those eight to ten hours at night, the drips keep coming, and by the next morning you've got yourself a puddle of fake urine."

Mr. Small brings a thumb and forefinger up to his nose, wiping the tip. "You've no idea what I'm dealing with."

"No, I don't. But this urinary incontinence thing was nothing more than an excuse to have her put to sleep. It's not the real reason."

"Huh. Now you know what I think?"

"Of course not. But I do know what it's like to be a child who feels slighted by someone I look up to, by someone I need to be a parent, by someone I want to love."

It's like the air goes out of him. He deflates, his body sagging a little. The beat of his woolen billy club suspended, he slowly drops his head and closes his eyelids. He looks spent, as though he's been ten rounds and he's ready to throw in the towel.

"Look, I never wanted kids, never have, but if you fall in love with the wrong woman, what're you gonna do?"

He keeps his head down, refusing to make eye contact. I hear the chime of the shopkeeper's bell. Another client?

"I've tried, but there's no instruction manual on how to get this right. I wanted to be a friend, to respect the memory of her father, but that dog was a constant reminder of him and what they had together. It's like we couldn't start over, begin as a new family, until Frieda was gone. I thought I could justify her being out of our life, because now she had a problem and chances were, given her age, it was something bad."

"And what were you going to tell Emily or your wife?"

"I wasn't going to tell them anything. That's why I'm here. Yeah, I dug into your past on the Internet, but I don't want to cause trouble. I just need you to keep quiet, to never call or come over again. I made a mistake. A big one, but please, give me a chance to be a stepfather."

"You didn't answer my question. What are they going to think happened to Frieda?"

"I don't know. She went missing. She knew she was dying and went off to die alone. She got lost and died in the cold. You and I are the only ones who know the truth, and at least we both know she didn't suffer."

The shopkeeper's bell rings again and then again and again. What's going on out there?

"Answer me this, and I urge you to think very carefully about what you say next. Knowing what you know about the broken fridge, knowing how it felt to walk out of this practice alone, how it felt pretending to help your wife and . . . daughter . . .

look for a missing dog, did you ever wish you could turn back the clock, still have Frieda and try again?"

He hesitates, and then his head snaps back and we lock eyes. "This parent. The one that let you down as a kid, did you make up? Did you learn to forgive?"

It's a perfectly timed punch under my chin. My turn to rock back on my heels.

"Yes. Yes I did. But I left it way too late because I never took the time to understand him and see how, in his own unique way, he really loved me."

I grind my molars together. After fourteen years, my dam of emotional suppression is up for another pounding, and I pray I can overpower the tears welling in my eyes. I stare back as hard as I can, willing my lids not to blink.

"Then my answer is yes. Yes. I wish I could take it back. Frieda's been gone for nearly a week and nothing has changed. I'm still unemployed. My house is still underwater, and we're still just as disconnected as a family. Now that I'm on this side, now that I can look back, I can see that this was never about a dog. My wife says I'm overwhelmed, I'm afraid of the responsibility, I'm jealous, all of the above. I know Emily misses her dad. I need to find a way to deal with her missing him, and getting rid of Frieda wasn't the answer."

Off in the waiting room I can hear the sound of conversation. And it sounds like a crowd.

The other door in the exam room, the one marked PRIVATE, swings open without a knock, and there's Lewis.

"Ah, there you are. Excellent timing."

I look at Lewis, look back at Brendon Small. "Excuse me, Mr. Small, I need to have a word with Dr. Lewis, in private." I usher Lewis back into the main work area.

"Is that Frieda's owner?"

"Yes," I say.

"But that's perfect. In fact, it couldn't be better."

Lewis darts over to the examination room to poke his head around the door. "Stay right where you are, Mr. Small. Be with you in a minute." Message delivered, he bounces back to me to ask, "Did you catch the article this morning?"

"What are you talking about?"

"The *Gazette*. Greer's article. It came out this morning."

I'm speechless.

"Praising you up and down over your handling of Tina the cat and Denise Laroche's untimely labor, but then he tosses in his coup de grâce, the promotional concept that no pet owner in Eden Falls could possibly ignore."

I'm still dumbstruck.

"A free health examination."

"A what?"

"Think about it. What's the one thing guaranteed to get people walking through our front door? The offer of something of value that is totally free. In fact Ginny Weidmeyer has been gracious enough to have the event catered—beer, wine, little meaty and cheesy things with crackers."

"Whoa, there. Event? Ginny Weidmeyer. She's in on this?"

Lewis beams.

"And don't you need a license or something to serve alcohol?"

"Course not. So long as you invite the Chief of Police."

"But Lewis, free exams?"

Lewis sighs, the old man frustrated because I'm not keeping up.

"You and I examine their pets at no cost

to the client. You get to meet a lot of new people. You get to know their animals, and you get to offer friendly advice about their pet's health care. Chances are you're going to pick up on a few minor ailments, make helpful suggestions about things to watch out for, things you would recommend doing in the future. And where do you think those people are going to go for follow-up on these particular recommendations?"

It's the teaser that gets the buyer into the showroom. They get to kick some tires and see what's on offer, rather than never stopping by. Greer's a smart man.

"That's all very well but we need money right now. Today. We're out of time and 'free' isn't going to cut it."

Lewis makes no attempt to hide how much he's loving this, showing off, not worrying that chipped incisor. "Calm yourself. Doris and I are on it."

Why would he think this assurance makes me feel anything close to calm?

The door keeps chiming. "How many people are you expecting?" I ask.

"No idea, but Ginny says she's ordered enough to keep a hundred people, and their pets, comfortably fed and watered. Sounds like it's already started."

Lewis acts as though this evening will be the turning point that keeps Bedside Manor alive and, by extension, ensures his ailing wife remains where she needs to be.

"Why didn't you let me in on this earlier?"

"I wanted it to be a surprise. And, I didn't want you to panic or overthink it."

"What's that supposed to mean?"

Lewis steps in, hands clutching my upper arms. "You need to live a little. Be more spontaneous. Start listening to your heart and stop deliberating and procrastinating in that mind of yours. Besides, you're going to have to say a few words of introduction, and Greer told me how you hate public speaking."

Lewis rushes through this last comment as though I might not notice it. I hear a high-pitched female laugh from the waiting room.

"No way. I'll play nice. I'll see the cases. But please don't make me speak in front of an audience."

"Cyrus, you've got no choice. You're the

new guy. They're going to want to know something about you."

"But what do I say?"

"Tell them as much or as little as you want. It's entirely up to you."

I think about this or should I say I try not to think, but rather allow myself to be led, influenced, and overwhelmed by what I feel and not by what I understand.

Lewis checks his watch. "It's nearly five. Greer's piece said we'd start seeing cases at five."

"Give me a minute. I need to grab a couple of things."

"You're not going to run out on me, are you?"

I shake my head, break his grip, and disappear upstairs.

Armed with the two props I've yet to hang in the exam room, I step into a waiting room that resembles a rowdy neighborhood party. A turbulent throng of chatty strangers is peeling off coats and scarves and hats as they surrender to their own warmth and bonhomie. Though the rumble of conversation is punctuated by the occasional yip and bark, even the canines on leashes and in arms appear to be enjoying themselves. I glimpse the back of a scarlet macaw on a shoulder, a trio of seated gray-haired ladies, cat carriers on laps, sipping glasses of white wine, and there's a young man in white shirt and black bow tie, working the crowd, offering finger food from a silver platter. There's no one I recognize and no one seems to be checking me out. I'm without a pet, a gatecrasher, and therefore best ignored.

"Ah, there you are." Lewis has me by the arm. "Let's make a little room for you at the far end. What have you got there?"

I'm about to tell him but someone's saying hello, wanting to shake his hand. Hovering and awkward, I turn to face the crowd and this time I recognize a bobbing blond beehive. Doris is everywhere, buzzing from one person to the next. And everywhere she goes she leans in close and whispers in ears, causing smiles to evaporate, causing hands to fumble for wallets and hunt for checkbooks. What is she saying? What is she up to?

Lewis is free again, guiding me through the masses and into what available space remains near the storage room door. He beckons me close. "You ready?" He leans back, studies my face. "Stupid question. You'll be fine. Remember, *don't think, feel.*"

I get raised eyebrows, his version of "am I right or am I right" and he's straight into, "Ladies and gentlemen . . ." The crowd begins to settle. "Ladies and gentlemen, dog lovers and cat lovers, thank you for—"

"Where's the love for the parrot?"

There's a ripple of laughter, and I wonder how many of them are already drunk.

"Let me try that over. Ladies and gentlemen . . . pet lovers . . ."—smiles, murmurs of approval—"thank you for joining us tonight as we celebrate a new beginning for your home town veterinary practice, Bedside Manor."

A round of applause and there's another *cha-ching* from the doorbell. I wish I could tell you it's another pet owner, but it's not. A few in the crowd notice my reaction and turn to see "what" not "who" must have walked in—my personal grim reaper, Mr. Critchley.

"Before I hand you over to a man who

has already proven himself capable of delivering a kitten and a baby with equal aplomb. . . ."

There's a whoop, a whistle, heads turn, and this time I follow the stares to find Denise Laroche, blushing but unable to conceal a proud smile as she rocks her swaddled baby on her shoulder.

". . . I must say a special thank-you to Peter Greer of the *Eden Falls Gazette*"— polite applause—"and the wonderful generosity of Ginny Weidmeyer for providing the drinks and snacks. Thanks, Ginny." Cheers all round, more vigorous clapping, and once again I follow the direction of nodding heads and jutting chins to find Greer and Ginny at the way back, waving away the gratitude.

"So, without further ado, it is my great pleasure to formally introduce to you Dr. Cyrus Mills."

Lewis gestures to me, backs away, and gives me a hearty go-get-'em thumbs-up before he disappears behind the door that leads directly to the central work area.

Nice time to abandon me. *Don't think; feel.* Feel what? Like I need to run? Like I need to vomit?

"Um, thank you for coming this evening . . ."

There's a cry of "speak up," a "can't hear you," and a throaty bark of disapproval that I instantly recognize as belonging to Greer's terrier, Toby.

". . . Obviously, I . . . um . . . I had no idea about . . ." I see heads tipping back to drain drinks, heads scanning left and right, looking for more mobile refreshments, the telltale murmur of people already losing interest. My knees are shaking, I don't know what to do with my hands, and I think I'm about to have a nosebleed.

"I wanted to . . . I'd like to take this opportunity to share something . . . something that might come as a surprise."

As if on cue, the examination room door bursts open and I catch sight of a stupefied and practically airborne Brendon Small hurtling into the masses followed by a collective gasp, followed by a squeal of delight and then cheering and laughing and finally more than enough chatter to totally drown me out.

I'm left hanging for a full minute before Lewis emerges from the mayhem. "Sorry, Dr. Mills, we couldn't keep your surprise waiting any longer." Then addressing the room, "This afternoon, Dr. Mills found a dog wandering the trails behind the practice. Mr. Small was kind enough to drop by and confirm that she is his missing retriever, Frieda."

A gap in the crowd opens up, enough for me to see Brendon Small holding the other end of the dog's leash, Anne Small, on her knees, hands in supplication, tears running down her cheeks, and Emily, her little arms wrapped around the neck of her golden, tiny fingers laced together, the grip sure, as though she will never let go.

Lewis glances over at me. "Looks like the lost dogs of Eden Falls have found themselves a new Patron Saint." And in his smug grin, his flashing brows, I suspect that finding Brendon in my exam room was the icing on the cake. Getting Anne and Emily Small to come this evening so he could return their lost dog had always been part of his master plan.

A new Patron Saint. If Lewis's intent is to pass the baton, no one notices my fumble. Everybody's back has turned my way and they miss my grimace of unworthiness, of remorse. There's the flash of a camera and the chink of glasses. It's as though my speech is over, as though finding Frieda was the surprise I spoke of, a surprise the citizens of Eden Falls would obviously prefer over listening to me stutter and ramble. It's time to set the record straight.

"I've got two things I need to share." I'm shouting, the noisy heckler, spoiling the show but impossible to ignore. "The first is a series of photographs." I hold up the collage from the basement, high over my head like a banner. For now I have their attention, though expressions appear more puzzled than interested. Mr. Critchley, standing at the way back, is the exception. His chin is raised, eyes narrowed, as though he is above all this, the excuses, the empty banter, because the time has come to pay up or suffer the consequences.

"Some of you will recognize the woman in the pictures, but I'm sure all of you know the man in the central photo with the little boy on his lap. Please, pass it around and take a closer look."

I hand out the collage, and there's another chime from the shopkeeper's bell, a collective glance back, but this time, when my eyes discover the target of their shared curiosity, I'm left staring and then they're left staring at me.

It's Amy.

Instantly three thoughts flutter across my mind. Mentally I grab the first, a question, a curious but nonchalant "hum, what's Amy doing here?" This gives way to an impulsive, "wow, Amy looks great—the way she's done her hair, that hint of makeup accentuating her eyes and lips." But this is rapidly followed by a scream of, *"oh my God, Amy's here, dressed for dinner, for dinner with me at seven thirty and I've totally forgotten about our date, and Mr. Critchley is here to claim his pound of flesh, and there are all these drunken people staring at me, expecting me to examine their pets for free."*

I look into the crowd. I look at Amy, the picture of me on my father's lap heading her way. I wanted to tell her tonight, tell her how wrong I have been, but not like this. I wanted to tell her in private, in increments, in carefully constructed sentences that give me my best chance to explain.

It's too late. There's no turning back. I reach for the FedEx package sent from

Charleston, open it up, and pull out a framed sheet of paper.

"They say . . . they say there's only one thing certain in life and that's death. I think they're wrong. I think there are two. Okay, death, but also, regret. You know what I'm talking about—the things you never did, the things you never said, the things you wish you'd never said. It's not a question of *if* you will regret, it's a question of *when*. Trouble is, for most of us, these two certainties—death and regret—come as a package deal, and by then it's too late.

"The other thing about regret is the way regret means you care. That's what makes Bedside Manor one of the biggest regrets of my life. I'm not talking about the way the building's falling apart or the outdated equipment or the bad debt or the financial screwups, I'm talking about what counts, the Bedside Manor that you know will be here every time you walk through that front door with a sick animal. That certain something is here because the woman in those photos, Dr. Ruth Mills, helped keep it alive. That certain something is here because the smiling man with the half-closed eyes, your Doc Cobb, always took his time, always made time, kept his focus on his patient and not on the dollar. As for that little boy on his lap, well, that little boy will always have regrets, but I want to assure you that he's committed to keeping that certain something you cannot see, cannot measure, cannot buy, cannot fake, and cannot ignore about Bedside Manor alive. That little boy is Bobby's son, Cyrus. It's time for that little boy to pay his respects. Here, tonight, I am so very proud to tell you, that little boy is me."

I hold up my framed veterinary degree for everyone to see, the one given to Dr. Cyrus *Cobb,* and despite everything that's happened, I brace for the collective gasp, for people to put down their glasses, drop their half-eaten chicken satay or shrimp cocktail in the trash, grab their leash or cat carrier and storm off in a show of solidarity to the former deity of Bedside Manor.

But as I look around the room, for the most part, people's expressions remain essentially unchanged. Maybe they already knew? Maybe they just don't care? Maybe it doesn't matter to them in the way that it matters to me. You see, it's not enough to be Bobby's son. When you've got this much catching up to do, you've got to flaunt it.

Among the masses I glimpse the shiny bullet head of Chief Matt. He turns my way, looking even more confused than normal. Then I notice the faces of three people in particular—Lewis, Peter Greer, and Ginny Weidmeyer—heads held high, eyes and lips connected by a smile I last saw in my mother, like the smile of a parent humbled by the achievements of someone they love.

Then, from one end of the room to the other, I bob and weave and get on tippy-toes until my eyes finally meet Amy's, trying to get a read on her reaction to my speech. Was she shocked by my change of heart about my father? Was she disappointed because I couldn't talk about it when the two of us were alone? The waiting stretches until she simply turns away, breaking the connection, pushing her way through the front door and out into the lot.

I'm after her, jostling through the crowd, throwing out random apologies and "excuse me's" and I'm halfway there when I'm jerked to a complete stop by none other than Lewis.

"Cyrus, your father would have been so proud of you. And . . ."

I should be thanking him, letting everyone know how much Lewis has done for me, but there's Critchley at the back of the room, beckoning me with an insistent claw, like it would be foolish of me to ignore him.

"Sorry, Lewis, but could you fend off Mr. Critchley for a few minutes? There's something I need to do."

I don't wait for a reply. I keep squeezing, nudging, and ultimately shoving my way through the crowd.

Out into the night and there she is, across the lot, unlocking her SUV.

"Amy. Amy, wait."

I'm shouting but Amy totally ignores me, hopping into the driver's seat.

"Please," I scream, halfway across the slick asphalt, doing my best Bambi impersonation. "Don't go. I screwed up. I should have faced my past. I should have talked things out with my father when I had the chance but I never did."

The driver's-side door is ajar, as though maybe she's listening. I survey the lot to make sure we're alone. "Thing is, I'm a loner. I'm . . . I'm not good at expressing what's inside. Sometimes I wish I were more direct, like you, but I'm not."

Get to the point, Cyrus.

"Look, I want you to know . . . I want you to know I've ditched my pride. If I could have kept Bedside Manor alive I would have stayed."

To my relief, Amy begins stepping back out of her truck. I push on. "I had . . . well . . . hoped, perhaps you and I could . . ."

That's when I notice that she's clutching a large plaid blanket in her hand. And, once again, I've jumped to the wrong conclusion.

"It's Clint's favorite blanket. We forgot it last night. I was just bringing it in for her. What do you mean, *you would have stayed*?"

"Cyrus."

The scratchy holler comes from behind me. I spin around and spy the familiar orange dot glowing in the darkness.

"Cyrus. Doc Lewis says he needs you. Says it's urgent."

I think Doris referring to me by my first name is more frightening than the prospect of confronting Mr. Critchley.

Turning back to Amy, I say, "Um . . .

look . . . I want to explain everything. You still want to grab something to eat, later?"

Amy hesitates, her expression giving nothing away. I'm rooted to the spot, more paralyzed than frozen, my heart in limbo.

"I'd love to," she says.

She could have said "of course" or "sounds like a plan," but she slipped in that word, *love*. For a reason?

"Assuming you stop gawking at me and get on with seeing all your new clients."

My tongue is Super Glued to the roof of my mouth. Then she smiles and I want to hug her, no, I want to kiss her, but I dare not push my luck.

"Cyrus, did you hear what I said?"

For a woman with what must be a limited lung capacity, Doris has a surprisingly commanding voice. I slip-slide my way back to the front door.

"Thanks, Doris."

Arms folded across her chest, cigarette bobbing between her lips, she almost lets me go. Almost. I'm halfway through the front door, and though her words are muffled by the sound of the crowd, I swear she says, "Nice speech."

I look back but fingers like tarantula legs alight on my shoulder.

"Dr. Mills, you had me worried," says Mr. Critchley. "I thought you might be running away from your responsibilities."

Neither of us smiles, and I realize he's not joking.

"Did working a Saturday make all the difference? Mr. Greer's article mentioned a free clinic, so I assume you must have already met your financial quota for the week."

Critchley's confidence that I have failed almost seeps from his pores. I feel the room full of pet lovers at my back. Yes, many of them will have been drawn by the freebies—the booze, the checkup—but, bottom line, they were drawn to Bedside Manor because this practice has always been rooted in how much it cares about the animals in their lives.

"Do we really have to do this here? Right now?" I'm almost whispering, wanting to spare my clients more than myself.

Critchley doesn't even deliberate. "I think it best to get this over, don't you?" Then, barely able to contain his smile, he says, "Don't make me ask for the check."

Anybody who tells you money is the root of all evil doesn't have any.

"What did you say?" Critchley asks.

I look away and feel the pull of the old imaginary itch at the back of my head. But this time I resist it, meet the attorney's weaselly eyes, and say, "I don't have it."

"I beg your pardon."

"I said I don't have it."

"Yes you do, Cyrus," says Lewis, suddenly at my side, handing me a check and a pen. "It's all filled out, you just need to sign it."

In a daze I scribble my signature and hand it over.

"What?" Lewis's question could be aimed at either Critchley or me. My expression is rooted in confusion. I imagine Critchley's is rooted in skepticism.

"Don't worry, the check won't bounce," says Lewis. Then he gestures to Doris as she steps back inside. "Our . . . office manager . . . assures me that she has taken in more than enough money in outstanding debt just this evening to easily cover our first payment." And then, though I'm sure Lewis means it in the nicest possible way, he slaps the defeated attorney on the back and says, "Cheer up, Mr. Critchley. If the folks of Eden Falls are happy to support Bedside Manor, perhaps you should as well."

Critchley looks like a man who bet all his money on black just as the roulette ball lands on red.

"Mr. Critchley, I didn't know you had a pet?" It's Ginny Weidmeyer to the rescue, and based on the speed of the attorney's recovery I can only assume that the Weidmeyer estate gets a lot of personal attention from the folks at Green State Bank. "Can I get you a drink? Something to eat?" She gestures to the waiter, but Peter Greer arrives first with Toby in his arms. Perhaps Greer has discovered Ginny is a free agent. Perhaps the Jack Russell will lunge for Mr. Critchley's jugular. Much as I'd love to find out, I step back and pull Lewis to one side.

"What are you doing? We don't have the money."

"Yes, we do," says Lewis. "I just made sure Doris worked a little harder on the bad debt."

"How?"

"By convincing her she'd be unemployed

if we didn't come up with the money. You said it yourself, no one knows better than Doris which clients are stalling, hoping we'll go belly up. And who do you think was feeding Bobby Cobb with all the details of daily life in Eden Falls, the ones he always seemed to know, the ones that made his care feel that much more personal?"

Doris. *Everybody knows everybody in Eden Falls.*

"If you know who's planning on buying a new car, if you know who can afford to get her nails done every week, you know who can pay their vet bill. And let's not forget the seedy details certain pet owners might prefer to keep quiet."

"Sounds a bit like blackmail." I catch a glimpse of Doris in the crowd. She must have heard me because her look says I will need to be punished. "But let's call it strategic commerce."

Suddenly the long arm of the law reaches out and grabs me.

"Okay, you're old Doc Cobb's son," says Chief Devito, "but I'm still having a hell of a time placing you."

I'm only half listening because to the

side and behind him, a group of individuals have most of my attention. There's Brendon Small, an unspoken thank-you written across his face. There's Anne Small, her eyes puffy and bloodshot, beginning to cry again, and between them and headed my way, Emily and her dog, Frieda.

I see a grinning golden retriever that made me think twice. I see a family getting a second chance. And, as I glance back at Devito, I see an opportunity I simply cannot resist. "Hey, Chief, *'say hello to my little friend!'*"

Then I spot Ethel Silverman and Kai, letting everyone around her know that I give away free dog food. There's Crystal Haggerty and Puck, honing in on a frightened young man with a chocolate Lab puppy cradled in his arms, and though Crystal is clearly on the prowl, I overhear her mentioning that I have a gift when it comes to their particular breed of dog.

My graduation certificate heads our way and Lewis makes a grab for it

"What are you going to do with this, now everyone's seen it?"

He passes it to me, and the name *Cobb* jumps out at me, but this time in a good way. "I'm going to hang it up in the exam room. Same with the photographs from the basement. I just wish . . . stupid . . . changing my name . . . it feels so . . . embarrassing, so overly dramatic and immature."

Lewis waves the notion away. "It's no different from Harry Carp calling every dog he's ever had Clint. It's a name. Who cares if you're Cobb or Mills? All that matters is the person behind the name. All that matters is you're here."

This shouldn't feel like forgiveness but it does, and I'm grateful.

"But," he adds, "you need to sort out this problem with your license."

"I know. And I'm going to. As soon as I find another way to pay my legal fees, now that I'm not selling this place."

Lewis cracks another smile, reaches into his jacket pocket, and, for the second time this evening, hands me a check. "Here. Do you think this will cover it?"

The word *surprise* does not do justice to my comprehension of the dollar amount scribbled in the little box and the signature of the person cutting the check—Ginny

Weidmeyer. I turn in her direction, but she's got her back to me, still talking to Mr. Critchley.

"I can't take this. It's a ridiculous amount."

"Of course it is and of course you can," says Lewis. "Ginny insists it's not a gift and it's not a loan. It's simply a prepayment on veterinary services she will require for her cat, Chelsea. Don't look so worried. She's going to make you work for every penny."

A week ago I would have been appalled by such a proposal. Now I'm prepared to do whatever it takes to keep Bedside Manor alive. Now I don't deliberate. I grab Lewis by the hand, not to shake it, but to pull him into me for a hug. And you know what, I don't feel the least bit awkward as I think about how this moment would have felt with my father, think about the name DR. CYRUS COBB, DVM, chiseled into my mother's tombstone.

I pull away and say, "If you can look after this place for a few days I'll head down to Charleston tomorrow. Get it all sorted out."

"Be my pleasure," says Lewis, "but, first things first." And with this he takes a step back and addresses the room. "Ladies and gentlemen. Dr. Mills and I would like to start."

And that's when my life starts over, when I know I've made the right choice, when this *real* veterinarian turns to *his* clientele and asks, "Who's first?"

« ACKNOWLEDGMENTS »

First of all, any implication that veterinary pathologists are not *real* veterinarians is, like the rest of this book, totally fictitious. The author apologizes for any misleading or erroneous content, medical or otherwise, but this material is intended to entertain, not provide guidance to pet owners who seek answers to animal health issues.

I must thank Deb Waterman and Ellie Millard for being kind enough to read early drafts and Kiki Koroshetz, Allyson Rudolph, and Diane Aronson for their many insightful comments on everything that followed. To all the fabulous folks at Hyperion: Ellen Archer, Elisabeth Dyssegaard, Kristin Kiser, Christine Ragasa, Kathryn Hough, Bryan Christian, and Jon Bernstein, a heartfelt thanks for your vision, enthusiasm, and dedication to this project.

Your collective buzz and passion for our book makes this writer feel very much at home.

Christine Pride, my editor, always believed I could make the difficult transition from nonfiction to fiction. Somehow she has shaped and transformed my writing into something that I am proud to call a novel. I continue to be blessed to have her on my side.

Jeff Kleinman, my agent, has been nothing less than amazing to work with. By turns he's the architect, the drill sergeant, and the magician who made the impossible possible. Cheers, Jeff. Here's to many more books together.

A big thank-you to my daughters, Emily and Whitney, and my wife, Kathy. I know I am a lucky man. Their love and support never wavers, even when I bring my laptop to the beach.

Finally, I must pay homage to our dogs, Sophie and Meg. Though I learned that Labradors eat first and ask questions later, only a fool underestimates the intelligence of a terrier; their best lesson was teaching me how these devoted creatures complete a family. You're still with us on every walk.

Nick Trout Graduated From Veterinary school at the University of Cambridge in 1989. He is a staff surgeon at the prestigious Angell Animal Medical Center in Boston; the author of three books, the *New York Times* bestseller *Tell Me Where It Hurts, Love Is the Best Medicine,* and *Ever By My Side*; and he is a contributing columnist for *The Bark* magazine. He lives in Massachusetts with his wife, Kathy, and their adopted Labradoodle, Thai.